DEAD
DRUNK

T0005994

DEAD DRUNK

Tales of Intoxication and Demon Drinks

Edited by

PAM LOCK

This collection first published in 2023 by
The British Library
96 Euston Road
London NW1 2DB

Selection, introduction and notes © 2023 Pam Lock
Volume copyright © 2023 The British Library Board

Dates attributed to each story relate to first publication.

Cataloguing in Publication Data
A catalogue record for this publication is available from the British Library

ISBN 978 0 7123 5409 7
e-ISBN 978 0 7123 6836 0

Frontispiece illustration: *Absinthe Drinker*, Viktor Oliva, 1901. Zlata Husa
Gallery Prague. The illustration on page 272 is based on a woodcut frontispiece
for Thomas Heywood's *Philocothonista, or, The drunkard, opened, dissected,
and anatomized*, from *Broadside Black-letter Ballads, printed in the sixteenth
and seventeenth centuries, etc.*, edited by J. P. Collier, London, 1868.

Cover design by Mauricio Villamayor with illustration by Sandra Gómez
Text design and typesetting by Tetragon, London
Printed in England by CPI Group (UK) Ltd, Croydon, CR0 4YY

CONTENTS

INTRODUCTION

"What's so unpleasant about being drunk?"
"You ask a glass of water."

DOUGLAS ADAMS,
The Hitchhiker's Guide to the Galaxy (1979)

Alcohol changes our perception of the world in delicious and dangerous ways. As Douglas Adams points out in the exchange between Ford Prefect and Arthur Dent above, the advantages and disadvantages of drinking and drunkenness are a matter of perspective. This collection of Tales of the Weird takes advantage of the uncertainty this ambiguity brings. Humans (and a few animals) have been seeking intoxication since—and as part of—our evolution.[*] Some anthropologists believe that the imaginative space that drunkenness and other forms of intoxication offer are partly responsible for our evolutionary "success".[†] From telling tales over a drink to help explain the world and pass on knowledge to trying new things as a result of a drink or two, the conversations, collaborations, and courage enhanced by alcohol can work wonders in our worlds. We also use alcohol for rest and relaxation at home and in close company. In the eighteenth century, Erasmus Darwin (Charles Darwin's uncle) described the benefits of alcohol at the end of the day. He said it calmed the drinker

---

[*] Although a recent study has demonstrated that the old myth of the drunken elephant eating fermented fruit from the ground is not credible, (<www.nationalgeographic.com/animals/article/news-elephants-drunk-wild-myth>), we do know that they and a range of primates enjoy human-made alcohols. (<www.discoverwildlife.com/news/why-monkeys-get-drunk>).

[†] See for example Edward Slingerland, *Drunk* (2021).

"in the approach of sleep" to allow them to ignore "external stimuli" and quieten their minds. He compared a drink in the evening to that sensation "produced in young children by rocking their cradles".* Further, one of the early words for alcohol was Aqua Vitae. Coined by the alchemists, Aqua Vitae means roughly "Water of Life" and has long been associated with magical things. The term, Aqua Vitae, went on to be used as a description for spirits (ardent spirits, as they used to be called)—in other words, strong drink. The original association with magic, medicine, and science remained, linking the Brits' favourite stimulant to the wondrous. And, of course, it can be very fun. In short, alcohol *can* make life better.

However, alcohol has a darker side and its effects span an unusually broad spectrum. In British culture we associate it with our most joyous celebrations (weddings, christenings, birthdays) and at the same time it is often held responsible for some of the worst acts in society. The following Tales of the Weird explore this darker side of alcohol. This is partly because the gothic (which usually includes the "weird") is a literary form that focuses on darkness to enlighten the reader, challenges social norms, and explores anxieties in contemporary society. As such, it is often a misunderstood force for good, or contemplation, or change. Drunkenness is an ideal tool for this kind of writing because heavy drinking can create a dark and frightening atmosphere in which normal, familiar things terrify the drinker or the witnesses. Further, drinkers can be violent, irrational beings. As Ellen Wood wrote in her temperance (anti-drink) novel, *Danesbury House* (1860), drinkers are often described in animalistic ways. Five-year-old Arthur's mother has recently been killed in a carriage accident caused by a drunken gatekeeper and he asks his aunt:

---

* Erasmus Darwin, "Of Drunkenness", *Zoonomia* (1794).

"Why did he drink?" he sobbed. "Why does anybody drink?"

"Because they are beasts," said Mrs. Philip. "And they *are* nothing else," she added, as if in apology, "when they drink themselves into that state."*

Poor Arthur bears the brunt of the explosion of negative effects that Wood links to alcohol in her prize-winning anti-drink novel. Drinking is not only responsible for bad deeds but is often used to repress bad memories. Yet, it also lowers our defence mechanisms so drinkers can be haunted by guilt. As a result, the drinker can be haunted by their misdeeds even as they try to hide from them. Think of the drinking of the pirates in *Treasure Island* (1883)—the "fifteen men on a dead man's chest" are their friends and colleagues, some murdered by them, and their response is... a bottle of rum and "yo ho ho". But the alcohol in which they seek solace deforms their bodies and minds in the process and they are visited by bad dreams and hallucinations.

I have collected for you a range of intoxicating and intoxicated weird tales from one of the peaks of British drinking in recorded history. We start with an old favourite of mine, Stevenson's "The Body-Snatcher" (1884). A re-telling of the infamous Burke and Hare murders, this short story explores how alcohol could lead a young and inexperienced man to commit crimes he would never contemplate when sober. Told from the point of view of the young medical student receiving the murdered bodies from Burke and Hare for dissection at the University, as the story continues, drunkenness torments him with a supernatural reminder of his own guilt. Rudyard Kipling and Wilkie Collins also play with the connection between drunkenness and guilt in their stories in this collection. Kipling's

---

* Ellen Wood, *Danesbury House* (1860).

"The Mark of the Beast" explores colonial guilt. Fuelled by a riotous evening of drinking, three men stagger home from a New Year's party and, on the way, one drunkenly desecrates a temple. Although told uncomfortably (particularly for a modern reader) from the white male coloniser's perspective, Kipling's story clearly concludes that in practice, colonisation is damaging everyone concerned in its disturbing conclusion. Collins's "The Ostler" (1855) explores the relationship between a married couple using a dream to cast suspicion on a wife whose dangerous behaviour includes drinking with dubious local characters. Anthony Trollope, George Cruikshank, and E. E. L. explore the dangers of the drunkard to the family and community. Trollope's "The Spotted Dog" reflects on drunkenness and class. It centres on an academic "brought low" by his drunken, working-class wife. He is entrusted with the only copy of a manuscript by the narrating editors with disastrous results. Rhoda Broughton's strange tale "Under the Cloak" is a tale of burglary on a train and features a small intoxicating bottle that is definitely not spirits. E. E. L's "Kitty's Dream" is the only gothic temperance story I have come across to date. Kitty, the child of drunken parents, recounts a dream haunted by devils and drunkenness, instantly converting her mother and father to sobriety. I have paired this with two of the most famous temperance stories of the century, George Cruikshank's "The Bottle" and "The Drunkard's Children" (1847 and 1848). The illustrations tell the bulk of the story and, as the eponymous bottle ruins the life of the family depicted, become increasingly gothic in appearance and plot. The final panel of "The Drunkard's Children" is a dramatic depiction of the daughter's suicide (she throws herself off the bridge) which has the hauntingly sad beauty of *Wuthering Heights* (1847). "How We Got Up the Glenmutchkin Railway" (1845) and "The Barber's Supper" (1837) are comic stories in which drinking is a driving force in the absurd plot, in both cases making it more rather than less believable. In William Aytoun's "Glenmutchkin Railway", drunkenness powers the plot of the story and of the railway scam the two protagonists are cooking up together. Aytoun goes as far as naming some of the invented supporters of the faux railway with drink-related names like Sir Polloxfen Tremens (a play on "delirium tremens", a contemporary name for alcoholism). In "The Barber's Supper", James White employs alcohol to both bump off the corrupt rich man of the town and to create a farcical feel as the reader follows the barber's grotesque adventures afterwards. I finish with the mythical poem by Byron, "Lines Inscribed Upon a Cup Formed from a Skull" (1808), also reflected on the cover of this collection. It is written about a real drinking cup which Byron had made for him from a skull discovered in the grounds of his home, in which he used to serve claret to his guests at dinner parties.

So cosy down in your favourite chair with a glass of something you enjoy and sample these delicious Tales of the Weird. But whatever you do, don't drink too deep, you wouldn't want to find yourself *Dead Drunk...*

PAM LOCK

A NOTE FROM THE PUBLISHER

The original short stories reprinted in the British Library Tales of the Weird series were written and published in a period ranging across the nineteenth and twentieth centuries. There are many elements of these stories which continue to entertain modern readers; however, in some cases there are also uses of language, instances of stereotyping and some attitudes expressed by narrators or characters which may not be endorsed by the publishing standards of today. We acknowledge therefore that some elements in the stories selected for reprinting may continue to make uncomfortable reading for some of our audience. With this series British Library Publishing aims to offer a new readership a chance to read some of the rare material of the British Library's collections in an affordable paperback format, to enjoy their merits and to look back into the worlds of the past two centuries as portrayed by their writers. It is not possible to separate these stories from the history of their writing and as such the following stories are presented as they were originally published with minor edits only, made for consistency of style and sense. We welcome feedback from our readers, which can be sent to the following address:

British Library Publishing
The British Library
96 Euston Road
London, NW1 2DB
United Kingdom

THE BODY-SNATCHER

Robert Louis Stevenson

Scottish author, Robert Louis Stevenson (1850–1894) wrote one of the most famous gothic stories in history: *Strange Case of Dr. Jekyll and Mr. Hyde* (1886). In a recent article, I argue that his other most famous novel, *Treasure Island* (1882), also contains essential gothic elements in the grotesque depiction of the pirates and especially their drunkenness. Stevenson was also the king of the short story and the majority of the fiction he wrote in his short lifetime was in this form. This long short story was written in between these two novels and although Stevenson wasn't sure about the story in later life, it was extremely popular at the time, and remains one of my favourites of his many short stories. On its release, the story's publication was advertised by men wearing sandwich boards bearing posters so horrible that they were banned by the Metropolitan Police.

First published in the *Pall Mall Gazette* in 1884, the story gives an alternative account of the real-life story of famous body-snatchers and murderers, Burke and Hare, who were said to have sold the corpses of 17 victims for use in the dissecting rooms of Edinburgh University between November 1827 and October 1828. The resulting criminal case was widely reported and became very famous as it intrigued, horrified, and titillated the Scottish public and the world. Sixty years later, Stevenson re-imagines the story from the point of view of the young medical students who received the stolen and murdered bodies for the dissection rooms of Edinburgh Medical School. Having studied both law and medicine briefly at Edinburgh University before his health (and disinclination?) forced him to stop, Stevenson brings the sometimes claustrophobic feeling of the small university world of that time to life in dark and disturbing ways. The doctor in charge, "Dr. K" in the story, is based on the infamous and powerful Dr. Knox of the real story, who arranged for the bodies to be purchased. Although he was never prosecuted, he lost his reputation and was eventually hounded out of Edinburgh as a result of his links with the case. He was later buried in an unmarked grave.*

As in many of his stories, Stevenson employs alcohol and intoxication to build up a believable and psychologically complex gothic atmosphere. The main character, Fettes, is a naïve medical student looking to help fund his studies with some work as an assistant in the medical school. Little does he know that he will be drawn into murder and grave-robbing in the wee small hours. Alcohol becomes a fuel to embolden him in his tasks and a balm to ease his guilty conscience until one night, the guilt becomes too much, and his intoxication leads him to a supernatural and terrifying experience.

---

* <www.nationalgalleries.org/art-and-artists/66808>.

Every night in the year, four of us sat in the small parlour of the George at Debenham—the undertaker, and the landlord, and Fettes, and myself. Sometimes there would be more; but blow high, blow low, come rain or snow or frost, we four would be each planted in his own particular arm-chair. Fettes was an old drunken Scotchman, a man of education obviously, and a man of some property, since he lived in idleness. He had come to Debenham years ago, while still young, and by a mere continuance of living had grown to be an adopted townsman. His blue camlet cloak was a local antiquity, like the church-spire. His place in the parlour at the George, his absence from church, his old, crapulous, disreputable vices, were all things of course in Debenham. He had some vague Radical opinions and some fleeting infidelities, which he would now and again set forth and emphasise with tottering slaps upon the table. He drank rum—five glasses regularly every evening; and for the greater portion of his nightly visit to the George sat, with his glass in his right hand, in a state of melancholy alcoholic saturation. We called him the Doctor, for he was supposed to have some special knowledge of medicine, and had been known, upon a pinch, to set a fracture or reduce a dislocation; but beyond these slight particulars, we had no knowledge of his character and antecedents.

One dark winter night—it had struck nine some time before the landlord joined us—there was a sick man in the George, a great neighbouring proprietor suddenly struck down with apoplexy on his way to Parliament; and the great man's still greater London doctor had been telegraphed to his bedside. It was the first time that such a thing had happened in Debenham, for the railway was but newly open, and we were all proportionately moved by the occurrence.

"He's come," said the landlord, after he had filled and lighted his pipe.

"He?" said I. "Who?—not the doctor?"

"Himself," replied our host.

"What is his name?"

"Doctor Macfarlane," said the landlord.

Fettes was far through his third tumbler, stupidly fuddled, now nodding over, now staring mazily around him; but at the last word he seemed to awaken, and repeated the name "Macfarlane" twice, quietly enough the first time, but with sudden emotion at the second.

"Yes," said the landlord, "that's his name, Doctor Wolfe Macfarlane."

Fettes became instantly sober; his eyes awoke, his voice became clear, loud, and steady, his language forcible and earnest. We were all startled by the transformation, as if a man had risen from the dead.

"I beg your pardon," he said, "I am afraid I have not been paying much attention to your talk. Who is this Wolfe Macfarlane?" And then, when he had heard the landlord out, "It cannot be, it cannot be," he added; "and yet I would like well to see him face to face."

"Do you know him, Doctor?" asked the undertaker, with a gasp.

"God forbid!" was the reply. "And yet the name is a strange one; it were too much to fancy two. Tell me, landlord, is he old?"

"Well," said the host, "he's not a young man, to be sure, and his hair is white; but he looks younger than you."

"He is older, though; years older. But," with a slap upon the table, "it's the rum you see in my face—rum and sin. This man, perhaps, may have an easy conscience and a good digestion. Conscience! Hear me speak. You would think I was some good, old, decent Christian, would you not? But no, not I; I never canted. Voltaire might have canted if he'd stood in my shoes; but the brains"—with a rattling fillip on his bald head—"the brains were clear and active, and I saw and made no deductions."

"If you know this doctor," I ventured to remark, after a somewhat awful pause, "I should gather that you do not share the landlord's good opinion."

Fettes paid no regard to me.

"Yes," he said, with sudden decision, "I must see him face to face."

There was another pause, and then a door was closed rather sharply on the first floor, and a step was heard upon the stair.

"That's the doctor," cried the landlord. "Look sharp, and you can catch him."

It was but two steps from the small parlour to the door of the old George Inn; the wide oak staircase landed almost in the street; there was room for a Turkey rug and nothing more between the threshold and the last round of the descent; but this little space was every evening brilliantly lit up, not only by the light upon the stair and the great signal-lamp below the sign, but by the warm radiance of the bar-room window. The George thus brightly advertised itself to passers-by in the cold street. Fettes walked steadily to the spot, and we, who were hanging behind, beheld the two men meet, as one of them had phrased it, face to face. Dr. Macfarlane was alert and vigorous. His white hair set off his pale and placid, although energetic, countenance. He was richly dressed in the finest of broadcloth and the whitest of linen, with a great gold watch-chain, and studs and spectacles of the same precious material. He wore a broad-folded tie, white and speckled with lilac, and he carried on his arm a comfortable driving-coat of fur. There was no doubt but he became his years, breathing, as he did, of wealth and consideration; and it was a surprising contrast to see our parlour sot—bald, dirty, pimpled, and robed in his old camlet cloak—confront him at the bottom of the stairs.

"Macfarlane!" he said somewhat loudly, more like a herald than a friend.

The great doctor pulled up short on the fourth step, as though the familiarity of the address surprised and somewhat shocked his dignity.

"Toddy Macfarlane!" repeated Fettes.

The London man almost staggered. He stared for the swiftest of seconds at the man before him, glanced behind him with a sort of scare, and then in a startled whisper, "Fettes!" he said, "You!"

"Ay," said the other, "me! Did you think I was dead too? We are not so easy shut of our acquaintance."

"Hush, hush!" exclaimed the doctor. "Hush, hush! this meeting is so unexpected—I can see you are unmanned. I hardly knew you, I confess, at first; but I am overjoyed—overjoyed to have this opportunity. For the present it must be how-d'ye-do and good-bye in one, for my fly is waiting, and I must not fail the train; but you shall—let me see—yes—you shall give me your address, and you can count on early news of me. We must do something for you, Fettes. I fear you are out at elbows; but we must see to that for auld lang syne, as once we sang at suppers."

"Money!" cried Fettes; "money from you! The money that I had from you is lying where I cast it in the rain."

Dr. Macfarlane had talked himself into some measure of superiority and confidence, but the uncommon energy of this refusal cast him back into his first confusion.

A horrible, ugly look came and went across his almost venerable countenance. "My dear fellow," he said, "be it as you please; my last thought is to offend you. I would intrude on none. I will leave you my address, however—"

"I do not wish it—I do not wish to know the roof that shelters you," interrupted the other. "I heard your name; I feared it might be you; I wished to know if, after all, there were a God; I know now that there is none. Begone!"

He still stood in the middle of the rug, between the stair and doorway; and the great London physician, in order to escape, would be forced to step to one side. It was plain that he hesitated before the thought of this humiliation. White as he was, there was a dangerous glitter in his spectacles; but while he still paused uncertain, he became aware that the driver of his fly was peering in from the street at this unusual scene and caught a glimpse at the same time of our little body from the parlour, huddled by the corner of the bar. The presence of so many witnesses decided him at once to flee. He crouched together, brushing on the wainscot, and made a dart like a serpent, striking for the door. But his tribulation was not yet entirely at an end, for even as he was passing Fettes clutched him by the arm and these words came in a whisper, and yet painfully distinct, "Have you seen it again?"

The great rich London doctor cried out aloud with a sharp, throttling cry; he dashed his questioner across the open space, and, with his hands over his head, fled out of the door like a detected thief. Before it had occurred to one of us to make a movement the fly was already rattling toward the station. The scene was over like a dream, but the dream had left proofs and traces of its passage. Next day the servant found the fine gold spectacles broken on the threshold, and that very night we were all standing breathless by the bar-room window, and Fettes at our side, sober, pale, and resolute in look.

"God protect us, Mr. Fettes!" said the landlord, coming first into possession of his customary senses. "What in the universe is all this? These are strange things you have been saying."

Fettes turned toward us; he looked us each in succession in the face. "See if you can hold your tongues," said he. "That man Macfarlane is not safe to cross; those that have done so already have repented it too late."

And then, without so much as finishing his third glass, far less waiting for the other two, he bade us good-bye and went forth, under the lamp of the hotel, into the black night.

We three turned to our places in the parlour, with the big red fire and four clear candles; and as we recapitulated what had passed, the first chill of our surprise soon changed into a glow of curiosity. We sat late; it was the latest session I have known in the old George. Each man, before we parted, had his theory that he was bound to prove; and none of us had any nearer business in this world than to track out the past of our condemned companion, and surprise the secret that he shared with the great London doctor. It is no great boast, but I believe I was a better hand at worming out a story than either of my fellows at the George; and perhaps there is now no other man alive who could narrate to you the following foul and unnatural events.

In his young days Fettes studied medicine in the schools of Edinburgh. He had talent of a kind, the talent that picks up swiftly what it hears and readily retails it for its own. He worked little at home; but he was civil, attentive, and intelligent in the presence of his masters. They soon picked him out as a lad who listened closely and remembered well; nay, strange as it seemed to me when I first heard it, he was in those days well favoured, and pleased by his exterior. There was, at that period, a certain extramural teacher of anatomy, whom I shall here designate by the letter K. His name was subsequently too well known. The man who bore it skulked through the streets of Edinburgh in disguise, while the mob that applauded at the execution of Burke called loudly for the blood of his employer. But Mr. K—— was then at the top of his vogue; he enjoyed a popularity due partly to his own talent and address, partly to the incapacity of his rival, the university professor. The students, at least, swore by his name, and Fettes believed himself, and was believed by others, to have laid the foundations of success when he had acquired the favour of this meteorically famous man. Mr. K—— was a *bon vivant* as well as an accomplished teacher; he liked a sly illusion no less than a careful preparation. In both capacities Fettes enjoyed and deserved his notice, and by the second year of his attendance he held the half-regular position of second demonstrator or sub-assistant in his class.

In this capacity the charge of the theatre and lecture-room devolved in particular upon his shoulders. He had to answer for the cleanliness of the premises and the conduct of the other students, and it was a part of his duty to supply, receive, and divide the various subjects. It was with a view to this last—at that time very delicate—affair that he was lodged by Mr. K—— in the same wynd, and at last in the same building, with the dissecting-rooms. Here, after a night of turbulent pleasures, his hand still tottering, his sight still misty and confused, he would be called out of bed in the black hours before the winter dawn by the unclean and desperate interlopers who supplied the table. He would open the door to these men, since infamous throughout the land. He would help them with their tragic burden, pay them their sordid price, and remain alone, when they were gone, with the unfriendly relics of humanity. From such a scene he would return to snatch another hour or two of slumber, to repair the abuses of the night, and refresh himself for the labours of the day.

Few lads could have been more insensible to the impressions of a life thus passed among the ensigns of mortality. His mind was closed against all general considerations. He was incapable of interest in the fate and fortunes of another, the slave of his own desires and low ambitions. Cold, light, and selfish in the last resort, he had that modicum of prudence, miscalled morality, which keeps a man from inconvenient drunkenness or punishable theft. He coveted, besides, a measure of consideration from his masters and his fellow-pupils, and he had no desire to fail conspicuously in the external parts of life. Thus he made it his pleasure to gain some distinction in his studies, and day after day rendered unimpeachable eye-service to his employer, Mr. K——. For his day of work he indemnified himself by nights of roaring, blackguardly enjoyment; and when that balance had been struck, the organ that he called his conscience declared itself content.

The supply of subjects was a continual trouble to him as well as to his master. In that large and busy class, the raw material of the anatomists kept perpetually running out; and the business thus rendered necessary was not only unpleasant in itself, but threatened dangerous consequences to all who were concerned. It was the policy of Mr. K—— to ask no questions in his dealings with the trade. "They bring the body, and we pay the price," he used to say, dwelling on the alliteration—"*quid pro quo*." And, again, and somewhat profanely, "Ask no questions," he would tell his assistants, "for conscience' sake." There was no understanding that the subjects were provided by the crime of murder. Had that idea been broached to him in words, he would have recoiled in horror; but the lightness of his speech upon so grave a matter was, in itself, an offence against good manners, and a temptation to the men with whom he dealt. Fettes, for instance, had often remarked to himself upon the singular freshness of the bodies. He had been struck again and again by the hang-dog, abominable looks of the ruffians who came to him before the dawn; and putting things together clearly in his private thoughts, he perhaps attributed a meaning too immoral and too categorical to the unguarded counsels of his master. He understood his duty, in short, to have three branches: to take what was brought, to pay the price, and to avert the eye from any evidence of crime.

One November morning this policy of silence was put sharply to the test. He had been awake all night with a racking toothache—pacing his room like a caged beast or throwing himself in fury on his bed—and had fallen at last into that profound, uneasy slumber that so often follows on a night of pain, when he was awakened by the third or fourth angry repetition of the concerted signal. There was a thin, bright moonshine; it was bitter cold, windy, and frosty; the town had not yet awakened, but an indefinable stir already preluded the noise and business of the day. The ghouls had come later than usual, and they seemed more than usually eager to be gone. Fettes, sick with sleep, lighted them upstairs. He heard their grumbling Irish voices through a dream; and as they stripped the sack from their sad merchandise he leaned dozing, with his shoulder propped against the wall; he had to shake himself to find the men their money. As he did so his eyes lighted on the dead face. He started; he took two steps nearer, with the candle raised.

"God Almighty!" he cried. "That is Jane Galbraith!"

The men answered nothing, but they shuffled nearer the door.

"I know her, I tell you," he continued. "She was alive and hearty yesterday. It's impossible she can be dead; it's impossible you should have got this body fairly."

"Sure, sir, you're mistaken entirely," said one of the men.

But the other looked Fettes darkly in the eyes, and demanded the money on the spot.

It was impossible to misconceive the threat or to exaggerate the danger. The lad's heart failed him. He stammered some excuses, counted out the sum, and saw his hateful visitors depart. No sooner were they gone than he hastened to confirm his doubts. By a dozen unquestionable marks he identified the girl he had jested with the day before. He saw, with horror, marks upon her body that might well betoken violence. A panic seized him, and he took refuge in his room. There he reflected at length over the discovery that he had made; considered soberly the bearing of Mr. K——'s instructions and the danger to himself of interference in so serious a business, and at last, in sore perplexity, determined to wait for the advice of his immediate superior, the class assistant.

This was a young doctor, Wolfe Macfarlane, a high favourite among all the reckless students, clever, dissipated, and unscrupulous to the last degree. He had travelled and studied abroad. His manners were agreeable and a little forward. He was an authority on the stage, skilful on the ice or the links with skate or golf-club; he dressed with nice audacity, and, to put the finishing touch upon his glory, he kept a gig and a strong trotting-horse. With Fettes he was on terms of intimacy; indeed, their relative positions called for some community of life; and when subjects were scarce the pair would drive far into the country in Macfarlane's gig, visit and desecrate some lonely graveyard, and return before dawn with their booty to the door of the dissecting-room.

On that particular morning Macfarlane arrived somewhat earlier than his wont. Fettes heard him, and met him on the stairs, told him his story, and showed him the cause of his alarm. Macfarlane examined the marks on her body.

"Yes," he said with a nod, "it looks fishy."

"Well, what should I do?" asked Fettes.

"Do?" repeated the other. "Do you want to do anything? Least said soonest mended, I should say."

"Some one else might recognise her," objected Fettes. "She was as well known as the Castle Rock."

"We'll hope not," said Macfarlane, "and if anybody does—well, you didn't, don't you see, and there's an end. The fact is, this has been going on too long. Stir up the mud, and you'll get K—— into the most unholy trouble; you'll be in a shocking box yourself. So will I, if you come to that. I should like to know how any one of us would look, or what the devil we should have to say for ourselves, in any Christian witness-box. For me, you know there's one thing certain—that, practically speaking, all our subjects have been murdered."

"Macfarlane!" cried Fettes.

"Come now!" sneered the other. "As if you hadn't suspected it yourself!"

"Suspecting is one thing—"

"And proof another. Yes, I know; and I'm as sorry as you are this should have come here," tapping the body with his cane. "The next best thing for me is not to recognise it; and," he added coolly, "I don't. You may, if you please. I don't dictate, but I think a man of the world would do as I do; and I may add, I fancy that is what K—— would look for at our hands. The question is, Why did he choose us two for his assistants? And I answer, because he didn't want old wives."

This was the tone of all others to affect the mind of a lad like Fettes. He agreed to imitate Macfarlane. The body of the unfortunate girl was duly dissected, and no one remarked or appeared to recognise her.

One afternoon, when his day's work was over, Fettes dropped into a popular tavern and found Macfarlane sitting with a stranger. This was a small man, very pale and dark, with coal-black eyes. The cut of his features gave a promise of intellect and refinement which was but feebly realised in his manners, for he proved, upon a nearer acquaintance, coarse, vulgar, and stupid. He exercised, however, a very remarkable control over Macfarlane; issued orders like the Great Bashaw; became inflamed at the least discussion or delay, and commented rudely on the servility with which he was obeyed. This most offensive person took a fancy to Fettes on the spot, plied him with drinks, and honoured him with unusual confidences on his past career. If a tenth part of what he confessed were true, he was a very loathsome rogue; and the lad's vanity was tickled by the attention of so experienced a man.

"I'm a pretty bad fellow myself," the stranger remarked, "but Macfarlane is the boy—Toddy Macfarlane I call him. Toddy, order your friend another glass." Or it might be, "Toddy, you jump up and shut the door." "Toddy hates me," he said again. "Oh yes, Toddy, you do!"

"Don't you call me that confounded name," growled Macfarlane.

"Hear him! Did you ever see the lads play knife? He would like to do that all over my body," remarked the stranger.

"We medicals have a better way than that," said Fettes. "When we dislike a dead friend of ours, we dissect him."

Macfarlane looked up sharply, as though this jest were scarcely to his mind.

The afternoon passed. Gray, for that was the stranger's name, invited Fettes to join them at dinner, ordered a feast so sumptuous that the tavern was thrown into commotion, and when all was done commanded Macfarlane to settle the bill. It was late before they separated; the man Gray was incapably drunk. Macfarlane, sobered by his fury, chewed the cud of the money he had been forced to squander and the slights he had been obliged to swallow. Fettes, with various liquors singing in his head, returned home with devious footsteps and a mind entirely in abeyance. Next day Macfarlane was absent from the class, and Fettes smiled to himself as he imagined him still squiring the intolerable Gray from tavern to tavern. As soon as the hour of liberty had struck he posted from place to place in quest of his last night's companions. He could find them, however, nowhere; so returned early to his rooms, went early to bed, and slept the sleep of the just.

At four in the morning he was awakened by the well-known signal. Descending to the door, he was filled with astonishment to find Macfarlane with his gig, and in the gig one of those long and ghastly packages with which he was so well acquainted.

"What?" he cried. "Have you been out alone? How did you manage?"

But Macfarlane silenced him roughly, bidding him turn to business. When they had got the body upstairs and laid it on the table, Macfarlane made at first as if he were going away. Then he paused and seemed to hesitate; and then, "You had better look at the face," said he, in tones of some constraint. "You had better," he repeated, as Fettes only stared at him in wonder.

"But where, and how, and when did you come by it?" cried the other.

"Look at the face," was the only answer.

Fettes was staggered; strange doubts assailed him. He looked from the young doctor to the body, and then back again. At last, with a start, he did as he was bidden. He had almost expected the sight that met his eyes, and yet the shock was cruel. To see, fixed in the rigidity of death and naked on that coarse layer of sackcloth, the man whom he had left well clad and full of meat and sin upon the threshold of a tavern, awoke, even in the thoughtless Fettes, some of the terrors of the conscience. It was a *cras tibi* which re-echoed in his soul, that two whom he had known should have come to lie upon these icy tables.

Yet these were only secondary thoughts. His first concern regarded Wolfe. Unprepared for a challenge so momentous, he knew not how to look his comrade in the face. He durst not meet his eye, and he had neither words nor voice at his command.

It was Macfarlane himself who made the first advance. He came up quietly behind and laid his hand gently but firmly on the other's shoulder.

"Richardson," said he, "may have the head."

Now Richardson was a student who had long been anxious for that portion of the human subject to dissect. There was no answer, and the murderer resumed: "Talking of business, you must pay me; your accounts, you see, must tally."

Fettes found a voice, the ghost of his own: "Pay you!" he cried. "Pay you for that?"

"Why, yes, of course you must. By all means and on every possible account, you must," returned the other. "I dare not give it for nothing, you dare not take it for nothing; it would compromise us both. This is another case like Jane Galbraith's. The more things are wrong the more we must act as if all were right. Where does old K—— keep his money?"

"There," answered Fettes hoarsely, pointing to a cupboard in the corner.

"Give me the key, then," said the other, calmly, holding out his hand.

There was an instant's hesitation, and the die was cast. Macfarlane could not suppress a nervous twitch, the infinitesimal mark of an immense relief, as he felt the key between his fingers. He opened the cupboard, brought out pen and ink and a paper-book that stood in one compartment, and separated from the funds in a drawer a sum suitable to the occasion.

"Now, look here," he said, "there is the payment made—first proof of your good faith: first step to your security. You have now to clinch it by a second. Enter the payment in your book, and then you for your part may defy the devil."

The next few seconds were for Fettes an agony of thought; but in balancing his terrors it was the most immediate that triumphed. Any future difficulty seemed almost welcome if he could avoid a present quarrel with Macfarlane. He set down the candle which he had been carrying all this time, and with a steady hand entered the date, the nature, and the amount of the transaction.

"And now," said Macfarlane, "it's only fair that you should pocket the lucre. I've had my share already. By the bye, when a man of the world falls into a bit of luck, has a few shillings extra in his pocket—I'm ashamed to speak of it, but there's a rule of conduct in the case. No treating, no purchase of expensive class-books, no squaring of old debts; borrow, don't lend."

"Macfarlane," began Fettes, still somewhat hoarsely, "I have put my neck in a halter to oblige you."

"To oblige me?" cried Wolfe. "Oh, come! You did, as near as I can see the matter, what you downright had to do in self-defence. Suppose I got into trouble, where would you be? This second little matter flows clearly from the first. Mr. Gray is the continuation of Miss Galbraith. You can't begin and then stop. If you begin, you must keep on beginning; that's the truth. No rest for the wicked."

A horrible sense of blackness and the treachery of fate seized hold upon the soul of the unhappy student.

"My God!" he cried, "but what have I done? and when did I begin? To be made a class assistant—in the name of reason, where's the harm in that? Service wanted the position; Service might have got it. Would *he* have been where *I* am now?"

"My dear fellow," said Macfarlane, "what a boy you are! What harm *has* come to you? What harm *can* come to you if you hold your tongue? Why, man, do you know what this life is? There are two squads of us—the lions and the lambs. If you're a lamb, you'll come to lie upon these tables like Gray or Jane Galbraith; if you're a lion, you'll live and drive a horse like me, like K——, like all the world with any wit or courage. You're staggered at the first. But look at K——! My dear fellow, you're clever, you have pluck. I like you, and K—— likes you. You were born to lead the hunt; and I tell you, on my honour and my experience of life, three days from now you'll laugh at all these scarecrows like a High School boy at a farce."

And with that Macfarlane took his departure and drove off up the wynd in his gig to get under cover before daylight. Fettes was thus left alone with his regrets. He saw the miserable peril in which he stood involved. He saw, with inexpressible dismay, that there was no limit to his weakness, and that, from concession to concession, he had fallen from the arbiter of Macfarlane's destiny to his paid and helpless accomplice. He would have given the world to have been a little braver at the time, but it did not occur to him that he might still be brave. The secret of Jane Galbraith and the cursed entry in the day-book closed his mouth.

Hours passed; the class began to arrive; the members of the unhappy Gray were dealt out to one and to another, and received without remark. Richardson was made happy with the head; and before the hour of freedom rang Fettes trembled with exultation to perceive how far they had already gone toward safety.

For two days he continued to watch, with increasing joy, the dreadful process of disguise.

On the third day Macfarlane made his appearance. He had been ill, he said; but he made up for lost time by the energy with which he directed the students. To Richardson in particular he extended the most valuable assistance and advice, and that student, encouraged by the praise of the demonstrator, burned high with ambitious hopes, and saw the medal already in his grasp.

Before the week was out Macfarlane's prophecy had been fulfilled. Fettes had outlived his terrors and had forgotten his baseness. He began to plume himself upon his courage, and had so arranged the story in his mind that he could look back on these events with an unhealthy pride. Of his accomplice he saw but little. They met, of course, in the business of the class; they received their orders together from Mr. K——. At times they had a word or two in private, and Macfarlane was from first to last particularly kind and jovial. But it was plain that he avoided any reference to their common secret; and even when Fettes whispered to him that he had cast in his lot with the lions and foresworn the lambs, he only signed to him smilingly to hold his peace.

At length an occasion arose which threw the pair once more into a closer union. Mr. K—— was again short of subjects; pupils were eager, and it was a part of this teacher's pretensions to be always well supplied. At the same time there came the news of a burial in the rustic graveyard of Glencorse. Time has little changed the place in question. It stood then, as now, upon a cross road, out of call of human habitations, and buried fathom deep in the foliage of six cedar trees. The cries of the sheep upon the neighbouring hills, the streamlets upon either hand, one loudly singing among pebbles, the other dripping furtively from pond to pond, the stir of the wind in mountainous old flowering chestnuts, and once in seven days the voice of the bell and the old tunes of the precentor, were the only sounds that disturbed the silence around the rural church. The Resurrection Man—to use a byname of the period—was not to be deterred by any of the sanctities of customary piety. It was part of his trade to despise and desecrate the scrolls and trumpets of old tombs, the paths worn by the feet of worshippers and mourners, and the offerings and the inscriptions of bereaved affection. To rustic neighbourhoods, where love is more than commonly tenacious, and where some bonds of blood or fellowship unite the entire society of a parish, the body-snatcher, far from being repelled by natural respect, was attracted by the ease and safety of the task. To bodies that had been laid in earth, in joyful expectation of a far different awakening, there came that hasty, lamp-lit, terror-haunted resurrection of the spade and mattock. The coffin was forced, the cerements torn, and the melancholy relics, clad in sackcloth, after being rattled for hours on moonless byways, were at length exposed to uttermost indignities before a class of gaping boys.

Somewhat as two vultures may swoop upon a dying lamb, Fettes and Macfarlane were to be let loose upon a grave in that green and quiet resting-place. The wife of a farmer, a woman who had lived for sixty years, and been known for nothing but good butter and a godly conversation, was to be rooted from her grave at midnight and carried, dead and naked, to that far-away city that she had always honoured with her Sunday's best; the place beside her family was to be empty till the crack of doom; her innocent and almost venerable members to be exposed to that last curiosity of the anatomist.

Late one afternoon the pair set forth, well wrapped in cloaks and furnished with a formidable bottle. It rained without remission—a cold, dense, lashing rain. Now and again there blew a puff of wind, but these sheets of falling water kept it down. Bottle and all, it was a sad and silent drive as far as Penicuik, where they were to spend the evening. They stopped once, to hide their implements in a thick bush not far from the churchyard, and once again at the Fisher's

Tryst, to have a toast before the kitchen fire and vary their nips of whisky with a glass of ale. When they reached their journey's end the gig was housed, the horse was fed and comforted, and the two young doctors in a private room sat down to the best dinner and the best wine the house afforded. The lights, the fire, the beating rain upon the window, the cold, incongruous work that lay before them, added zest to their enjoyment of the meal. With every glass their cordiality increased. Soon Macfarlane handed a little pile of gold to his companion.

"A compliment," he said. "Between friends these little d—d accommodations ought to fly like pipe-lights."

Fettes pocketed the money, and applauded the sentiment to the echo. "You are a philosopher," he cried. "I was an ass till I knew you. You and K—— between you, by the Lord Harry! but you'll make a man of me."

"Of course we shall," applauded Macfarlane. "A man? I tell you, it required a man to back me up the other morning. There are some big, brawling, forty-year-old cowards who would have turned sick at the look of the d—d thing; but not you—you kept your head. I watched you."

"Well, and why not?" Fettes thus vaunted himself. "It was no affair of mine. There was nothing to gain on the one side but disturbance, and on the other I could count on your gratitude, don't you see?" And he slapped his pocket till the gold pieces rang.

Macfarlane somehow felt a certain touch of alarm at these unpleasant words. He may have regretted that he had taught his young companion so successfully, but he had no time to interfere, for the other noisily continued in this boastful strain:—

"The great thing is not to be afraid. Now, between you and me, I don't want to hang—that's practical; but for all cant, Macfarlane,

I was born with a contempt. Hell, God, Devil, right, wrong, sin, crime, and all the old gallery of curiosities—they may frighten boys, but men of the world, like you and me, despise them. Here's to the memory of Gray!"

It was by this time growing somewhat late. The gig, according to order, was brought round to the door with both lamps brightly shining, and the young men had to pay their bill and take the road. They announced that they were bound for Peebles, and drove in that direction till they were clear of the last houses of the town; then, extinguishing the lamps, returned upon their course, and followed a by-road toward Glencorse. There was no sound but that of their own passage, and the incessant, strident pouring of the rain. It was pitch dark; here and there a white gate or a white stone in the wall guided them for a short space across the night; but for the most part it was at a foot pace, and almost groping, that they picked their way through that resonant blackness to their solemn and isolated destination. In the sunken woods that traverse the neighbourhood of the burying-ground the last glimmer failed them, and it became necessary to kindle a match and re-illumine one of the lanterns of the gig. Thus, under the dripping trees, and environed by huge and moving shadows, they reached the scene of their unhallowed labours.

They were both experienced in such affairs, and powerful with the spade; and they had scarce been twenty minutes at their task before they were rewarded by a dull rattle on the coffin lid. At the same moment Macfarlane, having hurt his hand upon a stone, flung it carelessly above his head. The grave, in which they now stood almost to the shoulders, was close to the edge of the plateau of the graveyard; and the gig lamp had been propped, the better to illuminate their labours, against a tree, and on the immediate verge of the steep bank descending to the stream. Chance had taken a sure aim with the stone. Then came a clang of broken glass; night fell upon them; sounds alternately dull and ringing announced the bounding of the lantern down the bank, and its occasional collision with the trees. A stone or two, which it had dislodged in its descent, rattled behind it into the profundities of the glen; and then silence, like night, resumed its sway; and they might bend their hearing to its utmost pitch, but naught was to be heard except the rain, now marching to the wind, now steadily falling over miles of open country.

They were so nearly at an end of their abhorred task that they judged it wisest to complete it in the dark. The coffin was exhumed and broken open; the body inserted in the dripping sack and carried between them to the gig; one mounted to keep it in its place, and the other, taking the horse by the mouth, groped along by wall and bush until they reached the wider road by the Fisher's Tryst. Here was a faint, diffused radiancy, which they hailed like daylight; by that they pushed the horse to a good pace and began to rattle along merrily in the direction of the town.

They had both been wetted to the skin during their operations, and now, as the gig jumped among the deep ruts, the thing that stood propped between them fell now upon one and now upon the other. At every repetition of the horrid contact each instinctively repelled it with the greater haste; and the process, natural although it was, began to tell upon the nerves of the companions. Macfarlane made some ill-favoured jest about the farmer's wife, but it came hollowly from his lips, and was allowed to drop in silence. Still their unnatural burden bumped from side to side; and now the head would be laid, as if in confidence, upon their shoulders, and now the drenching sackcloth would flap icily about their faces. A creeping chill began to possess the soul of Fettes. He peered at the bundle, and it seemed somehow larger than at first. All over the country-side, and from every degree of distance, the farm dogs accompanied their passage with tragic ululations; and it grew and grew upon his mind that some unnatural miracle had been accomplished, that some nameless change had befallen the dead body, and that it was in fear of their unholy burden that the dogs were howling.

"For God's sake," said he, making a great effort to arrive at speech, "for God's sake, let's have a light!"

Seemingly Macfarlane was affected in the same direction; for, though he made no reply, he stopped the horse, passed the reins to his companion, got down, and proceeded to kindle the remaining lamp. They had by that time got no farther than the cross-road down to Auchenclinny. The rain still poured as though the deluge were returning, and it was no easy matter to make a light in such a world of wet and darkness. When at last the flickering blue flame had been transferred to the wick and began to expand and clarify, and shed a wide circle of misty brightness round the gig, it became possible for the two young men to see each other and the thing they had along with them. The rain had moulded the rough sacking to the outlines of the body underneath; the head was distinct from the trunk, the shoulders plainly modelled; something at once spectral and human riveted their eyes upon the ghastly comrade of their drive.

For some time Macfarlane stood motionless, holding up the lamp. A nameless dread was swathed, like a wet sheet, about the body, and tightened the white skin upon the face of Fettes; a fear that was meaningless, a horror of what could not be, kept mounting to his brain. Another beat of the watch, and he had spoken. But his comrade forestalled him.

"That is not a woman," said Macfarlane, in a hushed voice.

"It was a woman when we put her in," whispered Fettes.

"Hold that lamp," said the other. "I must see her face."

And as Fettes took the lamp his companion untied the fastenings of the sack and drew down the cover from the head. The light fell very clear upon the dark, well-moulded features and smooth-shaven cheeks of a too familiar countenance, often beheld in dreams of both of these young men. A wild yell rang up into the night; each leaped from his own side into the roadway: the lamp fell, broke, and was extinguished; and the horse, terrified by this unusual commotion, bounded and went off toward Edinburgh at a gallop, bearing along with it, sole occupant of the gig, the body of the dead and long-dissected Gray.

THE SPOTTED DOG

Anthony Trollope

Anthony Trollope (1815–1882) predominantly wrote novels and is best known for the satirical *Chronicles of Barsetshire* series (adapted for television in 1982 as *The Barchester Chronicles*). Indeed, he was so prolific that new novels were still being published for several years after he died—a prospect that he looked forward to with amusement during his life. This short story was originally published in *Saint Paul's Magazine* in March–April 1870 and then included in his short story collection *Editor's Tales*, all written from the point of view of a pair of editors. Trollope was interested in the effects of heavy drinking and the relationship between drunkenness and social mobility (both "up" and "down"). He also explored the subject of suicide in his works, having considered taking his own life at 14 years old.[*] These characterisations of suicidal characters often feature heavy drinking, as a means of making the suicidal character more susceptible to their self-destructive thoughts and emboldening the suicide to act.[†]

"The Spotted Dog" chronicles their experiences with an academic whom they ask to index the large and sprawling work by a rural

---

[*] He writes about this in his *An Autobiography* (1883).
[†] See for example Roger Scatcherd's drunken despair in *Doctor Thorne* (1858) and Melmotte's drinking binge prior to his suicide in *The Way We Live Now* (1874).

clergyman. The academic has fallen on hard times after marrying a working-class woman disapproved of by his family who (apparently) leads him into drunkenness. Concerned about the safety of the manuscript, they agree that it will be guarded in his local public house. However, his relationship with alcohol becomes increasingly problematic and leads to disaster for him, his family, and the sole copy of the manuscript.

PART I
The Attempt

Some few years since we received the following letter;—

"Dear Sir,

"I write to you for literary employment, and I implore you to provide me with it if it be within your power to do so. My capacity for such work is not small, and my acquirements are considerable. My need is very great, and my views in regard to remuneration are modest. I was educated at ——, and was afterwards a scholar of —— College, Cambridge. I left the university without a degree, in consequence of a quarrel with the college tutor. I was rusticated, and not allowed to return. After that I became for awhile a student for the Chancery Bar. I then lived for some years in Paris, and I understand and speak French as though it were my own language. For all purposes of literature I am equally conversant with German. I read Italian. I am, of course, familiar with Latin. In regard to Greek I will only say that I am less ignorant of it than nineteen-twentieths of our national scholars. I am well read in modern and ancient history. I have especially studied political economy. I have not neglected other matters necessary to the education of an enlightened man,—unless it be natural philosophy. I can write English, and can write it with rapidity. I am a poet;—at least, I so esteem myself. I am not a believer. My character will not bear investigation;—in saying which, I mean you to understand, not that I steal or cheat, but that I live in a dirty lodging, spend many of my hours in a public-house, and cannot pay tradesmen's bills where tradesmen have been found to trust me. I have a wife and four children,—which burden forbids me to free myself from all care by a bare bodkin. I am just past forty, and since I quarrelled with my family because I could not understand The Trinity, I have never been the owner of a ten-pound note. My wife was not a lady. I married her because I was determined to take refuge from the conventional thraldom of so-called 'gentlemen' amidst the liberty of the lower orders. My life, of course, has been a mistake. Indeed, to live at all,—is it not a folly?

"I am at present employed on the staff of two or three of the 'Penny Dreadfuls.' Your august highness in literature has perhaps never heard of a 'Penny Dreadful.' I write for them matter, which we among ourselves call 'blood and nastiness,'—and which is copied from one to another. For this I am paid forty-five shillings a week. For thirty shillings a week I will do any work that you may impose upon me for the term of six months. I write this letter as a last effort to rescue myself from the filth of my present position, but I entertain no hope of any success. If you ask it I will come and see you; but do not send for me unless you mean to employ me, as I am ashamed of myself. I live at No. 3, Cucumber Court, Gray's Inn Lane;—but if you write, address to the care of Mr. Grimes, the Spotted Dog, Liquorpond Street. Now I have told you my whole life, and you may help me if you will. I do not expect an answer.

"YOURS TRULY,

"JULIUS MACKENZIE."

Indeed he had told us his whole life, and what a picture of a life he had drawn! There was something in the letter which compelled attention. It was impossible to throw it, half read, into the waste-paper basket, and to think of it not at all. We did read it, probably twice, and then put ourselves to work to consider how much of it might be true and how much false. Had the man been a boy at ——, and then a scholar of his college? We concluded that, so far, the narrative was true. Had he abandoned his dependence on wealthy friends from conscientious scruples, as he pretended; or had other and less creditable reasons caused the severance? On that point we did not quite believe him. And then, as to those assertions made by himself in regard to his own capabilities,—how far did they gain credence with us? We think that we believed them all, making some small discount,—with the exception of that one in which he proclaimed himself to be a poet. A man may know whether he understands French, and be quite ignorant whether the rhymed lines which he produces are or are not poetry. When he told us that he was an infidel, and that his character would not bear investigation, we went with him altogether. His allusion to suicide we regarded as a foolish boast. We gave him credit for the four children, but were not certain about the wife. We quite believed the general assertion of his impecuniosity. That stuff about "conventional thraldom" we hope we took at its worth. When he told us that his life had been a mistake he spoke to us Gospel truth.

Of the "Penny Dreadfuls," and of "blood and nastiness," so called, we had never before heard, but we did not think it remarkable that a man so gifted as our correspondent should earn forty-five shillings a week by writing for the cheaper periodicals. It did not, however, appear to us probable that any one so remunerated would be willing to leave that engagement for another which should give him only thirty shillings. When he spoke of the "filth of his present position," our heart began to bleed for him. We know what it is so well, and can fathom so accurately the degradation of the educated man who, having been ambitious in the career of literature, falls into that slough of despond by which the profession of literature is almost surrounded. There we were with him, as brothers together. When we came to Mr. Grimes and the Spotted Dog, in Liquorpond Street, we thought that we had better refrain from answering the letter,—by which decision on our part he would not, according to his own statement, be much disappointed. Mr. Julius Mackenzie! Perhaps at this very time rich uncles and aunts were buttoning up their pockets against the sinner because of his devotion to the Spotted Dog. There are well-to-do people among the Mackenzies. It might be the case that that heterodox want of comprehension in regard to The Trinity was the cause of it; but we have observed that in most families, grievous as are doubts upon such sacred subjects, they are not held to be cause of hostility so invincible as is a thorough-going devotion to a Spotted Dog. If the Spotted Dog had brought about these troubles, any interposition from ourselves would be useless.

For twenty-four hours we had given up all idea of answering the letter; but it then occurred to us that men who have become disreputable as drunkards do not put forth their own abominations when making appeals for aid. If this man were really given to drink he would hardly have told us of his association with the public-house. Probably he was much at the Spotted Dog, and hated himself for being there. The more we thought of it the more we fancied that the gist of his letter might be true. It seemed that the man had desired to tell the truth as he himself believed it.

It so happened that at that time we had been asked to provide an index to a certain learned manuscript in three volumes. The intended publisher of the work had already procured an index from a professional compiler of such matters; but the thing had been so badly done that it could not be used. Some knowledge of the classics was required, though it was not much more than a familiarity with the names of Latin and Greek authors, to which perhaps should be added some acquaintance, with the names also, of the better-known editors and commentators. The gentleman who had had the task in hand had failed conspicuously, and I had been told by my enterprising friend Mr. X——, the publisher, that £25 would be freely paid on the proper accomplishment of the undertaking. The work, apparently so trifling in its nature, demanded a scholar's acquirements, and could hardly be completed in less than two months. We had snubbed the offer, saying that we should be ashamed to ask an educated man to give his time and labour for so small a remuneration;—but to Mr. Julius Mackenzie £25 for two months' work would manifestly be a godsend. If Mr. Julius Mackenzie did in truth possess the knowledge for which he gave himself credit; if he was, as he said, "familiar with Latin," and was "less ignorant of Greek than nineteen-twentieths of our national scholars," he might perhaps be able to earn this £25. We certainly knew no one else who could and who would do the work properly for that money. We therefore wrote to Mr. Julius Mackenzie, and requested his presence. Our note was short, cautious, and also courteous. We regretted that a man so gifted should be driven by stress of circumstances to such need. We could undertake nothing, but if it would not put him to too much trouble to call upon us, we might perhaps be able to suggest something to him. Precisely at the hour named Mr. Julius Mackenzie came to us.

We well remember his appearance, which was one unutterably painful to behold. He was a tall man, very thin,—thin we might say as a whipping-post, were it not that one's idea of a whipping-post conveys erectness and rigidity, whereas this man, as he stood before us, was full of bends, and curves, and crookedness. His big head seemed to lean forward over his miserably narrow chest, His back was bowed, and his legs were crooked and tottering. He had told us that he was over forty, but we doubted, and doubt now, whether he had not added something to his years, in order partially to excuse the wan, worn weariness of his countenance. He carried an infinity of thick, ragged, wild, dirty hair, dark in colour, though not black, which age had not yet begun to grizzle. He wore a miserable attempt at a beard, stubbly, uneven, and half shorn,—as though it had been cut down within an inch of his chin with blunt scissors. He had two ugly projecting teeth, and his cheeks were hollow. His eyes were deep-set, but very bright, illuminating his whole face; so that it was impossible to look at him and to think him to be one wholly insig- nificant. His eyebrows were large and shaggy, but well formed, not meeting across the brow, with single, stiffly-projecting hairs,—a pair of eyebrows which added much strength to his countenance. His nose was long and well shaped,—but red as a huge carbuncle. The moment we saw him we connected that nose with the Spotted Dog. It was not a blotched nose, not a nose covered with many carbuncles, but a brightly red, smooth, well-formed nose, one glowing carbuncle in itself. He was dressed in a long brown great-coat, which was but- toned up round his throat, and which came nearly to his feet. The binding of the coat was frayed, the buttons were half uncovered, the button-holes were tattered, the velvet collar had become party- coloured with dirt and usage. It was in the month of December, and a great-coat was needed; but this great-coat looked as though it were worn because other garments were not at his command. Not an inch of linen or even of flannel shirt was visible. Below his coat we could only see his broken boots and the soiled legs of his trousers, which had reached that age which in trousers defies description. When we looked at him we could not but ask ourselves whether this man had been born a gentleman and was still a scholar. And yet there was that in his face which prompted us to believe the account he had given of himself. As we looked at him we felt sure that he possessed keen intellect, and that he was too much of a man to boast of acquirements which he did not believe himself to possess. We shook hands with him, asked him to sit down, and murmured something of our sorrow that he should be in distress.

"I am pretty well used to it," said he. There was nothing mean in his voice;—there was indeed a touch of humour in it, and in his manner there was nothing of the abjectness of supplication. We had his letter in our hands, and we read a portion of it again as he sat opposite to us. We then remarked that we did not understand how he, having a wife and family dependent on him, could offer to give up a third of his income with the mere object of changing the nature of his work. "You don't know what it is," said he, "to write for the 'Penny Dreadfuls.' I'm at it seven hours a day, and hate the very words that I write. I cursed myself afterwards for sending that letter. I know that to hope is to be an ass. But I did send it, and here I am."

We looked at his nose and felt that we must be careful before we suggested to our learned friend Dr. —— to put his manuscript into the hands of Mr. Julius Mackenzie. If it had been a printed book the attempt might have been made without much hazard, but our friend's work, which was elaborate, and very learned, had not yet reached the honours of the printing-house. We had had our own doubts whether it might ever assume the form of a real book; but our friend, who was a wealthy as well as a learned man, was, as yet, very determined. He desired, at any rate, that the thing should be perfected, and his publisher had therefore come to us offering £25 for the codification and index. Were anything other than good to befall his manuscript, his lamentations would be loud, not on his own score,—but on behalf of learning in general. It behoved us therefore to be cautious. We pretended to read the letter again, in order that we might gain time for a decision, for we were greatly frightened by that gleaming nose.

Let the reader understand that the nose was by no means Bardolphian. If we have read Shakespeare aright Bardolph's nose was a thing of terror from its size as well as its hue. It was a mighty vat, into which had ascended all the divinest particles distilled from the cellars of the hostelrie in Eastcheap. Such at least is the idea which stage representations have left upon all our minds. But the nose now before us was a well-formed nose, would have been a commanding nose,—for the power of command shows itself much in the nasal organ,—had it not been for its colour. While we were thinking of this, and doubting much as to our friend's manuscript, Mr. Mackenzie interrupted us. "You think I am a drunkard," said he. The man's mother-wit had enabled him to read our inmost thoughts.

As we looked up the man had risen from his chair, and was standing over us. He loomed upon us very tall, although his legs were crooked, and his back bent. Those piercing eyes, and that nose which almost assumed an air of authority as he carried it, were a great way above us. There seemed to be an infinity of that old brown greatcoat. He had divined our thoughts, and we did not dare to contradict him. We felt that a weak, vapid, unmanly smile was creeping over our face. We were smiling as a man smiles who intends to imply some contemptuous assent with the self-depreciating comment of his companion. Such a mode of expression is in our estimation most cowardly, and most odious. We had not intended it, but we knew that the smile had pervaded us. "Of course you do," said he. "I was a drunkard, but I am not one now. It doesn't matter;—only I wish you hadn't sent for me. I'll go away at once."

So saying, he was about to depart, but we stopped him. We assured him with much energy that we did not mean to offend him. He protested that there was no offence. He was too well used to that kind of thing to be made "more than wretched by it." Such was his heart-breaking phrase. "As for anger, I've lost all that long ago. Of course you take me for a drunkard, and I should still be a drunkard, only—"

"Only what?" I asked.

"It don't matter," said he. "I need not trouble you with more than I have said already. You haven't got anything for me to do, I suppose?" Then I explained to him that I had something he might do, if I could venture to entrust him with the work. With some trouble I got him to sit down again, and to listen while I explained to him the circumstances. I had been grievously afflicted when he alluded to his former habit of drinking,—a former habit as he himself now stated,—but I entertained no hesitation in raising questions as to his erudition. I felt almost assured that his answers would be satisfactory, and that no discomfiture would arise from such questioning. We were quickly able to perceive that we at any rate could not examine him in classical literature. As soon as we mentioned the name and nature of the work he went off at score, and satisfied us amply that he was familiar at least with the title-pages of editions. We began, indeed, to fear whether he might not be too caustic a critic on our own friend's performance. "Dr. —— is only an amateur himself," said we, deprecating in advance any such exercise of the red-nosed man's too severe erudition. "We never get much beyond dilettanteism here," said he, "as far as Greek and Latin are concerned." What a terrible man he would have been could he have got upon the staff of the Saturday Review, instead of going to the Spotted Dog!

We endeavoured to bring the interview to an end by telling him that we would consult the learned Doctor from whom the manuscript had emanated; and we hinted that a reference would be of course acceptable. His impudence,—or perhaps we should rather call it his straightforward sincere audacity,—was unbounded. "Mr. Grimes of the Spotted Dog knows me better than any one else," said he. We blew the breath out of our mouth with astonishment. "I'm not asking you to go to him to find out whether I know Latin and Greek," said Mr. Mackenzie. "You must find that out for yourself." We assured him that we thought we had found that out. "But he can tell you that I won't pawn your manuscript." The man was so grim and brave that he almost frightened us. We hinted, however, that literary reference should be given. The gentleman who paid him forty-five shillings a week,—the manager, in short, of the "Penny Dreadful,"—might tell us something of him. Then he wrote for us a name on a scrap of paper, and added to it an address in the close vicinity of Fleet Street, at which we remembered to have seen the title of a periodical which we now knew to be a "Penny Dreadful."

Before he took his leave he made us a speech, again standing up over us, though we also were on our legs. It was that bend in his neck, combined with his natural height, which gave him such an air of superiority in conversation. He seemed to overshadow us, and to have his own way with us, because he was enabled to look down upon us. There was a footstool on our hearth-rug, and we remember to have attempted to stand upon that, in order that we might escape this supervision; but we stumbled, and had to kick it from us, and something was added to our sense of inferiority by this little failure. "I don't expect much from this," he said. "I never do expect much. And I have misfortunes independent of my poverty which make it impossible that I should be other than a miserable wretch."

"Bad health?" we asked.

"No;—nothing absolutely personal;—but never mind. I must not trouble you with more of my history. But if you can do this thing for me, it may be the means of redeeming me from utter degradation." We then assured him that we would do our best, and he left us with a promise that he would call again on that day week.

The first step which we took on his behalf was one the very idea of which had at first almost moved us to ridicule. We made inquiry respecting Mr. Julius Mackenzie, of Mr. Grimes, the landlord of the Spotted Dog. Though Mr. Grimes did keep the Spotted Dog, he might be a man of sense and, possibly, of conscience. At any rate he would tell us something, or confirm our doubts by refusing to tell us anything. We found Mr. Grimes seated in a very neat little back parlour, and were peculiarly taken by the appearance of a lady in a little cap and black silk gown, whom we soon found to be Mrs. Grimes. Had we ventured to employ our intellect in personifying for ourselves an imaginary Mrs. Grimes as the landlady of a Spotted Dog public-house in Liquorpond Street, the figure we should have built up for ourselves would have been the very opposite of that which this lady presented to us. She was slim, and young, and pretty, and had pleasant little tricks of words, in spite of occasional slips in her grammar, which made us almost think that it might be our duty to come very often to the Spotted Dog to inquire about Mr. Julius Mackenzie. Mr. Grimes was a man about forty,—fully ten years the senior of his wife,—with a clear grey eye, and a mouth and chin from which we surmised that he would be competent to clear the Spotted Dog of unruly visitors after twelve o'clock, whenever it might be his wish to do so. We soon made known our request. Mr. Mackenzie had come to us for literary employment. Could they tell us anything about Mr. Mackenzie?

"He's as clever an author, in the way of writing and that kind of thing, as there is in all London," said Mrs. Grimes with energy. Perhaps her opinion ought not to have been taken for much, but it had its weight. We explained, however, that at the present moment we were specially anxious to know something of the gentleman's character and mode of life. Mr. Grimes, whose manner to us was quite courteous, sat silent, thinking how to answer us. His more impulsive and friendly wife was again ready with her assurance. "There ain't an honester gentleman breathing;—and I say he is a gentleman, though he's that poor he hasn't sometimes a shirt to his back."

"I don't think he's ever very well off for shirts," said Mr. Grimes.

"I wouldn't be slow to give him one of yours, John, only I know he wouldn't take it," said Mrs. Grimes. "Well now, look here, sir;— we've that feeling for him that our young woman there would draw anything for him he'd ask,—money or no money. She'd never venture to name money to him if he wanted a glass of anything,—hot or cold, beer or spirits. Isn't that so, John?"

"She's fool enough for anything as far as I know," said Mr. Grimes.

"She ain't no fool at all; and I'd do the same if I was there;—and so'd you, John. There is nothing Mackenzie'd ask as he wouldn't give him," said Mrs. Grimes, pointing with her thumb over her shoulder to her husband, who was standing on the hearth-rug;—"that is, in the way of drawing liquor, and refreshments, and such like. But he never raised a glass to his lips in this house as he didn't pay for, nor yet took a biscuit out of that basket. He's a gentleman all over, is Mackenzie."

It was strong testimony; but still we had not quite got at the bottom of the matter. "Doesn't he raise a great many glasses to his lips?" we asked.

"No he don't," said Mrs. Grimes,—"only in reason."

"He's had misfortunes," said Mr. Grimes.

"Indeed he has," said the lady,—"what I call the very trouble-somest of troubles. If you was troubled like him, John, where'd you be?"

"I know where you'd be," said John.

"He's got a bad wife, sir; the worst as ever was," continued Mrs. Grimes. "Talk of drink;—there is nothing that woman wouldn't do for it. She'd pawn the very clothes off her children's back in mid-winter to get it. She'd rob the food out of her husband's mouth for a drop of gin. As for herself,—she ain't no woman's notions left of keeping herself any way. She'd as soon be picked out of the gutter as not;—and as for words out of her mouth or clothes on her back, she hasn't got, sir, not an item of a female's feelings left about her."

Mrs. Grimes had been very eloquent, and had painted the "troublesomest of all troubles" with glowing words. This was what the wretched man had come to by marrying a woman who was not a lady in order that he might escape the "conventional thraldom" of gentility! But still the drunken wife was not all. There was the evidence of his own nose against himself, and the additional fact that he had acknowledged himself to have been formerly a drunkard. "I suppose he has drunk, himself?" we said.

"He has drunk, in course," said Mrs. Grimes.

"The world has been pretty rough with him, sir," said Mr. Grimes.

"But he don't drink now," continued the lady. "At least if he do, we don't see it. As for her, she wouldn't show herself inside our door."

"It ain't often that man and wife draws their milk from the same cow," said Mr. Grimes.

"But Mackenzie is here every day of his life," said Mrs. Grimes. "When he's got a sixpence to pay for it, he'll come in here and have a glass of beer and a bit of something to eat. We does make him a little extra welcome, and that's the truth of it. We knows what he is, and we knows what he was. As for book learning, sir;—it don't matter what language it is, it's all as one to him. He knows 'em all round just as I know my catechism."

"Can't you say fairer than that for him, Polly?" asked Mr. Grimes.

"Don't you talk of catechisms, John; nor yet of nothing else as a man ought to set his mind to;—unless it is keeping the Spotted Dog. But as for Mackenzie;—he knows off by heart whole books full of learning. There was some furreners here as come from,—I don't know where it was they come from, only it wasn't France, nor yet Germany, and he talked to them just as though he hadn't been born in England at all. I don't think there ever was such a man for knowing things. He'll go on with poetry out of his own head till you think it comes from him like web from a spider." We could not help thinking of the wonderful companionship which there must have been in that parlour while the reduced man was spinning his web and Mrs. Grimes, with her needlework lying idle in her lap, was sitting by, listening with rapt admiration. In passing by the Spotted Dog one would not imagine such a scene to have its existence within. But then so many things do have existence of which we imagine nothing!

Mr. Grimes ended the interview. "The fact is, sir, if you can give him employment better than what he has now, you'll be helping a man who has seen better days, and who only wants help to see 'em again. He's got it all there," and Mr. Grimes put his finger up to his head.

"He's got it all here too," said Mrs. Grimes, laying her hand upon her heart. Hereupon we took our leave, suggesting to these excellent friends that if it should come to pass that we had further dealings with Mr. Mackenzie we might perhaps trouble them again. They assured us that we should always be welcome, and Mr. Grimes himself saw us to the door, having made profuse offers of such good cheer as the house afforded. We were upon the whole much taken with the Spotted Dog.

From thence we went to the office of the "Penny Dreadful," in the vicinity of Fleet Street. As we walked thither we could not but think of Mrs. Grimes' words. The troublesomest of troubles! We acknowledged to ourselves that they were true words. Can there be any trouble more troublesome than that of suffering from the shame inflicted by a degraded wife? We had just parted from Mr. Grimes,—not, indeed, having seen very much of him in the course of our interview;—but little as we had seen, we were sure that he was assisted in his position by a buoyant pride in that he called himself the master, and owner, and husband of Mrs. Grimes. In the very step with which he passed in and out of his own door you could see that there was nothing that he was ashamed of about his household. When abroad he could talk of his "missus" with a conviction that the picture which the word would convey to all who heard him would redound to his honour. But what must have been the reflections of Julius Mackenzie when his mind dwelt upon his wife? We remembered the words of his letter. "I have a wife and four children, which burden forbids me to free myself from all care with a bare bodkin." As we thought of them, and of the story which had been told to us at the Spotted Dog, they lost that tone of rhodomontade with which they had invested themselves when we first read them. A wife who is indifferent to being picked out of the gutter, and who will pawn her children's clothes for gin, must be a trouble than which none can be more troublesome.

We did not find that we ingratiated ourselves with the people at the office of the periodical for which Mr. Mackenzie worked; and yet we endeavoured to do so, assuming in our manner and tone something of the familiarity of a common pursuit. After much delay we came upon a gentleman sitting in a dark cupboard, who twisted round his stool to face us while he spoke to us. We believe that he was the editor of more than one "Penny Dreadful," and that as many as a dozen serial novels were being issued to the world at the same time under his supervision. "Oh!" said he, "so you're at that game, are you?" We assured him that we were at no game at all, but were simply influenced by a desire to assist a distressed scholar. "That be blowed," said our brother. "Mackenzie's doing as well here as he'll do anywhere. He's a drunken blackguard, when all's said and done. So you're going to buy him up, are you? You won't keep him long,—and then he'll have to starve." We assured the gentleman that we had no desire to buy up Mr. Mackenzie; we explained our ideas as to the freedom of the literary profession, in accordance with which Mr. Mackenzie could not be wrong in applying to us for work; and we especially deprecated any severity on our brother's part towards the man, more especially begging that nothing might be decided, as we were far from thinking it certain that we could provide Mr. Mackenzie with any literary employment. "That's all right," said our brother, twisting back his stool. "He can't work for both of us;—that's all. He has his bread here regular, week after week; and I don't suppose you'll do as much as that for him." Then we went away, shaking the dust off our feet, and wondering much at the great development of literature which latter years have produced. We had not even known of the existence of these papers;—and yet there they were, going forth into the hands of hundreds of thousands of readers, all of whom were being, more or less, instructed in their modes of life and manner of thinking by the stories which were thus brought before them.

But there might be truth in what our brother had said to us. Should Mr. Mackenzie abandon his present engagement for the sake of the job which we proposed to put in his hands, might he not thereby injure rather than improve his prospects? We were acquainted with only one learned doctor desirous of having his manuscripts codified and indexed at his own expense. As for writing for the periodical with which we were connected, we knew enough of the business to be aware that Mr. Mackenzie's gifts of erudition would very probably not so much assist him in attempting such work as would his late training act against him. A man might be able to read and even talk a dozen languages,—"just as though he hadn't been born in England at all,"—and yet not write the language with which we dealt after the fashion which suited our readers. It might be that he would fly much above our heads, and do work infinitely too big for us. We did not regard our own heads as being very high. But, for such altitude as they held, a certain class of writing was adapted. The gentleman whom we had just left would require, no doubt, altogether another style. It was probable that Mr. Mackenzie had already fitted himself to his present audience. And, even were it not so, we could not promise him forty-five shillings a week, or even that thirty shillings for which he asked. There is nothing more dangerous than the attempt to befriend a man in middle life by transplanting him from one soil to another.

When Mr. Mackenzie came to us again we endeavoured to explain all this to him. We had in the meantime seen our friend the Doctor, whose beneficence of spirit in regard to the unfortunate man of letters was extreme. He was charmed with our account of the man, and saw with his mind's eye the work, for the performance of which he was pining, perfected in a manner that would be a blessing to the scholars of all future ages. He was at first anxious to ask Julius Mackenzie down to his rectory, and, even after we had explained to him that this would not at present be expedient, was full of a dream of future friendship with a man who would be able to discuss the digamma with him, who would have studied Greek metres, and have an opinion of his own as to Porson's canon. We were in possession of the manuscript, and had our friend's authority for handing it over to Mr. Mackenzie.

He came to us according to appointment, and his nose seemed to be redder than ever. We thought that we discovered a discouraging flavour of spirits in his breath. Mrs. Grimes had declared that he drank,—only in reason; but the ideas of the wife of a publican,—even though that wife were Mrs. Grimes,—might be very different from our own as to what was reasonable in that matter. And as we looked at him he seemed to be more rough, more ragged, almost more wretched than before. It might be that, in taking his part with my brother of the "Penny Dreadful," with the Doctor, and even with myself in thinking over his claims, I had endowed him with higher qualities than I had been justified in giving to him. As I considered him and his appearance I certainly could not assure myself that he looked like a man worthy to be trusted. A policeman, seeing him at a street corner, would have had an eye upon him in a moment. He rubbed himself together within his old coat, as men do when they come out of gin-shops. His eye was as bright as before, but we thought that his mouth was meaner, and his nose redder. We were almost disenchanted with him. We said nothing to him at first about the Spotted Dog, but suggested to him our fears that if he undertook work at our hands he would lose the much more permanent employment which he got from the gentleman whom we had seen in the cupboard. We then explained to him that we could promise to him no continuation of employment.

The violence with which he cursed the gentleman who had sat in the cupboard appalled us, and had, we think, some effect in bringing back to us that feeling of respect for him which we had almost lost. It may be difficult to explain why we respected him because he cursed and swore horribly. We do not like cursing and swearing, and were any of our younger contributors to indulge themselves after that fashion in our presence we should, at the very least,—frown upon them.

We did not frown upon Julius Mackenzie, but stood up, gazing into his face above us, again feeling that the man was powerful. Perhaps we respected him because he was not in the least afraid of us. He went on to assert that he cared not,—not a straw, we will say,—for the gentleman in the cupboard. He knew the gentleman in the cupboard very well; and the gentleman in the cupboard knew him. As long as he took his work to the gentleman in the cupboard, the gentleman in the cupboard would be only too happy to purchase that work at the rate of sixpence for a page of manuscript containing two hundred and fifty words. That was his rate of payment for prose fiction, and at that rate he could earn forty-five shillings a week. He wasn't afraid of the gentleman in the cupboard. He had had some words with the gentleman in the cupboard before now, and they two understood each other very well. He hinted, moreover, that there were other gentlemen in other cupboards; but with none of them could he advance beyond forty-five shillings a week. For this he had to sit, with his pen in his hand, seven hours seven days a week, and the very paper, pens, and ink came to fifteenpence out of the money. He had struck for wages once, and for a halcyon month or two had carried his point of sevenpence halfpenny a page; but the gentlemen in the cupboards had told him that it could not be. They, too, must live. His matter was no doubt attractive; but any price above sixpence a page unfitted it for their market. All this Mr. Julius Mackenzie explained to us with much violence of expression. When I named Mrs. Grimes to him the tone of his voice was altered. "Yes;" said he,—"I thought they'd say a word for me. They're the best friends I've got now. I don't know that you ought quite to believe her, for I think she'd perhaps tell a lie to do me a service." We assured him that we did believe every word Mrs. Grimes had said to us.

After much pausing over the matter we told him that we were empowered to trust him with our friend's work, and the manuscript was produced upon the table. If he would undertake the work and perform it, he should be paid £8: 6s.: 8d. for each of the three volumes as they were completed. And we undertook, moreover, on our own responsibility, to advance him money in small amounts through the hands of Mrs. Grimes, if he really settled himself to the task. At first he was in ecstasies, and as we explained to him the way in which the index should be brought out and the codification performed, he turned over the pages rapidly, and showed us that he understood at any rate the nature of the work to be done. But when we came to details he was less happy. In what workshop was this new work to be performed? There was a moment in which we almost thought of telling him to do the work in our own room; but we hesitated, luckily, remembering that his continual presence with us for two or three months would probably destroy us altogether. It appeared that his present work was done sometimes at the Spotted Dog, and sometimes at home in his lodgings. He said not a word to us about his wife, but we could understand that there would be periods in which to work at home would be impossible to him. He did not pretend to deny that there might be danger on that score, nor did he ask permission to take the entire manuscript at once away to his abode. We knew that if he took part he must take the whole, as the work could not be done in parts. Counter references would be needed. "My circumstances are bad;—very bad indeed," he said. We expressed the great trouble to which we should be subjected if any evil should happen to the manuscript. "I will give it up," he said, towering over us again, and shaking his head. "I cannot expect that I should be trusted." But we were determined that it should not be given up. Sooner than give the matter up we would make some arrangement by hiring a place in which he might work. Even though we were to pay ten shillings a week for a room for him out of the money, the bargain would be a good one for him. At last we determined that we would pay a second visit to the Spotted Dog, and consult Mrs. Grimes. We felt that we should have a pleasure in arranging together with Mrs. Grimes any scheme of benevolence on behalf of this unfortunate and remarkable man. So we told him that we would think over the matter, and send a letter to his address at the Spotted Dog, which he should receive on the following morning. He then gathered himself up, rubbed himself together again inside his coat, and took his departure.

As soon as he was gone we sat looking at the learned Doctor's manuscript, and thinking of what we had done. There lay the work of years, by which our dear and venerable old friend expected that he would take rank among the great commentators of modern times. We, in truth, did not anticipate for him all the glory to which he looked forward. We feared that there might be disappointment. Hot discussion on verbal accuracies or on rules of metre are perhaps not so much in vogue now as they were a hundred years ago. There might be disappointment and great sorrow; but we could not with equanimity anticipate the prevention of this sorrow by the possible loss or destruction of the manuscript which had been entrusted to us. The Doctor himself had seemed to anticipate no such danger. When we told him of Mackenzie's learning and misfortunes, he was eager at once that the thing should be done, merely stipulating that he should have an interview with Mr. Mackenzie before he returned to his rectory.

That same day we went to the Spotted Dog, and found Mrs. Grimes alone. Mackenzie had been there immediately after leaving our room, and had told her what had taken place. She was full of the subject and anxious to give every possible assistance. She confessed at once that the papers would not be safe in the rooms inhabited by Mackenzie and his wife. "He pays five shillings a week," she said, "for a wretched place round in Cucumber Court. They are all huddled together, any way; and how he manages to do a thing at all there,—in the way of author-work,—is a wonder to everybody. Sometimes he can't, and then he'll sit for hours together at the little table in our tap-room." We went into the tap-room and saw the little table. It was a wonder indeed that any one should be able to compose and write tales of imagination in a place so dreary, dark, and ill-omened. The little table was hardly more than a long slab or plank, perhaps eighteen inches wide. When we visited the place there were two brewers' draymen seated there, and three draggled, wretched-looking women. The carters were eating enormous hunches of bread and bacon, which they cut and put into their mouths slowly, solemnly, and in silence. The three women were seated on a bench, and when I saw them had no signs of festivity before them. It must be presumed that they had paid for something, or they would hardly have been allowed to sit there. "It's empty now," said Mrs. Grimes, taking no immediate notice of the men or of the women; "but sometimes he'll sit writing in that corner, when there's such a jabber of voices as you wouldn't hear a cannon go off over at Reid's, and that thick with smoke you'd a'most cut it with a knife. Don't he, Peter?" The man whom she addressed endeavoured to prepare himself for answer by swallowing at the moment three square inches of bread and bacon, which he had just put into his mouth. He made an awful effort, but failed; and, failing, nodded his head three times. "They all know him here, sir," continued Mrs. Grimes. "He'll go on writing, writing, writing, for hours together; and nobody'll say nothing to him. Will they, Peter?" Peter, who was now half-way through the work he had laid out for himself, muttered some inarticulate grunt of assent.

We then went back to the snug little room inside the bar. It was quite clear to me that the man could not manipulate the Doctor's manuscript, of which he would have to spread a dozen sheets before him at the same time, in the place I had just visited. Even could he have occupied the chamber alone, the accommodation would not have been sufficient for the purpose. It was equally clear that he could not be allowed to use Mrs. Grimes' snuggery. "How are we to get a place for him?" said I, appealing to the lady. "He shall have a place," she said, "I'll go bail; he shan't lose the job for want of a workshop." Then she sat down and began to think it over. I was just about to propose the hiring of some decent room in the neighbourhood, when she made a suggestion, which I acknowledge startled me. "I'll have a big table put into my own bedroom," said she, "and he shall do it there. There ain't another hole or corner about the place as'd suit; and he can lay the gentleman's papers all about on the bed, square and clean and orderly. Can't he now? And I can see after 'em, as he don't lose 'em. Can't I now?"

By this time there had sprung up an intimacy between ourselves and Mrs. Grimes which seemed to justify an expression of the doubt which I then threw on the propriety of such a disarrangement of her most private domestic affairs. "Mr. Grimes will hardly approve of that," we said.

"Oh, John won't mind. What'll it matter to John as long as Mackenzie is out in time for him to go to bed? We ain't early birds, morning or night,—that's true. In our line folks can't be early. But from ten to six there's the room, and he shall have it. Come up and see, sir." So we followed Mrs. Grimes up the narrow staircase to the marital bower. "It ain't large, but there'll be room for the table, and for him to sit at it;—won't there now?"

It was a dark little room, with one small window looking out under the low roof, and facing the heavy high dead wall of the brewery opposite. But it was clean and sweet, and the furniture in it was all solid and good, old-fashioned, and made of mahogany. Two or three of Mrs. Grimes' gowns were laid upon the bed, and other portions of her dress were hung on pegs behind the doors. The only untidy article in the room was a pair of "John's" trousers, which he had failed to put out of sight. She was not a bit abashed, but took them up and folded them and patted them, and laid them in the capacious wardrobe. "We'll have all these things away," she said, "and then he can have all his papers out upon the bed just as he pleases."

We own that there was something in the proposed arrangement which dismayed us. We also were married, and what would our wife have said had we proposed that a contributor,—even a contributor not red-nosed and seething with gin,—that any best-disciplined contributor should be invited to write an article within the precincts of our sanctum? We could not bring ourselves to believe that Mr. Grimes would authorise the proposition. There is something holy about the bedroom of a married couple; and there would be a special desecration in the continued presence of Mr. Julius Mackenzie. We thought it better that we should explain something of all this to her. "Do you know," we said, "this seems to be hardly prudent?"

"Why not prudent?" she asked.

"Up in your bedroom, you know! Mr. Grimes will be sure to dislike it."

"What,—John! Not he. I know what you're a-thinking of, Mr. ——," she said. "But we're different in our ways than what you are. Things to us are only just what they are. We haven't time, nor yet money, nor perhaps edication, for seemings and thinkings as you have. If you was travelling out amongst the wild Injeans, you'd ask any one to have a bit in your bedroom as soon as look at 'em, if you'd got a bit for 'em to eat. We're travelling among wild Injeans all our lives, and a bedroom ain't no more to us than any other room. Mackenzie shall come up here, and I'll have the table fixed for him, just there by the window." I hadn't another word to say to her, and I could not keep myself from thinking for many an hour afterwards, whether it may not be a good thing for men, and for women also, to believe that they are always travelling among wild Indians.

When we went down Mr. Grimes himself was in the little parlour. He did not seem at all surprised at seeing his wife enter the room from above accompanied by a stranger. She at once began her story, and told the arrangement which she proposed,—which she did, as I observed, without any actual request for his sanction. Looking at Mr. Grimes' face, I thought that he did not quite like it; but he accepted it, almost without a word, scratching his head and raising his eyebrows. "You know, John, he could no more do it at home than he could fly," said Mrs. Grimes.

"Who said he could do it at home?"

"And he couldn't do it in the tap-room;—could he? If so, there ain't no other place, and so that's settled." John Grimes again scratched his head, and the matter was settled. Before we left the house Mackenzie himself came in, and was told in our presence of the accommodation which was to be prepared for him. "It's just like you, Mrs. Grimes," was all he said in the way of thanks. Then Mrs. Grimes made her bargain with him somewhat sternly. He should have the room for five hours a day,—ten till three, or twelve till five; but he must settle which, and then stick to his hours. "And I won't have nothing up there in the way of drink," said John Grimes.

"Who's asking to have drink there?" said Mackenzie.

"You're not asking now, but maybe you will. I won't have it, that's all."

"That shall be all right, John," said Mrs. Grimes, nodding her head.

"Women are that soft,—in the way of judgment,—that they'll go and do a'most anything, good or bad, when they've got their feelings up." Such was the only rebuke which in our hearing Mr. Grimes administered to his pretty wife. Mackenzie whispered something to the publican, but Grimes only shook his head. We understood it all thoroughly. He did not like the scheme, but he would not contradict his wife in an act of real kindness. We then made an appointment with the scholar for meeting our friend and his future patron at our rooms, and took our leave of the Spotted Dog. Before we went, however, Mrs. Grimes insisted on producing some cherry-bounce, as she called it, which, after sundry refusals on our part, was brought in on a small round shining tray, in a little bottle covered all over with gold sprigs, with four tiny glasses similarly ornamented. Mrs. Grimes poured out the liquor, using a very sparing hand when she came to the glass which was intended for herself. We find it, as a rule, easier to talk with the Grimeses of the world than to eat with them or to drink with them. When the glass was handed to us we did not know whether or no we were expected to say something. We waited, however, till Mr. Grimes and Mackenzie had been provided with their glasses. "Proud to see you at the Spotted Dog, Mr. ——," said Grimes. "That we are," said Mrs. Grimes, smiling at us over her almost imperceptible drop of drink. Julius Mackenzie just bobbed his head, and swallowed the cordial at a gulp,—as a dog does a lump of meat, leaving the impression on his friends around him that he has not got from it half the enjoyment which it might have given him had he been a little more patient in the process. I could not but think that had Mackenzie allowed the cherry-bounce to trickle a little in his palate, as I did myself, it would have gratified him more than it did in being chucked down his throat with all the impetus which his elbow could give to the glass. "That's tidy tipple," said Mr. Grimes, winking his eye. We acknowledged that it was tidy. "My mother made it, as used to keep the Pig and Magpie, at Colchester," said Mrs. Grimes.

In this way we learned a good deal of Mrs. Grimes' history. Her very earliest years had been passed among wild Indians.

Then came the interview between the Doctor and Mr. Mackenzie. We must confess that we greatly feared the impression which our younger friend might make on the elder. We had of course told the Doctor of the red nose, and he had accepted the information with a smile. But he was a man who would feel the contamination of contact with a drunkard, and who would shrink from an unpleasant association. There are vices of which we habitually take altogether different views in accordance with the manner in which they are brought under our notice. This vice of drunkenness is often a joke in the mouths of those to whom the thing itself is a horror. Even before our boys we talk of it as being rather funny, though to see one of them funny himself would almost break our hearts. The learned commentator had accepted our account of the red nose as though it were simply a part of the undeserved misery of the wretched man; but should he find the wretched man to be actually redolent of gin his feelings might be changed. The Doctor was with us first, and the volumes of the MS. were displayed upon the table. The compiler of them, as he lifted here a page and there a page, handled them with the gentleness of a lover. They had been exquisitely arranged, and were very fair. The pagings, and the margins, and the chapterings, and all the complementary paraphernalia of authorship, were perfect. "A lifetime, my friend; just a lifetime!" the Doctor had said to us, speaking of his own work while we were waiting for the man to whose hands was to be entrusted the result of so much labour and scholarship. We wished at that moment that we had never been called on to interfere in the matter.

Mackenzie came, and the introduction was made. The Doctor was a gentleman of the old school, very neat in his attire,—dressed in perfect black, with knee-breeches and black gaiters, with a closely-shorn chin, and an exquisitely white cravat. Though he was in truth simply the rector of his parish, his parish was one which entitled him to call himself a dean, and he wore a clerical rosette on his hat. He was a well-made, tall, portly gentleman, with whom to take the slightest liberty would have been impossible. His well-formed full face was singularly expressive of benevolence, but there was in it too an air of command which created an involuntary respect. He was a man whose means were ample, and who could afford to keep two curates, so that the appanages of a Church dignitary did in some sort belong to him. We doubt whether he really understood what work meant,—even when he spoke with so much pathos of the labour of his life; but he was a man not at all exacting in regard to the work of others, and who was anxious to make the world as smooth and rosy to those around him as it had been to himself. He came forward, paused a moment, and then shook hands with Mackenzie. Our work had been done, and we remained in the background during the interview. It was now for the Doctor to satisfy himself with the scholarship,—and, if he chose to take cognisance of the matter, with the morals of his proposed assistant.

Mackenzie himself was more subdued in his manner than he had been when talking with ourselves. The Doctor made a little speech, standing at the table with one hand on one volume and the other on another. He told of all his work, with a mixture of modesty as to the thing done, and self-assertion as to his interest in doing it, which was charming. He acknowledged that the sum proposed for the aid which he required was inconsiderable;—but it had been fixed by the proposed publisher. Should Mr. Mackenzie find that the labour was long he would willingly increase it. Then he commenced a conversation respecting the Greek dramatists, which had none of the air or tone of an examination, but which still served the purpose of enabling Mackenzie to show his scholarship. In that respect there was no doubt that the ragged, red-nosed, disreputable man, who stood there longing for his job, was the greater proficient of the two. We never discovered that he had had access to books in later years; but his memory of the old things seemed to be perfect. When it was suggested that references would be required, it seemed that he did know his way into the library of the British Museum. "When I wasn't quite so shabby," he said boldly, "I used to be there." The Doctor instantly produced a ten-pound note, and insisted that it should be taken in advance. Mackenzie hesitated, and we suggested that it was premature; but the Doctor was firm. "If an old scholar mayn't assist one younger than himself," he said, "I don't know when one man may aid another. And this is no alms. It is simply a pledge for work to be done." Mackenzie took the money, muttering something of an assurance that as far as his ability went, the work should be done well. "It should certainly," he said, "be done diligently."

When money had passed, of course the thing was settled; but in truth the bank-note had been given, not from judgment in settling the matter, but from the generous impulse of the moment. There was, however, no receding. The Doctor expressed by no hint a doubt as to the safety of his manuscript. He was by far too fine a gentleman to give the man whom he employed pain in that direction. If there were risk, he would now run the risk. And so the thing was settled.

We did not, however, give the manuscript on that occasion into Mackenzie's hands, but took it down afterwards, locked in an old despatch box of our own, to the Spotted Dog, and left the box with the key of it in the hands of Mrs. Grimes. Again we went up into that lady's bedroom, and saw that the big table had been placed by the window for Mackenzie's accommodation. It so nearly filled the room, that, as we observed, John Grimes could not get round at all to his side of the bed. It was arranged that Mackenzie was to begin on the morrow.

PART II
The Result

During the next month we saw a good deal of Mr. Julius Mackenzie, and made ourselves quite at home in Mrs. Grimes' bedroom. We went in and out of the Spotted Dog as if we had known that establishment all our lives, and spent many a quarter of an hour with the hostess in her little parlour, discussing the prospects of Mr. Mackenzie and his family. He had procured for himself decent, if not exactly new, garments out of the money so liberally provided by my learned friend the Doctor, and spent much of his time in the library of the British Museum. He certainly worked very hard, for he did not altogether abandon his old engagement. Before the end of the first month the index of the first volume, nearly completed, had been sent down for the inspection of the Doctor, and had been returned with ample eulogium and some little criticism. The criticisms Mackenzie answered by letter, with true scholarly spirit, and the Doctor was delighted. Nothing could be more pleasant to him than a correspondence, prolonged almost indefinitely, as to the respective merits of a *rò* or a *rōv,* or on the demand for a spondee or an iamb. When he found that the work was really in industrious hands, he ceased to be clamorous for early publication, and gave us to understand privately that Mr. Mackenzie was not to be limited to the sum named. The matter of remuneration was, indeed, left very much to ourselves, and Mackenzie had certainly found a most efficient friend in the author whose works had been confided to his hands.

All this was very pleasant, and Mackenzie throughout that month worked very hard. According to the statements made to me by Mrs. Grimes he took no more gin than what was necessary for a hard-working man. As to the exact quantity of that cordial which she imagined to be beneficial and needful, we made no close inquiry. He certainly kept himself in a condition for work, and so far all went on happily. Nevertheless, there was a terrible skeleton in the cupboard,—or rather out of the cupboard, for the skeleton could not be got to hide itself. A certain portion of his prosperity reached the hands of his wife, and she was behaving herself worse than ever. The four children had been covered with decent garments under Mrs. Grimes' care, and then Mrs. Mackenzie had appeared at the Spotted Dog, loudly demanding a new outfit for herself. She came not only once, but often, and Mr. Grimes was beginning to protest that he saw too much of the family. We had become very intimate with Mrs. Grimes, and she did not hesitate to confide to us her fears lest "John should cut up rough" before the thing was completed. "You see," she said, "it is against the house, no doubt, that woman coming nigh it." But still she was firm, and Mackenzie was not disturbed in the possession of the bedroom. At last Mrs. Mackenzie was provided with some articles of female attire;—and then, on the very next day, she and the four children were again stripped almost naked. The wretched creature must have steeped herself in gin to the shoulders, for in one day she made a sweep of everything. She then came in a state of furious intoxication to the Spotted Dog, and was removed by the police under the express order of the landlord.

We can hardly say which was the most surprising to us, the loyalty of Mrs. Grimes or the patience of John. During that night, as we were told two days afterwards by his wife, he stormed with passion. The papers she had locked up in order that he should not get at them and

73

destroy them. He swore that everything should be cleared out on the following morning. But when the morning came he did not even say a word to Mackenzie, as the wretched, downcast, broken-hearted creature passed upstairs to his work. "You see I knows him, and how to deal with him," said Mrs. Grimes, speaking of her husband. "There ain't another like himself nowheres;—he's that good. A softer-hearteder man there ain't in the public line. He can speak dreadful when his dander is up, and can look—; oh, laws, he just can look at you! But he could no more put his hands upon a woman, in the way of hurting,—no more than be an archbishop." Where could be the man, thought we to ourselves as this was said to us, who could have put a hand, in the way of hurting,—upon Mrs. Grimes?

On that occasion, to the best of our belief, the policeman contented himself with depositing Mrs. Mackenzie at her own lodgings. On the next day she was picked up drunk in the street, and carried away to the lock-up house. At the very moment in which the story was being told to us by Mrs. Grimes, Mackenzie had gone to the police office to pay the fine, and to bring his wife home. We asked with dismay and surprise why he should interfere to rescue her,—why he did not leave her in custody as long as the police would keep her? "Who'd there be to look after the children?" asked Mrs. Grimes, as though she were offended at our suggestion. Then she went on to explain that in such a household as that of poor Mackenzie the wife is absolutely a necessity, even though she be an habitual drunkard. Intolerable as she was, her services were necessary to him. "A husband as drinks is bad," said Mrs. Grimes;—with something, we thought, of an apologetic tone for the vice upon which her own prosperity was partly built,—"but when a woman takes to it, it's the —— devil." We thought that she was right, as we pictured to ourselves that man of letters satisfying the magistrate's demand for his wife's misconduct,

and taking the degraded, half-naked creature once more home to
his children.

We saw him about twelve o'clock on that day, and he had then,
too evidently, been endeavouring to support his misery by the free
use of alcohol. We did not speak of it down in the parlour; but even
Mrs. Grimes, we think, would have admitted that he had taken more
than was good for him. He was sitting up in the bedroom with his head
hanging upon his hand, with a swarm of our learned friend's papers
spread on the table before him. Mrs. Grimes, when he entered the
house, had gone upstairs to give them out to him; but he had made no
attempt to settle himself to his work. "This kind of thing must come to
an end," he said to us with a thick, husky voice. We muttered something to him as to the need there was that he should exert a manly
courage in his troubles. "Manly!" he said. "Well, yes; manly. A man
should be a man, of course. There are some things which a man can't
bear. I've borne more than enough, and I'll have an end of it."

We shall never forget that scene. After awhile he got up, and
became almost violent. Talk of bearing! Who had borne half as much
as he? There were things a man should not hear. As for manliness,
he believed that the truly manly thing would be to put an end to the
lives of his wife, his children, and himself at one swoop. Of course
the judgment of a mealy-mouthed world would be against him, but
what would that matter to him when he and they had vanished out of
this miserable place into the infinite realms of nothingness? Was he
fit to live, or were they? Was there any chance for his children but
that of becoming thieves and prostitutes? And for that poor wretch,
of a woman, from out of whose bosom even her human instincts had
been washed by gin,—would not death to her be, indeed, a charity? There was but one drawback to all this. When he should have
destroyed them, how would it be with him if he should afterwards fail

to make sure work with his own life? In such case it was not hanging that he would fear, but the self-reproach that would come upon him in that he had succeeded in sending others out of their misery, but had flinched when his own turn had come. Though he was drunk when he said these horrid things, or so nearly drunk that he could not perfect the articulation of his words, still there was a marvellous eloquence with him. When we attempted to answer, and told him of that canon which had been set against self-slaughter, he laughed us to scorn. There was something terrible to us in the audacity of the arguments which he used, when he asserted for himself the right to shuffle off from his shoulders a burden which they had not been made broad enough to bear. There was an intensity and a thorough hopelessness of suffering in his case, an openness of acknowledged degradation, which robbed us for the time of all that power which the respectable ones of the earth have over the disreputable. When we came upon him with our wise saws, our wisdom was shattered instantly, and flung back upon us in fragments. What promise could we dare to hold out to him that further patience would produce any result that could be beneficial? What further harm could any such doing on his part bring upon him? Did we think that were he brought out to stand at the gallows' foot with the knowledge that ten minutes would usher him into what folks called eternity, his sense of suffering would be as great as it had been when he conducted that woman out of court and along the streets to his home, amidst the jeering congratulations of his neighbours? "When you have fallen so low," said he, "that you can fall no lower, the ordinary trammels of the world cease to bind you." Though his words were knocked against each other with the dulled utterances of intoxication, his intellect was terribly clear, and his scorn for himself, and for the world that had so treated him, was irrepressible.

We must have been over an hour with him up there in the bedroom, and even then we did not leave him. As it was manifest that he could do no work on that day, we collected the papers together, and proposed that he should take a walk with us. He was patient as we shovelled together the Doctor's pages, and did not object to our suggestion. We found it necessary to call up Mrs. Grimes to assist us in putting away the "Opus magnum," and were astonished to find how much she had come to know about the work. Added to the Doctor's manuscript there were now the pages of Mackenzie's indexes,—and there were other pages of reference, for use in making future indexes,—as to all of which Mrs. Grimes seemed to be quite at home. We have no doubt that she was familiar with the names of Greek tragedians, and could have pointed out to us in print the performances of the chorus. "A little fresh air'll do you a deal of good, Mr. Mackenzie," she said to the unfortunate man,—"only take a biscuit in your pocket." We got him out into the street, but he angrily refused to take the biscuit which she endeavoured to force into his hands.

That was a memorable walk. Turning from the end of Liquorpond Street up Gray's Inn Lane towards Holborn, we at once came upon the entrance into a miserable court. "There," said he; "it is down there that I live. She is sleeping it off now, and the children are hanging about her, wondering whether mother has got money to have another go at it when she rises. I'd take you down to see it all, only it'd sicken you." We did not offer to go down the court, abstaining rather for his sake than for our own. The look of the place was as of a spot squalid, fever-stricken, and utterly degraded. And this man who was our companion had been born and bred a gentleman,—had been nourished with that soft and gentle care which comes of wealth and love combined,—had received the education which the country gives to her most favoured sons, and had taken such advantage of that education as is seldom taken by any of those favoured ones;—and Cucumber Court, with a drunken wife and four half-clothed, half-starved children, was the condition to which he had brought himself! The world knows nothing higher nor brighter than had been his outset in life,—nothing lower nor more debased than the result. And yet he was one whose time and intellect had been employed upon the pursuit of knowledge,—who even up to this day had high ideas of what should be a man's career,—who worked very hard and had always worked,—who as far as we knew had struck upon no rocks in the pursuit of mere pleasure. It had all come to him from that idea of his youth that it would be good for him "to take refuge from the conventional thraldom of so-called gentlemen amidst the liberty of the lower orders." His life, as he had himself owned, had indeed been a mistake.

We passed on from the court, and crossing the road went through the squares of Gray's Inn, down Chancery Lane, through the little iron gate into Lincoln's Inn, round through the old square,—than which we know no place in London more conducive to suicide; and the new square,—which has a gloom of its own, not so potent, and savouring only of madness, till at last we found ourselves in the Temple Gardens. I do not know why we had thus clung to the purlieus of the Law, except it was that he was telling us how in his early days, when he had been sent away from Cambridge,—as on this occasion he acknowledged to us, for an attempt to pull the tutor's nose, in revenge for a supposed insult,—he had intended to push his fortunes as a barrister. He pointed up to a certain window in a dark corner of that suicidal old court, and told us that for one year he had there sat at the feet of a great Gamaliel in Chancery, and had worked with all his energies. Of course we asked him why he had left a prospect so alluring. Though his answers to us were not quite explicit, we think that he did not attempt to conceal the truth. He learned to drink, and that Gamaliel took upon himself to rebuke the failing, and by the end of that year he had quarrelled irreconcilably with his family. There had been great wrath at home when he was sent from Cambridge, greater wrath when he expressed his opinion upon certain questions of religious faith, and wrath to the final severance of all family relations when he told the chosen Gamaliel that he should get drunk as often as he pleased. After that he had "taken refuge among the lower orders," and his life, such as it was, had come of it.

In Fleet Street, as we came out of the Temple, we turned into an eating-house and had some food. By this time the exercise and the air had carried off the fumes of the liquor which he had taken, and I knew that it would be well that he should eat. We had a mutton chop and a hot potato and a pint of beer each, and sat down to table for the first and last time as mutual friends. It was odd to see how in his converse with us on that day he seemed to possess a double identity. Though the hopeless misery of his condition was always present to him, was constantly on his tongue, yet he could talk about his own career and his own character as though they belonged to a third person. He could even laugh at the wretched mistake he had made in life, and speculate as to its consequences. For himself he was well aware that death was the only release that he could expect. We did not dare to tell him that if his wife should die, then things might be better with him. We could only suggest to him that work itself, if he would do honest work, would console him for many sufferings. "You don't know the filth of it," he said to us. Ah, dear; how well we remember the terrible word, and the gesture with which he pronounced it, and the gleam of his eyes as he said it! His manner to us on this occasion was completely changed, and we had a gratification in feeling that a sense had come back upon him of his old associations. "I remember this room so well," he said,—"when I used to have friends and money." And, indeed, the room was one which has been made memorable by Genius. "I did not think ever to have found myself here again." We observed, however, that he could not eat the food that was placed before him. A morsel or two of the meat he swallowed, and struggled to eat the crust of his bread, but he could not make a clean plate of it, as we did,—regretting that the nature of chops did not allow of ampler dimensions. His beer was quickly finished, and we suggested to him a second tankard. With a queer, half-abashed twinkle of the eye, he accepted our offer, and then the second pint disappeared also. We had our doubts on the subject, but at last decided against any further offer. Had he chosen to call for it he must have had a third; but he did not call for it. We left him at the door of the tavern, and he then promised that in spite of all that he had suffered and all that he had said he would make another effort to complete the Doctor's work. "Whether I go or stay," he said, "I'd like to earn the money that I've spent." There was something terrible in that idea of his going! Whither was he to go?

The Doctor heard nothing of the misfortune of these three or four inauspicious days; and the work was again going on prosperously when he came up again to London at the end of the second month. He told us something of his banker, and something of his lawyer, and murmured a word or two as to a new curate whom he needed; but we knew that he had come up to London because he could not bear a longer absence from the great object of his affections. He could not endure to be thus parted from his manuscript, and was again childishly anxious that a portion of it should be in the printer's hands. "At sixty-five, sir," he said to us, "a man has no time to dally with his work." He had been dallying with his work all his life, and we sincerely believed that it would be well with him if he could be contented to dally with it to the end. If all that Mackenzie said of it was true, the Doctor's erudition was not equalled by his originality, or by his judgment. Of that question, however, we could take no cognisance. He was bent upon publishing, and as he was willing and able to pay for his whim and was his own master, nothing that we could do would keep him out of the printer's hands.

He was desirous of seeing Mackenzie, and was anxious even to see him once at his work. Of course he could meet his assistant in our editorial room, and all the papers could easily be brought backwards and forwards in the old despatch-box. But in the interest of all parties we hesitated as to taking our revered and reverend friend to the Spotted Dog. Though we had told him that his work was being done at a public-house, we thought that his mind had conceived the idea of some modest inn, and that he would be shocked at being introduced to a place which he would regard simply as a gin-shop. Mrs. Grimes, or if not Mrs. Grimes, then Mr. Grimes, might object to another visitor to their bedroom; and Mackenzie himself would be thrown out of gear by the appearance of those clerical gaiters upon the humble scene of his labours. We, therefore, gave him such reasons as were available for submitting, at any rate for the present, to having the papers brought up to him at our room. And we ourselves went down to the Spotted Dog to make an appointment with Mackenzie for the following day. We had last seen him about a week before, and then the task was progressing well. He had told us that another fortnight would finish it. We had inquired also of Mrs. Grimes about the man's wife. All she could tell us was that the woman had not again troubled them at the Spotted Dog. She expressed her belief, however, that the drunkard had been more than once in the hands of the police since the day on which Mackenzie had walked with us through the squares of the Inns of Court.

It was late when we reached the public-house on the occasion to which we now allude, and the evening was dark and rainy. It was then the end of January, and it might have been about six o'clock. We knew that we should not find Mackenzie at the public-house; but it was probable that Mrs. Grimes could send for him, or, at least, could make the appointment for us. We went into the little parlour, where she was seated with her husband, and we could immediately see, from the countenance of both of them, that something was amiss. We began by telling Mrs. Grimes that the Doctor had come to town. "Mackenzie ain't here, sir," said Mrs. Grimes, and we almost thought that the very tone of her voice was altered. We explained that we had not expected to find him at that hour, and asked if she could send for him. She only shook her head. Grimes was standing with his back to the fire and his hands in his trousers pockets. Up to this moment he had not spoken a word. We asked if the man was drunk. She again shook her head. Could she bid him to come to us to-morrow, and bring the box and the papers with him? Again she shook her head.

"I've told her that I won't have no more of it," said Grimes; "nor yet I won't. He was drunk this morning,—as drunk as an owl."

"He was sober, John, as you are, when he came for the papers this afternoon at two o'clock." So the box and the papers had all been taken away!

"And she was here yesterday rampaging about the place, without as much clothes on as would cover her nakedness," said Mr. Grimes. "I won't have no more of it. I've done for that man what his own flesh and blood wouldn't do. I know that; and I won't have no more of it. Mary Anne, you'll have that table cleared out after breakfast to-morrow." When a man, to whom his wife is usually Polly, addresses her as Mary Anne, then it may be surmised that that man is in earnest. We knew that he was in earnest, and she knew it also.

"He wasn't drunk, John,—no, nor yet in liquor, when he come and took away that box this afternoon." We understood this reiterated assertion. It was in some sort excusing to us her own breach of trust in having allowed the manuscript to be withdrawn from her own charge, or was assuring us that, at the worst, she had not been guilty of the impropriety of allowing the man to take it away when he was unfit to have it in his charge. As for blaming her, who could have thought of it? Had Mackenzie at any time chosen to pass downstairs with the box in his hands, it was not to be expected that she should stop him violently. And now that he had done so we could not blame her; but we felt that a great weight had fallen upon our own hearts. If evil should come to the manuscript would not the Doctor's wrath fall upon us with a crushing weight? Something must be done at once. And we suggested that it would be well that somebody should go round to Cucumber Court. "I'd go as soon as look," said Mrs. Grimes, "but he won't let me."

"You don't stir a foot out of this to-night;—not that way," said Mr. Grimes.

"Who wants to stir?" said Mrs. Grimes.

We felt that there was something more to be told than we had yet heard, and a great fear fell upon us. The woman's manner to us was altered, and we were sure that this had come not from altered feelings on her part, but from circumstances which had frightened her. It was not her husband that she feared, but the truth of something that her husband had said to her. "If there is anything more to tell, for God's sake tell it," we said, addressing ourselves rather to the man than to the woman. Then Grimes did tell us his story. On the previous evening Mackenzie had received three or four sovereigns from Mrs. Grimes, being, of course, a portion of the Doctor's payments; and early on that morning all Liquorpond Street had been in a state of excitement with the drunken fury of Mackenzie's wife. She had found her way into the Spotted Dog, and was being actually extruded by the strength of Grimes himself,—of Grimes, who had been brought down, half dressed, from his bedroom by the row,—when Mackenzie himself, equally drunk, appeared upon the scene. "No, John;—not equally drunk," said Mrs. Grimes. "Bother!" exclaimed her husband, going on with his story. The man had struggled to take the woman by the arm, and the two had fallen and rolled in the street together. "I was looking out of the window, and it was awful to see," said Mrs. Grimes. We felt that it was "awful to hear." A man,—and such a man, rolling in the gutter with a drunken woman,—himself drunk,—and that woman his wife! "There ain't to be no more of it at the Spotted Dog; that's all," said John Grimes, as he finished his part of the story.

Then, at last, Mrs. Grimes became voluble. All this had occurred before nine in the morning. "The woman must have been at it all night," she said. "So must the man," said John. "Anyways he came back about dinner, and he was sober then. I asked him not to go up, and offered to make him a cup of tea. It was just as you'd gone out after dinner, John."

"He won't have no more tea here," said John.

"And he didn't have any then. He wouldn't, he said, have any tea, but went upstairs. What was I to do? I couldn't tell him as he shouldn't. Well;—during the row in the morning John had said something as to Mackenzie not coming about the premises any more."

"Of course I did," said Grimes.

"He was a little cut, then, no doubt," continued the lady; "and I didn't think as he would have noticed what John had said."

"I mean it to be noticed now."

"He had noticed it then, sir, though he wasn't just as he should be at that hour of the morning. Well;—what does he do? He goes

84

upstairs and packs up all the papers at once. Leastways, that's as I suppose. They ain't there now. You can go and look if you please, sir. Well; when he came down, whether I was in the kitchen,—though it isn't often as my eyes is off the bar, or in the tap-room, or busy drawing, which I do do sometimes, sir, when there are a many calling for liquor, I can't say;—but if I ain't never to stand upright again, I didn't see him pass out with the box. But Miss Wilcox did. You can ask her." Miss Wilcox was the young lady in the bar, whom we did not think ourselves called upon to examine, feeling no doubt whatever as to the fact of the box having been taken away by Mackenzie. In all this Mrs. Grimes seemed to defend herself, as though some serious charge was to be brought against her; whereas all that she had done had been done out of pure charity; and in exercising her charity towards Mackenzie she had shown an almost exaggerated kindness towards ourselves.

"If there's anything wrong, it isn't your fault," we said.

"Nor yet mine," said John Grimes.

"No, indeed," we replied.

"It ain't none of our faults," continued he; "only this;—you can't wash a blackamoor white, nor it ain't no use trying. He don't come here any more, that's all. A man in drink we don't mind. We has to put up with it. And they ain't that tarnation desperate as is a woman. As long as a man can keep his legs he'll try to steady hisself; but there is women who, when they've liquor, gets a fury for rampaging. There ain't a many as can beat this one, sir. She's that strong, it took four of us to hold her; though she can't hardly do a stroke of work, she's that weak when she's sober."

We had now heard the whole story, and, while hearing it, had determined that it was our duty to go round into Cucumber Court and seek the manuscript and the box. We were unwilling to pry into the wretchedness of the man's home; but something was due to the Doctor; and we had to make that appointment for the morrow, if it were still possible that such an appointment should be kept. We asked for the number of the house, remembering well the entrance into the court. Then there was a whisper between John and his wife, and the husband offered to accompany us. "It's a roughish place," he said, "but they know me." "He'd better go along with you," said Mrs. Grimes. We, of course, were glad of such companionship, and glad also to find that the landlord, upon whom we had inflicted so much trouble, was still sufficiently our friend to take this trouble on our behalf.

"It's a dreary place enough," said Grimes, as he led us up the narrow archway. Indeed it was a dreary place. The court spread itself a little in breadth, but very little, when the passage was passed, and there were houses on each side of it. There was neither gutter nor, as far as we saw, drain, but the broken flags were slippery with moist mud, and here and there, strewed about between the houses, there were the remains of cabbages and turnip-tops. The place swarmed with children, over whom one ghastly gas-lamp at the end of the court threw a flickering and uncertain light. There was a clamour of scolding voices, to which it seemed that no heed was paid; and there was a smell of damp, rotting nastiness, amidst which it seemed to us to be almost impossible that life should be continued. Grimes led the way, without further speech, to the middle house on the left hand of the court, and asked a man who was sitting on the low threshold of the door whether Mackenzie was within. "So that be you, Muster Grimes; be it?" said the man, without stirring. "Yes; he's there I guess, but they've been and took her." Then we passed on into the house. "No matter about that," said the man, as we apologised for kicking him in our passage. He had not moved, and it had been impossible to enter without kicking him.

86

It seemed that Mackenzie held the two rooms on the ground floor, and we entered them at once. There was no light, but we could see the glimmer of a fire in the grate; and presently we became aware of the presence of children. Grimes asked after Mackenzie, and a girl's voice told us that he was in the inner room. The publican then demanded a light, and the girl, with some hesitation, lit the end of a farthing candle, which was fixed in a small bottle. We endeavoured to look round the room by the glimmer which this afforded, but could see nothing but the presence of four children, three of whom seemed to be seated in apathy on the floor. Grimes, taking the candle in his hand, passed at once into the other room, and we followed him. Holding the bottle something over his head, he contrived to throw a gleam of light upon one of the two beds with which the room was fitted, and there we saw the body of Julius Mackenzie stretched in the torpor of dead intoxication. His head lay against the wall, his body was across the bed, and his feet dangled on to the floor. He still wore his dirty boots, and his clothes as he had worn them in the morning. No sight so piteous, so wretched, and at the same time so eloquent had we ever seen before. His eyes were closed, and the light of his face was therefore quenched. His mouth was open, and the slaver had fallen upon his beard. His dark, clotted hair had been pulled over his face by the unconscious movement of his hands. There came from him a stertorous sound of breathing, as though he were being choked by the attitude in which he lay; and even in his drunkenness there was an uneasy twitching as of pain about his face. And there sat, and had been sitting for hours past, the four children in the other room, knowing the condition of the parent whom they most respected, but not even endeavouring to do anything for his comfort. What could they do? They knew, by long training and thorough experience, that a fit of drunkenness had to be got out of by sleep. To them there was nothing shocking in it. It was but a periodical misfortune. "She'll have to own he's been and done it now," said Grimes, looking down upon the man, and alluding to his wife's good-natured obstinacy. He handed the candle to us, and, with a mixture of tenderness and roughness, of which the roughness was only in the manner and the tenderness was real, he raised Mackenzie's head and placed it on the bolster, and lifted the man's legs on to the bed. Then he took off the man's boots, and the old silk handkerchief from the neck, and pulled the trousers straight, and arranged the folds of the coat. It was almost as though he were laying out one that was dead. The eldest girl was now standing by us, and Grimes asked her how long her father had been in that condition. "Jack Hoggart brought him in just afore it was dark," said the girl. Then it was explained to us that Jack Hoggart was the man whom we had seen sitting on the doorstep.

"And your mother?" asked Grimes.

"The perlice took her afore dinner."

"And you children;—what have you had to eat?" In answer to this the girl only shook her head. Grimes took no immediate notice of this, but called the drunken man by his name, and shook his shoulder, and looked round to a broken ewer which stood on the little table, for water to dash upon him;—but there was no water in the jug. He called again, and repeated the shaking, and at last Mackenzie opened his eyes, and in a dull, half-conscious manner looked up at us. "Come, my man," said Grimes, "shake this off and have done with it."

"Hadn't you better try to get up?" we asked.

There was a faint attempt at rising, then a smile,—a smile which was terrible to witness, so sad was all which it said; then a look of utter, abject misery, coming, as we thought, from a momentary remembrance of his degradation; and after that he sank back in the dull, brutal, painless, death-like apathy of absolute unconsciousness.

"It'll be morning afore he'll move," said the girl.

"She's about right," said Grimes. "He's got it too heavy for us to do anything but just leave him. We'll take a look for the box and the papers."

And the man upon whom we were looking down had been born a gentleman, and was a finished scholar,—one so well educated, so ripe in literary acquirement, that we knew few whom we could call his equal. Judging of the matter by the light of our reason, we cannot say that the horror of the scene should have been enhanced to us by these recollections. Had the man been a shoemaker or a coalheaver there would have been enough of tragedy in it to make an angel weep,—that sight of the child standing by the bedside of her drunken father, while the other parent was away in custody,—and in no degree shocked at what she saw, because the thing was so common to her! But the thought of what the man had been, of what he was, of what he might have been, and the steps by which he had brought himself to the foul degradation which we witnessed, filled us with a dismay which we should hardly have felt had the gifts which he had polluted and the intellect which he had wasted been less capable of noble uses.

Our purpose in coming to the court was to rescue the Doctor's papers from danger, and we turned to accompany Grimes into the other room. As we did so the publican asked the girl if she knew anything of a black box which her father had taken away from the Spotted Dog. "The box is here," said the girl.

"And the papers?" asked Grimes. Thereupon the girl shook her head, and we both hurried into the outer room. I hardly know who first discovered the sight which we encountered, or whether it was shown to us by the child. The whole fire-place was strewn with half-burnt sheets of manuscript. There were scraps of pages of which almost the whole had been destroyed, others which were hardly more than scorched, and heaps of paper-ashes all lying tumbled together about the fender. We went down on our knees to examine them, thinking at the moment that the poor creature might in his despair have burned his own work and have spared that of the Doctor. But it was not so. We found scores of charred pages of the Doctor's elaborate handwriting. By this time Grimes had found the open box, and we perceived that the sheets remaining in it were tumbled and huddled together in absolute confusion. There were pages of the various volumes mixed with those which Mackenzie himself had written, and they were all crushed, and rolled, and twisted, as though they had been thrust thither as waste-paper,—out of the way. "'Twas mother as done it," said the girl, "and we put 'em back again when the perlice took her."

There was nothing more to learn,—nothing more by the hearing which any useful clue could be obtained. What had been the exact course of the scenes which had been enacted there that morning it little booted us to inquire. It was enough and more than enough that we knew that the mischief had been done. We went down on our knees before the fire, and rescued from the ashes with our hands every fragment of manuscript that we could find. Then we put the mass all together into the box, and gazed upon the wretched remnants almost in tears. "You'd better go and get a bit of some'at to eat," said Grimes, handing a coin to the elder girl. "It's hard on them to starve 'cause their father's drunk, sir." Then he took the closed box in his hand, and we followed him out into the street. "I'll send or step up and look after him to-morrow," said Grimes, as he put us and the box into a cab. We little thought, when we made to the drunkard that foolish request to arise, that we should never speak to him again.

As we returned to our office in the cab that we might deposit the box there ready for the following day, our mind was chiefly occupied in thinking over the undeserved grievances which had fallen upon ourselves. We had been moved by the charitable desire to do services to two different persons,—to the learned Doctor and to the red-nosed drunkard, and this had come of it! There had been nothing for us to gain by assisting either the one or the other. We had taken infinite trouble, attempting to bring together two men who wanted each other's services,—working hard in sheer benevolence;—and what had been the result? We had spent half an hour on our knees in the undignified and almost disreputable work of raking among Mrs. Mackenzie's cinders, and now we had to face the anger, the dismay, the reproach, and,—worse than all,—the agony of the Doctor. As to Mackenzie,—we asserted to ourselves again and again that nothing further could be done for him. He had made his bed, and he must lie upon it; but, oh! why,—why had we attempted to meddle with a being so degraded? We got out of the cab at our office door, thinking of the Doctor's countenance as we should see it on the morrow. Our heart sank within us, and we asked ourselves, if it was so bad with us now, how it would be with us when we returned to the place on the following morning.

But on the following morning we did return. No doubt each individual reader to whom we address ourselves has at some period felt that indescribable load of personal, short-lived care, which causes the heart to sink down into the boots. It is not great grief that does it;—nor is it excessive fear; but the unpleasant operation comes from the mixture of the two. It is the anticipation of some imperfectly-understood evil that does it,—some evil out of which there might perhaps be an escape if we could only see the way. In this case we saw no way out of it. The Doctor was to be with us at one o'clock, and he would come with smiles, expecting to meet his learned colleague. How should we break it to the Doctor? We might indeed send to him, putting off the meeting, but the advantage coming from that would be slight, if any. We must see the injured Grecian sooner or later; and we had resolved, much, as we feared, that the evil hour should not be postponed. We spent an hour that morning in arranging the fragments. Of the first volume about a third had been destroyed. Of the second nearly every page had been either burned or mutilated. Of the third but little had been injured. Mackenzie's own work had fared better than the Doctor's; but there was no comfort in that. After what had passed I thought it quite improbable that the Doctor would make any use of Mackenzie's work. So much of the manuscript as could still be placed in continuous pages, we laid out upon the table, volume by volume,—that in the middle sinking down from its original goodly bulk almost to the dimensions of a poor sermon;—and the half-burned bits we left in the box. Then we sat ourselves down at our accustomed table, and pretended to try to work. Our ears were very sharp, and we heard the Doctor's step upon our stairs within a minute or two of the appointed time. Our heart went to the very toes of our boots. We shuffled in our chair, rose from it, and sat down again,—and were conscious that we were not equal to the occasion. Hitherto we had, after some mild literary form, patronised the Doctor,—as a man of letters in town will patronise his literary friend from the country;—but we now feared him as a truant school-boy fears his master. And yet it was so necessary that we should wear some air of self-assurance!

In a moment he was with us, wearing that bland smile which we knew so well, and which at the present moment almost overpowered us. We had been sure that he would wear that smile, and had especially feared it. "Ah," said he, grasping us by the hand, "I thought I should have been late. I see that our friend is not here yet."

"Doctor," we replied, "a great misfortune has happened."

"A great misfortune! Mr. Mackenzie is not dead?"

"No;—he is not dead. Perhaps it would have been better that he had died long since. He has destroyed your manuscript." The Doctor's face fell, and his hands at the same time, and he stood looking at us. "I need not tell you, Doctor, what my feelings are, and how great my remorse."

"Destroyed it!" Then we took him by the hand and led him to the table. He turned first upon the appetising and comparatively uninjured third volume, and seemed to think that we had hoaxed him. "This is not destroyed," he said, with a smile. But before I could explain anything, his hands were among the fragments in the box. "As I am a living man, they have burned it!" he exclaimed. "I—I—I—" Then he turned from us, and walked twice the length of the room, backwards and forwards, while we stood still, patiently waiting the explosion of his wrath. "My friend," he said, when his walk was over, "a great man underwent the same sorrow. Newton's manuscript was burned. I will take it home with me, and we will say no more about it." I never thought very much of the Doctor as a divine, but I hold him to have been as good a Christian as I ever met.

But that plan of his of saying no more about it could not quite be carried out. I was endeavouring to explain to him, as I thought it necessary to do, the circumstances of the case, and he was protesting his indifference to any such details, when there came a knock at the door, and the boy who waited on us below ushered Mrs. Grimes into the room. As the reader is aware, we had, during the last two months, become very intimate with the landlady of the Spotted Dog, but we had never hitherto had the pleasure of seeing her outside her own house. "Oh, Mr. ——" she began, and then she paused, seeing the Doctor.

We thought it expedient that there should be some introduction. "Mrs. Grimes," we said, "this is the gentleman whose invaluable manuscript has been destroyed by that unfortunate drunkard."

"Oh, then;—you're the Doctor, sir?" The Doctor bowed and smiled. His heart must have been very heavy, but he bowed politely and smiled sweetly. "Oh, dear," she said, "I don't know how to tell you!"

"To tell us what?" asked the Doctor.

"What has happened since?" we demanded. The woman stood shaking before us, and then sank into a chair. Then arose to us at the moment some idea that the drunken woman, in her mad rage, had done some great damage to the Spotted Dog,—had set fire to the house, or injured Mr. Grimes personally, or perhaps run a muck amidst the jugs and pitchers, window glass, and gas lights. Something had been done which would give the Grimeses a pecuniary claim on me or on the Doctor, and the woman had been sent hither to make the first protest. Oh,—when should I see the last of the results of my imprudence in having attempted to befriend such a one as Julius Mackenzie! "If you have anything to tell, you had better tell it," we said, gravely.

"He's been, and—"

"Not destroyed himself?" asked the Doctor.

"Oh yes, sir. He have indeed,—from ear to ear,—and is now a lying at the Spotted Dog!"

And so, after all, that was the end of Julius Mackenzie! We need hardly say that our feelings, which up to that moment had been very hostile to the man, underwent a sudden revulsion. Poor, overburdened, struggling, ill-used, abandoned creature! The world had been hard upon him, with a severity which almost induced one to make complaint against Omnipotence. The poor wretch had been willing to work, had been industrious in his calling, had had capacity for work; and he had also struggled gallantly against his evil fate, had recognised and endeavoured to perform his duty to his children and to the miserable woman who had brought him to his ruin! And that sin of drunkenness had seemed to us to be in him rather the reflex of her vice than the result of his own vicious tendencies. Still it might be doubtful whether she had not learned the vice from him. They had both in truth been drunkards as long as they had been known in the neighbourhood of the Spotted Dog; but it was stated by all who had known them there that he was never seen to be drunk unless when she had disgraced him by the public exposure of her own abomination. Such as he was he had now come to his end! This was the upshot of his loud claims for liberty from his youth upwards;—liberty as against his father and family; liberty as against his college tutor; liberty as against all pastors, masters, and instructors; liberty as against the conventional thraldom of the world! He was now lying a wretched corpse at the Spotted Dog, with his throat cut from ear to ear, till the coroner's jury should have decided whether or not they would call him a suicide!

Mrs. Grimes had come to tell us that the coroner was to be at the Spotted Dog at four o'clock, and to say that her husband hoped that we would be present. We had seen Mackenzie so lately, and had so much to do with the employment of the last days of his life, that we could not refuse this request, though it came accompanied by no legal summons. Then Mrs. Grimes again became voluble, and poured out to us her biography of Mackenzie as far as she knew it. He had been married to the woman ten years, and certainly had been a drunkard before he married her. "As for her, she'd been well-nigh suckled on gin," said Mrs. Grimes, "though he didn't know it, poor fellow." Whether this was true or not, she had certainly taken to drink soon after her marriage, and then his life had been passed in alternate fits of despondency and of desperate efforts to improve his own condition and that of his children. Mrs. Grimes declared to us that when the fit came on them,—when the woman had begun and the man had followed,—they would expend upon drink in two days what would have kept the family for a fortnight. "They say as how it was nothing for them to swallow forty shillings' worth of gin in forty-eight hours." The Doctor held up his hands in horror. "And it didn't, none of it, come our way," said Mrs. Grimes. "Indeed, John wouldn't let us serve it for 'em."

She sat there for half an hour, and during the whole time she was telling us of the man's life; but the reader will already have heard more than enough of it. By what immediate demon the woman had been instigated to burn the husband's work almost immediately on its production within her own home, we never heard. Doubtless there had been some terrible scene in which the man's sufferings must have been carried almost beyond endurance. "And he had feelings, sir, he had," said Mrs. Grimes; "he knew as a woman should be decent, and a man's wife especial; I'm sure we pitied him so, John and I, that we could have cried over him. John would say a hard word to him at times, but he'd have walked round London to do him a good turn. John ain't to say edicated hisself, but he do respect learning."

When she had told us all, Mrs. Grimes went, and we were left alone with the Doctor. He at once consented to accompany us to the Spotted Dog, and we spent the hour that still remained to us in discussing the fate of the unfortunate man. We doubt whether an allusion was made during the time to the burned manuscript. If so, it was certainly not made by the Doctor himself. The tragedy which had occurred in connection with it had made him feel it to be unfitting even to mention his own loss. That such a one should have gone to his account in such a manner, without hope, without belief, and without fear,—as Burley said to Bothwell, and Bothwell boasted to Burley,—that was the theme of the Doctor's discourse. "The mercy of God is infinite," he said, bowing his head, with closed eyes and folded hands. To threaten while the life is in the man is human. To believe in the execution of those threats when the life has passed away is almost beyond the power of humanity.

At the hour fixed we were at the Spotted Dog, and found there a crowd assembled. The coroner was already seated in Mrs. Grimes' little parlour, and the body as we were told had been laid out in the tap-room. The inquest was soon over. The fact that he had destroyed himself in the low state of physical suffering and mental despondency which followed his intoxication was not doubted. At the very time that he was doing it, his wife was being taken from the lock-up house to the police office in the police van. He was not penniless, for he had sent the children out with money for their breakfasts, giving special caution as to the youngest, a little toddling thing of three years old;—and then he had done it. The eldest girl, returning to the house, had found him lying dead upon the floor. We were called upon for our evidence, and went into the tap-room accompanied by the Doctor. Alas! the very table which had been dragged upstairs into the landlady's bedroom with the charitable object of assisting Mackenzie in his work,—the table at which we had sat with him conning the Doctor's pages,—had now been dragged down again and was used for another purpose. We had little to say as to the matter, except that we had known the man to be industrious and capable, and that we had, alas! seen him utterly prostrated by drink on the evening before his death.

The saddest sight of all on this occasion was the appearance of Mackenzie's wife,—whom we had never before seen. She had been brought there by a policeman, but whether she was still in custody we did not know. She had been dressed, either by the decency of the police or by the care of her neighbours, in an old black gown, which was a world too large and too long for her. And on her head there was a black bonnet which nearly enveloped her. She was a small woman, and, as far as we could judge from the glance we got of her face, pale, and worn, and wan. She had not such outward marks of a drunkard's career as those which poor Mackenzie always carried with him. She was taken up to the coroner, and what answers she gave to him were spoken in so low a voice that they did not reach us. The policeman, with whom we spoke, told us that she did not feel it much,—that she was callous now and beyond the power of mental suffering. "She's frightened just this minute, sir; but it isn't more than that," said the policeman. We gave one glance along the table at the burden which it bore, but we saw nothing beyond the outward lines of that which had so lately been the figure of a man. We should have liked to see the countenance once more. The morbid curiosity to see such horrid sights is strong with most of us. But we did not wish to be thought to wish to see it,—especially by our friend the Doctor,—and we abstained from pushing our way to the head of the table. The Doctor himself remained quiescent in the corner of the room the farthest from the spectacle. When the matter was submitted to them, the jury lost not a moment in declaring their verdict. They said that the man had destroyed himself while suffering under temporary insanity produced by intoxication. And that was the end of Julius Mackenzie, the scholar.

On the following day the Doctor returned to the country, taking with him our black box, to the continued use of which, as a sarcophagus, he had been made very welcome. For our share in bringing upon him the great catastrophe of his life, he never uttered to us, either by spoken or written word, a single reproach. That idea of suffering as the great philosopher had suffered seemed to comfort him. "If Newton bore it, surely I can," he said to us with his bland smile, when we renewed the expression of our regret. Something passed between us, coming more from us than from him, as to the expediency of finding out some youthful scholar who could go down to the rectory, and reconstruct from its ruins the edifice of our friend's learning. The Doctor had given us some encouragement, and we had begun to make inquiry, when we received the following letter:—

"—— RECTORY, ——, 18—.

"Dear Mr. ——, —You were so kind as to say that you would endeavour to find for me an assistant in arranging and reconstructing the fragments of my work on The Metres of the Greek Dramatists. Your promise has been an additional kindness." Dear, courteous, kind old gentleman! For we knew well that no slightest sting of sarcasm was intended to be conveyed in these words. "Your promise has been an additional kindness; but looking upon the matter carefully, and giving to it the best consideration in my power, I have determined to relinquish the design. That which has been destroyed cannot be replaced; and it may well be that it was not worth replacing. I am old now, and never could do again that which perhaps I was never fitted to do with any fair prospect of success. I will never turn again to the ashes of my unborn child; but will console myself with the memory of my grievance, knowing well, as I do so, that consolation from the severity of harsh but just criticism might have been more difficult to find. When I think of the end of my efforts as a scholar, my mind reverts to the terrible and fatal catastrophe of one whose scholarship was infinitely more finished and more ripe than mine.

"Whenever it may suit you to come into this part of the country, pray remember that it will give very great pleasure to myself and to my daughter to welcome you at our parsonage.

"BELIEVE ME TO BE,

"MY DEAR MR. ———,

"YOURS VERY SINCERELY,

"——— ———."

We never have found the time to accept the Doctor's invitation, and our eyes have never again rested on the black box containing the ashes of the unborn child to which the Doctor will never turn again. We can picture him to ourselves standing, full of thought, with his hand upon the lid, but never venturing to turn the lock. Indeed, we do not doubt but that the key of the box is put away among other secret treasures, a lock of his wife's hair, perhaps, and the little shoe of the boy who did not live long enough to stand at his father's knee. For a tender, soft-hearted man was the Doctor, and one who fed much on the memories of the past.

We often called upon Mr. and Mrs. Grimes at the Spotted Dog, and would sit there talking of Mackenzie and his family. Mackenzie's widow soon vanished out of the neighbourhood, and no one there knew what was the fate of her or of her children. And then also Mr. Grimes went and took his wife with him. But they could not be said to vanish. Scratching his head one day, he told me with a dolorous voice that he had made his fortune. "We've got as snug a little place as ever you see, just two mile out of Colchester," said Mrs. Grimes triumphantly,—"with thirty acres of land just to amuse John. And as for the Spotted Dog, I'm that sick of it, another year'd wear me to a dry bone." We looked at her, and saw no tendency that way. And we looked at John, and thought that he was not triumphant.

Who followed Mr. and Mrs. Grimes at the Spotted Dog we have never visited Liquorpond Street to see.

KITTY'S DREAM AND ITS RESULTS

E. E. L.

"Kitty's Dream" is a temperance (anti-drink) story designed to warn the reader about the dangers of alcohol and drunkenness. The temperance movement was a wide-ranging campaign against the production, trade, and consumption of alcohol in Britain, made up of hundreds of local and national groups and linked to a range of international associations. Some groups were pro-moderation and advocated for some medical or moderate consumption of alcohol, or focused their efforts on the avoidance of spirits rather than all forms of alcoholic drink. Others, usually known as teetotal or total abstinence groups, were against alcohol in all its forms and advocated against all types of consumption. These temperance and teetotal groups published hundreds of thousands of stories and articles from the 1820s to the end of the century. Published anonymously in the *Temperance Mirror* in 1886, it is likely that the author of this story, known here only as "E. E. L.", was a woman. This is an educated guess from me as an experienced Victorianist, partly because so many women of this period published anonymously and partly because so many writers for temperance publications were female.

Although temperance illustrations like George Cruikshank's were often gothic (see the next story in this collection), its literature was not. Though often populated with grotesque drinkers, murders, and suicides, temperance stories generally shy away from the Weird. "Kitty's Dream" is one of the only temperance tales I have come across that includes a supernatural representation of "the demon drink" as it was commonly known by campaigners. "Kitty's Dream" is the story of an idealised and angelic child converting their drunken parent(s). This was very common in this genre of fiction: the temperance movement had an extremely active youth movement, known as Blue Ribbon, created specifically to recruit children as young as possible and persuade them to recruit others, adults and children alike.* Temperance stories tended to be melodramatic so you might think the gothic would be an ideal genre for their writers, but this often conservative movement tended to favour confessional style narratives and moral tales designed to make their readers weep over the fates of the doomed drinkers whose ruined bodies and devastated families littered their pages. The demonic dream Kitty re-tells to persuade her parents to abstain makes it very unusual. Drink is personified, or rather demonified, when it literally becomes "the demon drink" and gloats over her parents' helplessness and threatens her with its grotesque "creepin'" hands and fingers.

* For more information, see Annemarie McAllister's work on the Blue Ribbon society and the temperance movement more broadly. A good place to start is her e-book, *On the Temperance Movement*.

The new district visitor, Mrs. Marsh, had nearly completed her round of calls on a certain Tuesday morning, when she suddenly thought of one old couple whom she had not yet seen, but who, she heard, were accounted eccentric, and "a little bit queer" by their neighbours. Having just half-an-hour to spare, Mrs. Marsh retraced the steps she had taken in an opposite direction, and knocked at the door of No. 9, Prospect Row; it was immediately opened by a pleasant-looking old man, who gazed enquiringly at the strange lady before him.

"Are you Mr. May?" she said, in her cheery, winning voice.

"That's me, ma'am, Thomas May, at your service."

"May I come in, then?" she enquired. "I am the new district visitor, and I want to get to know all my people well."

The old man opened the door wider, and said, "Walk in lady, by all means; the missus is out, but I am pleased to see yer."

Mrs. Marsh went in and sat down, and chatted away brightly to old May, with the ready sympathy and tact that won her many real friends in all ranks of life, and she was just coming away when her eyes fell on something on the mantel-piece, and she turned and gave an earnest look at the old man.

It was not strange that her attention had been rivetted, for the centre ornament on the mantel-shelf was an old black bottle, placed conspicuously forward, and labelled "Unsweetened Gin."

"Yer be wonderin', ma'am," said Thomas, "what that there curious ornament means; and it's puzzled many a one afore yer; but sometime, if yer like to 'ear the reason o't, I'll tell yer with real pleasure."

"Are you and your wife teetotallers, Mr. May?" said Mrs. Marsh, gently.

"Indeed we be, ma'am, thank the Lord, though it was not always so."

"Will you tell me the story now? I have time to listen," said Mrs. Marsh.

"Right willin'ly, ma'am, and 'ere comes the missus," he added, as he went to the door and opened it for his wife, who was a tidy, but delicate and weak-looking woman.

As she came in, he said, "This is the new district lady, Mary Ann, and I'm just a-goin' to tell 'er the meanin' o' that bottle up there, so come and sit yer down, and stop me if I go wrong in the tellin' o' it."

Mrs. Marsh shook hands with the poor woman, who smiled, and looked ashamed and glad and sad, all at once.

"It was like this, ma'am," began old Thomas, delighted to spin his yarn to a fresh listener, "it was like this; years ago when our Kitty—that's our only child, who's married now to the foreman of the steel-works yonder, and a likelier lass I'll be bound yer never see—well, as I was a-sayin', our Kitty was only twelve years old come the next Januwary, when one October night, I was at 'ome alone along o' 'er; the wife there was out. Ah, ma'am, in those days we wasn't what we is now, was we, Mary Ann? We both drank 'ard, ma'am, 'ard and allus, and the wife there was worse than me, wasn't yer, wife? Allus, allus drunk, and the poor little maid afeard for 'er life of us; well, ma'am, one night she there," pointing to his wife, "was out on the drink, and I was at 'ome, already 'arf seas over, when I sees Kitty come in, and I says, 'Kitty, fetch me that ere bottle off the top shelf in the cupboard, and a glass; you know the one I mean, quick now.' The child looked all startled like, and she says, 'Oh, father, won't yer do without it? do'ee now.' 'What do yer mean, child?' says I, angrily, 'a-talking to yer father like that; fetch it this instant,' says I, 'or I'll break every bone in yer body, I will.' 'No, dad,' says she, quite firm like, 'I can't; yer must get it yerself if yer want it.' Then, ma,am, I 'urls such words at 'er as I can't repeat to the likes o' yer, for yer see, ma'am, as 'ow I knew I couldn't walk straight across that ere floor, and in my worst times I was allus kind o' shamed like for the child to see me reel and stagger with the drink; so I says awful words to 'er, and with a fearful threat I orders 'er to bring the gin or suffer for it. Ma'am, that ere little maid of mine, she stood it all quite quiet, and then she just come and knelt down by me as I was sittin' by the table, and, 'Dad,' says she, lookin' up into my face, 'will yer listen to a dream I 'ad last night, and you'll know then why I can't fetch the gin for yer.' Somethin' in the child's face made me quiet, and I lays down my 'ead and says, 'Go on, Kitty, I'll listen, out with it.' Oh, ma'am, never will I forget that night; it was just awful to 'ear the child speak so solemn as she did, and so earnest too; forgive me, ma'am, it undoes me even now," and the poor old man had to wipe the tears off his wrinkled cheeks before he could go on.

"'Dad,' says she, 'Dad, I'd only been asleep a little while, I think, when I dreamt as 'ow yer told me to fetch the bottle as I've often done afore, just as yer did to-night; and I went, and when I opened the cupboard door I 'eard a awful laugh, a awful chucklin' laugh, which set me all of a tremble with its terrible sound, and when I looked at the bottle, oh, father! There was a awful blue face glaring at me out of it, and a dreadful grin it 'ad, and I was so 'orror-struck I couldn't move, and the fearful face kep' grinnin' and I could 'ear a mutterin' like till I couldn't stand it no longer, and in awful fear I clutched 'old of the bottle, and pulled out the cork, and the face seemed to come right up out of the bottle, and then long skinny arms with lean 'ands and fingers all came creepin' out, and the dreadful laugh rang out loud, and the lips moved, and I plainly 'eard the words "I've got 'im, I've got 'im, and 'er too, safe and sound; they're mine, they've sold themselves, body and soul, to the devil, and my work is not lost this time! come on, come on, both of yer—ye're mine, ye're mine." And then came the awful laugh again, and I thought I fainted right away, and when I come to, with yer a throwin' some cold water on my face, I was a sittin' up in bed in a cold sweat all over; and I can't forget, and I'll never forget that awful dream; oh, father! it was so fearful; it seems just as fearful now. Now yer know why I couldn't fetch the bottle—oh, father! dear father!' And poor Kitty just wailed and sobbed, and as she knelt there I just sobbed too, and when she 'eard me, she grew quiet, and prayed out loud in her little childish words for 'er mother and for me. Then, ma'am, she got on my knee, and with 'er arms round my neck, she just begged and prayed of me to give up the drink, and be a good father to 'er; and, ma'am, I did love 'er, though the drink made such a beast of me, and I promised, and we prayed again, and then we said we'd do what we could with mother there too, and, ma'am, the Lord be praised, I've never touched no drink since that night, and under God 'tis Kitty's work. Many's the struggle we 'ad, ma'am; the poor wife's was the 'ardest; you see I'd never been quite so bad, for some'ow the women seem to drink deeper than us when they do begin, but she's all square now, ain't yer, wife? Kitty's 'appiness and joy with us kep' us as much as anythin', especially when any old companions come in a jeerin', and tauntin', and a tryin' to make us give in and begin again; Kitty'd sit by with 'er bright face, and lookin' so confident like, that we'd a'scorned to give in, I do believe, with 'er eye upon us. Well! ma'am, when I'd kep' it a month, and the poor wife was a strugglin' 'ard, and a succeedin' too, I takes that very same bottle, and I seals it up, and I sticks it up there on that shelf, and there it's been ever since, and it reminds us of God's goodness, and o' what Kitty done, and I'm prouder o't standing there, ma'am, than anythin' else we've got."

Mrs. Marsh was wiping sympathetic tears away, and now she said earnestly, "You must tell this story to help others, who are tempted as you were—but do you never feel now, either of you, any fear of giving way to the love of drink again?"

"Never, ma'am," said the old man; "for myself I ain't a bit afeard, I can *smell* it, and not feel no inclination to drink it, but Mary Ann there, she can't do that yet, can yer?"

"No, ma'am," said the wife earnestly, "I'm all right 'ere, but I'm downright afeard of goin' within smell or sight of drink, or of bein' without Thomas 'ere to 'elp me."

"Well, ma'am," said Thomas, with a fond look at his wife, "she's fought wonderful 'ard, and I don't believe as 'ow the Lord will take me away until she's strong enough to be left alone."

Mrs. Marsh's gentle voice said, "Don't be afraid, Mrs. May: as long as you pray and try, our dear Saviour will help you," and with many more encouraging and cheering words, she left the little house, where she had learnt still more of the immense struggle to be gone through by those who have once succumbed to the awful love of drink, and of the sympathy needed to encourage them to persevere in giving it up.

Years afterwards Mrs. Marsh, who, soon after hearing the Mays' story, had to go abroad, revisited Prospect Row, and found that the old man was dead, and that his widow lived with Kitty and her children, and that she was now strong and thorough in her hatred and renunciation of drink, and never tired of telling her grandchildren the story of their mother's dream, and God's blessing on it.

THE BOTTLE
and
THE DRUNKARD'S CHILDREN

George Cruikshank

Popular illustrator and caricaturist George Cruikshank's (1792–1878) gradual conversion to temperance in the 1840s was partly inspired by his father's death from delirium tremens (a drink-related set of symptoms which was at that time identified as a specific disease) and partly by his worries about his own increasingly extreme drinking bouts. This conversion led him to produce one of the most influential anti-drink stories of the century, *The Bottle* (1847). A few years later, he signed a pledge to stop drinking entirely (a common thing among members of temperance groups until the mid-twentieth century). Although his fame as Charles Dickens's illustrator no doubt added to the success of the series, Cruikshank's conversion disgusted his friend and caused them to permanently part ways. In particular, Cruikshank's temperance versions of classic fairy tales in George Cruikshank's Fairy Library (1853) prompted Dickens to publish a public objection titled "Fraud on the Fairies" (1853) in his own popular periodical, *Household Words* (1850–1859). Dickens opposed teetotalism because of his basic objection to universal abstinence (i.e. the idea that everyone should stop drinking alcohol). He saw drinking as an important source of relief and conviviality for the majority of the population, particularly the working and middle classes. In one of several vitriolic anti-temperance articles, he argues: "Because Bill Brute, the robber in Newgate, and Mr. Brallaghan of Killalloo, resident down the next court, make wild beasts of themselves under the influence of strong liquor, therefore Jones, the decent and industrious mechanic, going to Hampton Court for a summer day with his wife and family is not to have his pint of beer and his glass of gin and water".[*] The fleeting characterisation of these working-class men—"Bill Brute" representing the criminal classes and "Jones" the "industrious" skilled worker—is a direct response to the equally extreme caricatures of Cruikshank and other temperance writers in their focus on the drinking of the working classes.

[*]   Charles Dickens, "Demoralisation and Total Abstinence", *The Examiner*, 27 Oct 1849.

THE BOTTLE

PLATE I   The bottle is brought out for the first time: the
husband induces his wife "just to take a drop".

PLATE II   He is discharged from his employment for
drunkenness: they pawn their clothes to supply the bottle.

PLATE III   An execution sweeps off the greater part of their furniture: they comfort themselves with the bottle.

PLATE IV   Unable to obtain employment, they are driven by poverty into the streets to beg, and by this means they still supply the bottle.

PLATE V Cold, misery, and want, destroy their youngest
child: they console themselves with the bottle.

PLATE VI Fearful quarrels, and brutal violence, are the
natural consequences of the frequent use of the bottle.

PLATE VII   The husband, in a state of furious drunkenness,
kills his wife with the instrument of all their misery.

PLATE VIII   The bottle has done its work—it has destroyed the
infant and the mother, it has brought the son and daughter to vice
and to the streets, and has left the father a hopeless maniac.

THE DRUNKARD'S CHILDREN

PLATE I Neglected by their parents, educated only in the streets, and falling into the hands of wretches who live upon the vices of others, they are led to the gin-shop, to drink at that fountain which nourishes every species of crime.

PLATE II Between the fine flaring gin-palace and the low dirty beer-shop, the boy-thief squanders and gambles away his ill-gotten gains.

PLATE III From the gin-shop to the dancing-rooms, from the dancing-rooms to the gin-shop, the poor girl is driven on in that course which ends in misery.

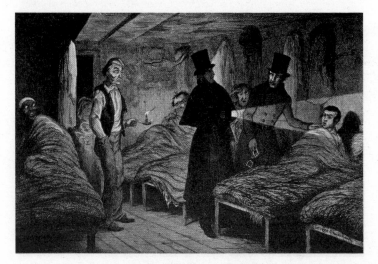

PLATE IV Urged on by his ruffian companions, and excited by drink, he commits a desperate robbery. He is taken by the police at the three-penny lodging house.

PLATE V From the bar of the gin-shop to the bar
of the Old Bailey it is but one step.

PLATE VI The drunkard's son is sentenced to the transportation
for life; the daughter, suspected of participation in the robbery, is
acquitted. The brother and sister part for ever in this world.

PLATE VII Early dissipation has destroyed the neglected
boy. The wretched convict droops, and dies.

PLATE VIII The maniac father and the convict brother
are gone. The poor girl, homeless, friendless, deserted,
destitute, and gin-mad, commits self-murder.

THE OSTLER

Wilkie Collins

Wilkie Collins (1824–1889) is best known for writing some of the earliest sensation novels including *The Woman in White* (1859) and *The Moonstone* (1868). Sensation fiction was named by one of its harshest critics, Henry Mansel, in an article that called for a stop to the genre, arguing that the novels morally corrupted their readers. The genre was short lived and petered out in the 1870s but it was influential on the development of important modern forms like the detective novel. Also known as the "enigma novel", sensation stories were designed to give a physical thrill (sensation) to the reader and were filled with mysteries, murders, and morally questionable characters. Collins's earlier works, including this short story, carried the seeds of this new genre, and this short story includes many of the key features we would now associate with sensation fiction.

In the 1850s, Collins's short stories and articles appeared regularly in his friend Charles Dickens's publications and they often collaborated on stories and theatrical performances. This story was first published in December 1855 in Dickens's popular periodical titled *Household Words* which featured his own work, fiction and non-fiction, and that of a wide range of new and celebrated authors of the time. "The Ostler" featured in one of the most famous collaborative Christmas collections published in *Household Words*. Although the seven stories were published anonymously, as was usual for this periodical, we now know from Dickens's notes and the brilliant free online repository for Dickens's journals (djo.org.uk) that these interconnecting stories were written by different authors, carefully curated by Dickens.* Although Collins was dissatisfied with the story and re-wrote it as "The Dream-Woman" some years later, I consider "The Ostler" to be the most complete and psychologically complex version of his tale. Drink features in its most disreputable form according to Victorian paternalistic rhetoric: the drunken woman. As you begin to read the story, I ask you to consider a question: does his overbearing mother really believe that Isaac's new wife is the terrifying woman from his dream or does her malignant suggestion drive a wedge between the newlyweds?

* See their page on this Christmas edition for more information: <www.djo. org.uk/indexes/magazines/1855-christmas.html>.

I find an old man, fast asleep, in one of the stalls of the stable. It is mid-day, and rather a strange time for an ostler to devote to sleep. Something curious, too, about the man's face. A withered woe-begone face. The eyebrows painfully contracted; the mouth fast set, and drawn down at the corners; the hollow cheeks sadly, and, as I cannot help fancying, prematurely wrinkled; the scanty, grizzled hair, telling weakly its own tale of some past sorrow or suffering. How fast he draws his breath, too, for a man asleep! He is talking in his sleep.

"Wake up!" I hear him say, in a quick whisper through his fast-clenched teeth. "Wake up there! Murder! O Lord help me! Lord help me, alone in this place!"

He stops, and sighs again—moves one lean arm slowly, till it rests over his throat—shudders a little, and turns on his straw—the arm leaves his throat—the hand stretches itself out, and clutches at the side towards which he has turned, as if he fancies himself to be grasping at the edge of something. Is he waking? No—there is the whisper again; he is still talking in his sleep.

"Light grey eyes," he says now, "and a droop in the left eyelid. Yes! yes!—flaxen hair with a gold-yellow streak in it—all right, mother—fair, white arms with a down on them—little lady's hand, with a reddish look under the finger-nails—and the knife—always the cursed knife—first on one side, then on the other. Aha! you she-devil, where's the knife? Never mind, mother—too late now. I've promised to marry, and marry I must. Murder! wake up there! for God's sake, wake up!"

At the last words his voice rises, and he grows so restless on a sudden, that I draw back quietly to the door. I see him shudder on the straw—his withered face grows distorted—he throws up both his hands with a quick, hysterical gasp; they strike against the bottom of the manger under which he lies; the blow awakens him; I have just time to slip through the door, before his eyes are fairly open and his senses are his own again.

What I have seen and heard has so startled and shocked me, that I feel my heart beating fast, as I softly and quickly retrace my steps across the inn-yard. The discomposure that is going on within me, apparently shows itself in my face; for, as I get back to the covered way leading to the inn stairs, the landlord, who is just coming out of the house to ring some bell in the yard, stops astonished, and asks what is the matter with me? I tell him what I have just seen.

"Aha!" says the landlord, with an air of relief. "I understand now. Poor old chap! He was only dreaming his old dream over again. There's the queerest story—of a dreadful kind, too, mind you—connected with him and his dream, that ever was told."

I entreat the landlord to tell me the story. After a little hesitation, he complies with my request.

Some years ago, there lived in the suburbs of a large sea-port town, on the west coast of England, a man in humble circumstances, by name Isaac Scatchard. His means of subsistence were derived from any employment that he could get, as an ostler; and, occasionally, when times went well with him, from temporary engagements in service, as stable-helper in private houses. Though a faithful, steady, and honest man, he got on badly in his calling. His ill-luck was proverbial among his neighbours. He was always missing good opportunities, by no fault of his own; and always living longest in service with amiable people who were not punctual payers of wages. "Unlucky Isaac" was his nickname in his own neighbourhood—and no one could say that he did not richly deserve it.

With far more than one man's fair share of adversity to endure, Isaac had but one consolation to support him—and that was of the dreariest and most negative kind. He had no wife and children to increase his anxieties and add to the bitterness of his various failures in life. It might have been from mere insensibility, or it might have been from generous unwillingness to involve another in his own unlucky destiny—but the fact undoubtedly was, that he arrived at the middle term of life without marrying; and, what is much more remarkable, without once exposing himself, from eighteen to eight and thirty, to the genial imputation of ever having had a sweetheart. When he was out of service, he lived alone with his widowed mother. Mrs. Scatchard was a woman above the average in her lowly station, as to capacities and manners. She had seen better days, as the phrase is; but she never referred to them in the presence of curious visitors; and, though perfectly polite to every one who approached her, never cultivated any intimacies among her neighbours. She contrived to provide, hardly enough, for her simple wants, by doing rough work for the tailors; and always managed to keep a decent home for her son to return to, whenever his ill-luck drove him out helpless into the world.

One bleak autumn, when Isaac was getting on fast towards forty, and when he was, as usual, out of place, through no fault of his own, he set forth from his mother's cottage on a long walk inland to a gentleman's seat, where he had heard that a stable-helper was required. It wanted then but two days of his birthday; and Mrs. Scatchard, with her usual fondness, made him promise, before he started, that he would be back in time to keep that anniversary with her, in as festive a way as their poor means would allow. It was easy for him to comply with this request, even supposing he slept a night each way on the road. He was to start from home on Monday morning; and, whether he got the new place or not, he was to be back for his birthday dinner on Wednesday at two o'clock.

Arriving at his destination too late on the Monday night to make application for the stable-helper's place, he slept at the village-inn, and, in good time on the Tuesday morning, presented himself at the gentleman's house, to fill the vacant situation. Here, again, his ill-luck pursued him as inexorably as ever. The excellent written testimonials, as to character, which he was able to produce, availed him nothing; his long walk had been taken in vain—only the day before, the stable-helper's place had been given to another man.

Isaac accepted this new disappointment resignedly, and as a matter of course. Naturally slow in capacity, he had the bluntness of sensibility and phlegmatic patience of disposition which frequently distinguish men with sluggishly-working mental powers. He thanked the gentleman's steward, with his usual quiet civility, for granting him an interview, and took his departure with no appearance of unusual depression in his face or manner. Before starting on his homeward walk, he made some enquiries at the inn, and ascertained that he might save a few miles, on his return, by following a new road. Furnished with full instructions, several times repeated, as to the various turnings he was to take, he set forth for his homeward journey, and walked on all day with only one stoppage for bread and cheese. Just as it was getting towards dark, the rain came on and the wind began to rise; and he found himself, to make matters worse, in a part of the country with which he was entirely unacquainted, though he knew himself to be some fifteen miles from home. The first house he found to inquire at was a lonely roadside inn, standing on the outskirts of a thick wood. Solitary as the place looked, it was welcome to a lost man who was also hungry, thirsty, footsore, and wet. The landlord was a civil, respectable-looking man; and the price he asked for a bed was reasonable enough. Isaac, therefore, decided on stopping comfortably at the inn for that night.

He was constitutionally a temperate man. His supper simply consisted of two rashers of bacon, a slice of home-made bread, and a pint of ale. He did not go to bed immediately after this moderate meal, but sat up with the landlord talking about his bad prospects and his long run of ill-luck, and diverging from these topics to the subject of horse-flesh and racing. Nothing was said either by himself, his host, or the few labourers who strayed into the tap-room, which could, in the slightest degree, excite the very small and very dull imaginative faculty which Isaac Scatchard possessed.

At a little after eleven the house was closed. Isaac went round with the landlord and held the candle while the doors and lower-windows were being secured: He noticed with surprise the strength of the bolts, bars, and iron-sheathed shutters.

"You see, we are rather lonely here," said the landlord. "We never have had any attempts made to break in yet, but it's always as well to be on the safe side. When nobody is sleeping here, I am the only man in the house. My wife and daughter are timid, and the servant-girl takes after her missusses: Another glass of ale, before you turn in?—No!—Well, how such a sober man as you comes to be out of place is more than I can make out, for one.—Here's where you're to sleep. You're our only lodger to-night, and I think you'll say my missus has done her best to make you comfortable. You're quite sure you won't have another glass of ale?—Very well. Good night."

It was half-past eleven by the clock in the passage as they went up stairs to the bedroom, the window of which looked on to the wood at the back of the house. Isaac locked the door, set his candle on the chest of drawers, and wearily got ready for bed. The bleak autumn wind was still blowing, and the solemn, monotonous, surging moan of it in the wood was dreary and awful to hear through the night-silence. Isaac felt strangely wakeful, and resolved, as he lay down in bed, to keep the candle alight until he began to grow sleepy; for there was something unendurably depressing in the bare idea of lying awake in the darkness, listening to the dismal, ceaseless moaning of the wind in the wood.

Sleep stole on him before he was aware of it. His eyes closed, and he fell off insensibly to rest, without having so much as thought of extinguishing the candle.

The first sensation of which he was conscious after sinking into slumber, was a strange shivering that ran through him suddenly from head to foot, and a dreadful sinking pain at the heart, such as he had never felt before. The shivering only disturbed his slumbers—the pain woke him instantly. In one moment he passed from a state of sleep to a state of wakefulness—his eyes wide open—his mental perceptions cleared on a sudden as if by a miracle.

The candle had burnt down nearly to the last morsel of tallow; but the top of the unsnuffed wick had just fallen off, and the light in the little room was, for the moment, fair and full. Between the foot of his bed and the closed door there stood a woman with a knife in her hand, looking at him. He was stricken speechless with terror, but he did not lose the preternatural clearness of his faculties; and he never took his eyes off the woman. She said not one word as they stared each other in the face; but she began to move slowly towards the left-hand side of the bed.

His eyes followed her. She was a fair, fine woman, with yellowish flaxen hair, and light grey eyes, with a droop in the left eyelid. He noticed those things and fixed them on his mind, before she was round at the side of the bed. Speechless, with no expression in her face, with no noise following her footfall,—she came closer and closer—stopped—and slowly raised the knife. He laid his right arm over his throat to save it; but; as he saw the knife coming down, threw his hand across the bed to the right side, and jerked his body over that way, just as the knife descended on the mattress within an inch of his shoulder.

His eyes fixed on her arm and hand, as she slowly drew the knife out of the bed. A white, well-shaped arm, with a pretty down lying lightly over the fair skin. A delicate, lady's hand, with the crowning beauty of a pink flush under and round the finger-nails.

She drew the knife out, and passed back again slowly to the foot of the bed; stopped there for a moment looking at him; then came on—still speechless, still with no expression on the blank, beautiful face, still with no sound following the stealthy footfalls—came on to the right side of the bed where he now lay. As she approached, she raised the knife again, and he drew himself away to the left side. She struck, as before, right into the mattress, with a deliberate, perpendicularly-downward action of the arm. This time his eyes wandered from her to the knife. It was like the large clasp knives which he had often seen labouring men use to cut their bread and bacon with. Her delicate little fingers did not conceal more than two thirds of the handle; he noticed that it was made of buck-horn, clean and shining as the blade was, and looking like new.

For the second time she drew the knife out, concealed it in the wide sleeve of her gown, then stopped by the bedside, watching him. For an instant he saw her standing in that position—then the wick of the spent candle fell over into the socket. The flame diminished to a little blue point, and the room grew dark. A moment, or less, if possible, passed so—and then the wick flamed up, smokily, for the last time. His eyes were still looking eagerly over the right-hand side of the bed when the final flash of light came, but they discerned nothing. The fair woman with the knife was gone.

The conviction that he was alone again, weakened the hold of the terror that had struck him dumb up to this time. The preternatural sharpness which the very intensity of his panic had mysteriously imparted to his faculties, left them suddenly. His brain grew confused—his heart beat wildly—his ears opened for the first time since the appearance of the woman, to a sense of the woful, ceaseless moaning of the wind among the trees. With the dreadful conviction of the reality of what he had seen, still strong within him, he leapt out of bed, and screaming—"Murder!—Wake up, there, wake up!"—dashed headlong through the darkness to the door.

It was fast locked, exactly as he had left it on going to bed.

His cries on starting up, had alarmed the house. He heard the terrified, confused, exclamations of women; he saw the master of the house approaching along the passage, with his burning rush-candle in one hand and his gun in the other.

"What is it?" asked the landlord, breathlessly.

Isaac could only answer in a whisper: "A woman, with a knife in her hand," he gasped out. "In my room—a fair, yellow-haired woman; she jobbed at me with the knife, twice over."

The landlord's pale cheeks grew paler. He looked at Isaac eagerly by the flickering light of his candle; and his face began to get red again—his voice altered, too, as well as his complexion.

"She seems to have missed you twice," he said.

"I dodged the knife as it came down," Isaac went on, in the same scared whisper. "It struck the bed each time."

The landlord took his candle into the bedroom immediately. In less than a minute he came out again into the passage in a violent passion.

"The devil fly away with you and your woman with the knife! What do you mean by coming into a man's place and frightening his family out of their wits about a dream?"

"I'll leave your house," said Isaac, faintly. "Better out on the road, in rain and dark, on my way home, than back again in that room after what I've seen in it. Lend me a light to get on my clothes by, and tell me what I'm to pay."

"Pay!" cried the landlord, leading the way with his light sulkily into the bedroom. "You'll find your score on the slate when you go down stairs. I wouldn't have taken you in for all the money you've got about you, if I'd known your dreaming, screeching ways before-hand. Look at the bed. Where's the cut of a knife in it? Look at the window—is the lock bursted? Look at the door (which I heard you fasten myself)—is it broke in? A murdering woman with a knife in my house! You ought to be ashamed of yourself!"

Isaac answered not a word. He huddled on his clothes; and then they went down stairs together.

"Nigh on twenty minutes past two!" said the landlord, as they passed the clock. "A nice time in the morning to frighten honest people out of their wits!"

Isaac paid his bill, and the landlord let him out at the front door, asking, with a grin of contempt, as he undid the strong fastenings, whether "the murdering woman got in that way?" They parted without a word on either side. The rain had ceased; but the night was dark, and the wind bleaker than ever. Little did the darkness, or the cold, or the uncertainty about his way home, matter to Isaac. If he had been turned out into a wilderness in a thunder-storm, it would have been a relief, after what he had suffered in the bedroom of the inn.

What was the fair woman with the knife? The creature of a dream, or that other creature from the unknown world called among men by the name of ghost? He could make nothing of the mystery—had made nothing of it, even when it was mid-day on Wednesday, and when he stood, at last, after many times missing his road, once more on the doorstep of home.

His mother came out eagerly to receive him. His face told her in a moment that something was wrong.

"I've lost the place; but that's my luck. I dreamed an ill dream last night, mother—or, may be, I saw a ghost. Take it either way, it scared me out of my senses, and I'm not my own man again yet."

"Isaac! your face frightens me. Come in to the fire. Come in, and tell mother all about it."

He was as anxious to tell as she was to hear; for it had been his hope, all the way home, that his mother, with her quicker capacity and superior knowledge, might be able to throw some light on the mystery which he could not clear up for himself. His memory of the dream was still mechanically vivid, though his thoughts were entirely confused by it.

His mother's face grew paler and paler as he went on. She never interrupted him by so much as a single word; but when he had done, she moved her chair close to his, put her arm round his neck, and said to him:

"Isaac, you dreamed your ill dream on this Wednesday morning. What time was it when you saw the fair woman with the knife in her hand?"

Isaac reflected on what the landlord had said when they passed by the clock on his leaving the inn—allowed as nearly as he could for the time that must have elapsed between the unlocking of his bedroom door and the paying of his bill just before going away, and answered:

"Somewhere about two o'clock in the morning."

His mother suddenly quitted her hold of his neck, and struck her hands together with a gesture of despair.

"This Wednesday is your birthday Isaac; and two o'clock in the morning was the time when you were born!"

Isaac's capacities were not quick enough to catch the infection of his mother's superstitious dread. He was amazed and a little startled also, when she suddenly rose from her chair, opened her old writing-desk, took out pen and ink and paper, and then said to him:

"Your memory is but a poor one, Isaac, and now I'm an old woman, mine's not much better. I want all about this dream of yours to be as well known to both of us, years hence, as it is now. Tell me over again all you told me a minute ago, when you spoke of what the woman with the knife looked like."

Isaac obeyed, and marvelled much as he saw his mother carefully set down on paper the very words that he was saying. "Light grey eyes," she wrote, as they came to the descriptive part, "with a droop, in the left eyelid. Flaxen hair, with a gold-yellow streak in it. White arms, with a down on them. Little lady's hand, with a reddish look about the finger-nails. Clasp knife with a buck-horn handle, that seemed as good as new." To these particulars, Mrs. Scatchard added the year, month, day of the week, and time in the morning, when the woman of the dream appeared to her son. She then locked up the paper carefully in her writing-desk.

Neither on that day, nor on any day after, could her son induce her to return to the matter of the dream. She obstinately kept her thoughts about it to herself, and even refused to refer again to the paper in her writing-desk. Ere long, Isaac grew weary of attempting to make her break her resolute silence; and time, which sooner or later, wears out all things, gradually wore out the impression produced on him by the dream. He began by thinking of it carelessly, and he ended by not thinking of it at all. This result was the more easily brought about by the advent of some important changes for the better in his prospects, which commenced not long after his terrible night's experience at the inn. He reaped at last the reward of his long and patient suffering under adversity, by getting an excellent place, keeping it for seven years, and leaving it, on the death of his master, not only with an excellent character, but also with a comfortable annuity bequeathed to him as a reward for saving his mistress's life in a carriage accident. Thus it happened that Isaac Scatchard returned to his old mother, seven years after the time of the dream at the inn, with an annual sum of money at his disposal, sufficient to keep them both in ease and independence for the rest of their lives.

The mother, whose health had been bad of late years, profited so much by the care bestowed on her and by freedom from money anxieties, that when Isaac's next birthday came round, she was able to sit up comfortably at table and dine with him.

On that day, as the evening drew on, Mrs. Scatchard discovered that a bottle of tonic medicine—which she was accustomed to take, and in which she had fancied that a dose or more was still left— happened to be empty. Isaac immediately volunteered to go to the chemist's, and get it filled again. It was as rainy and bleak an autumn night as on the memorable past occasion when he lost his way and slept at the roadside inn.

On going into the chemist's shop, he was passed hurriedly by a poorly-dressed woman coming out of it. The glimpse he had of her face struck him, and he looked back after her as she descended the door-steps.

"You're noticing that woman?" said the chemist's apprentice behind the counter. "It's my opinion there's something wrong with her. She's been asking for laudanum to put to a bad tooth. Master's out for half an hour; and I told her I wasn't allowed to sell poison to strangers in his absence. She laughed in a queer way, and said she would come back in half an hour. If she expects master to serve her, I think she'll be disappointed. It's a case of suicide, sir, if ever there was one yet."

These words added immeasurably to the sudden interest in the woman which Isaac had felt at the first sight of her face. After he had got the medicine-bottle filled, he looked about anxiously for her, as soon as he was out in the street. She was walking slowly up and down on the opposite side of the road. With his heart, very much to his own surprise, beating fast, Isaac crossed over and spoke to her.

He asked if she was in any distress. She pointed to her torn shawl, her scanty dress, her crushed, dirty bonnet—then moved under a lamp so as to let the light fall on her stern, pale, but still most beautiful face.

"I look like a comfortable, happy woman—don't I?" she said with a bitter laugh.

She spoke with a purity of intonation which Isaac had never heard before from other than ladies' lips. Her slightest actions seemed to have the easy negligent grace of a thorough-bred woman. Her skin, for all its poverty-stricken paleness, was as delicate as if her life had been passed in the enjoyment of every social comfort that wealth can purchase. Even her small, finely-shaped hands, gloveless as they were, had not lost their whiteness.

Little by little, in answer to his question, the sad story of the woman came out. There is no need to relate it here; it is told over and over again in Police Reports and paragraphs about Attempted Suicides.

"My name is Rebecca Murdoch," said the woman, as she ended. "I have ninepence left, and I thought of spending it at the chemist's over the way in securing a passage to the other world. Whatever it is, it can't be worse to me than this—so why should I stop here?"

Besides the natural compassion and sadness moved in his heart by what he heard, Isaac felt within him some mysterious influence at work all the time the woman was speaking, which utterly confused his ideas and almost deprived him of his powers of speech. All that he could say in answer to her last reckless words was, that he would prevent her from attempting her own life, if he followed her about all night to do it. His rough, trembling earnestness seemed to impress her.

"I won't occasion you that trouble," she answered, when he repeated his threat. "You have given me a fancy for living by speaking kindly to me. No need for the mockery of protestations and promises. You may believe me without them. Come to Fuller's Meadow to-morrow at twelve, and you will find me alive, to answer for myself. No!—no money. My ninepence will do to get me as good a night's lodging as I want."

She nodded and left him. He made no attempt to follow—he felt no suspicion that she was deceiving him.

"It's strange, but I can't help believing her," he said to himself—and walked away, bewildered, towards home.

On entering the house his mind was still so completely absorbed by its new subject of interest, that he took no notice of what his mother was doing when he came in with the bottle of medicine. She had opened her old writing-desk in his absence, and was now reading a paper attentively that lay inside it. On every birthday of Isaac's since she had written down the particulars of his dream from his own lips, she had been accustomed to read that same paper, and ponder over it in private.

The next day he went to Fuller's Meadow. He had done only right in believing her so implicitly—she was there, punctual to a minute, to answer for herself. The last-left faint defences in Isaac's heart against the fascination which a word or look from her began inscrutably to exercise over him, sank down and vanished before her for ever on that memorable morning.

When a man, previously insensible to the influence of women, forms an attachment in middle life, the instances are rare indeed, let the warning circumstances be what they may, in which he is found capable of freeing himself from the tyranny of the new ruling passion. The charm of being spoken to familiarly, fondly, and gratefully by a woman whose language and manners still retained enough of their early refinement to hint at the high social station that she had lost, would have been a dangerous luxury to a man of Isaac's rank at the age of twenty. But it was far more than that—it was certain ruin to him—now that his heart was opening unworthily to a new influence, at that middle time of life when strong feelings of all kinds, once implanted, strike root most stubbornly in a man's moral nature, A few more stolen interviews after that first morning in Fuller's Meadow completed his infatuation. In less than a month from the time when he first met her, Isaac Scatchard had consented to give Rebecca Murdoch a new interest in existence, and a chance of recovering the character she had lost, by promising to make her his wife.

She had taken possession, not of his passions only, but of his faculties as well. All arrangements for the present and all plans for the future were of her devising. All the mind he had he put into her keeping. She directed him on every point; even instructing him how to break the news of his approaching marriage in the safest manner to his mother.

"If you tell her how you met me and who I am at first," said the cunning woman, "she will move heaven and earth to prevent our marriage. Say I am the sister of one of your fellow-servants—ask her to see me before you go into any more particulars—and leave it to me to do the rest. I want to make her love me next best to you, Isaac, before she knows anything of who I really am."

The motive of the deceit was sufficient to sanctify it to Isaac. The stratagem proposed relieved him of his one great anxiety, and quieted his uneasy conscience on the subject, of his mother. Still, there was something wanting to perfect his happiness, something that he could not realise, something mysteriously untraceable, and yet, something that perpetually made itself felt; not when he was absent from Rebecca Murdoch, but, strange to say, when he was actually in her presence! She was kindness itself with him; she never made him feel his inferior capacities, and inferior manners,—she showed the sweetest anxiety to please him in the smallest trifles; but, in spite of all these attractions, he never could feel quite at his ease with her. At their first meeting, there had mingled with his admiration when he looked in her face, a faint involuntary feeling of doubt whether that face was entirely strange to him. No after familiarity had the slightest effect on this inexplicable, wearisome uncertainty.

Concealing the truth as he had been directed, he announced his marriage engagement precipitately and confusedly to his mother, on the day when he contracted it. Poor Mrs. Scatchard showed her perfect confidence in her son by flinging her arms round his neck, and giving him joy of having found at last, in the sister of one of his fellow-servants, a woman to comfort and care for him after his mother was gone. She was all eagerness to see the woman of her son's choice; and the next day was fixed for the introduction.

It was a bright sunny morning, and the little cottage parlour was full of light, as Mrs. Scatchard, happy and expectant, dressed for the occasion in her Sunday gown, sat waiting for her son and her future daughter-in-law. Punctual to the appointed time, Isaac hurriedly and nervously led his promised wife into the room. His mother rose to receive her—advanced a few steps, smiling—looked Rebecca full in the eyes—and suddenly stopped. Her face, which had been flushed the moment before, turned white in an instant—her eyes lost their expression of softness and kindness, and assumed a blank look of terror—her outstretched hands fell to her sides, and she staggered back a few steps with a low cry to her son.

"Isaac!" she whispered, clutching him fast by the arm, when he asked alarmedly if she was taken ill. "Isaac! Does that woman's face remind you of nothing?"

Before he could answer; before he could look round to where Rebecca, astonished and angered by her reception, stood, at the lower end of the room; his mother pointed impatiently to her writing-desk, and gave him the key.

"Open it," she said, in a quick, breathless whisper.

"What does this mean? Why am I treated as if I had no business here? Does your mother want to insult me?" asked Rebecca, angrily.

"Open it, and give me the paper in the left-hand drawer. Quick! quick, for Heaven's sake!" said Mrs. Scatchard, shrinking further back in terror. Isaac gave her the paper. She looked it over eagerly for a moment—then followed Rebecca, who was now turning away haughtily to leave the room, and caught her by the shoulder—abruptly raised the long, loose sleeve of her gown, and glanced at her hand and arm. Something like fear began to steal over the angry expression of Rebecca's face as she shook herself free from the old woman's grasp. "Mad!" she said to herself; "and Isaac never told me." With these few words she left the room.

Isaac was hastening after her when his mother turned and stopped his further progress. It wrung his heart to see the misery and terror in her face as she looked at him.

"Light grey eyes," she said, in low, mournful, awe-struck tones, pointing towards the open door. "A droop in the left eyelid. Flaxen hair with a gold-yellow streak in it. White arms with a down on them. Little, lady's hand, with a reddish look under the finger-nails. *The woman of the dream!*—Oh, Heaven! Isaac, the woman of the dream!"

That faint cleaving doubt which he had never been able to shake off in Rebecca Murdoch's presence, was fatally set at rest for ever. He *had* seen her face, then, before—seven years before, on his birthday, in the bedroom of the lonely inn. "The woman of the dream!"

"Be warned, Oh, my son! be warned! Isaac! Isaac! let her go, and do you stop with me!"

Something darkened the parlour window, as those words were said. A sudden chill ran through him; and he glanced sidelong at the shadow. Rebecca Murdoch had come back. She was peering incuriously at them over the low window blind.

"I have promised to marry, mother," he said, "and marry I must."

The tears came into his eyes as he spoke, and dimmed his sight; but he could just discern the fatal face outside moving away again from the window.

His mother's head sank lower.

"Are you faint?" he whispered.

"Broken-hearted, Isaac."

He stooped down and kissed her. The shadow, as he did so, returned to the window; and the fatal face peered in curiously once more.

Three weeks after that day, Isaac and Rebecca were man and wife. All that was hopelessly dogged and stubborn in the man's moral nature, seemed to have closed round his fatal passion, and to have fixed it unassailably in his heart.

After that first interview in the cottage parlour, no consideration would induce Mrs. Scatchard to see her son's wife again, or even to talk of her when Isaac tried hard to plead her cause after their marriage. This course of conduct was not in any degree occasioned by a discovery of the degradation in which Rebecca had lived. There was no question of that between mother and son. There was no question of anything but the fearfully exact resemblance between the living breathing woman and the spectre woman of Isaac's dream. Rebecca, on her side, neither felt nor expressed the slightest sorrow at the estrangement between herself and her mother-in-law. Isaac, for the sake of peace, had never contradicted her first idea that age and long illness had affected Mrs. Scatchard's mind. He even allowed his wife to upbraid him for not having confessed this to her at the time of their marriage engagement, rather than risk anything by hinting at the truth. The sacrifice of his integrity before his one all-mastering delusion, seemed but a small thing, and cost his conscience but little, after the sacrifices he had already made.

The time of waking from his delusion—the cruel and the rueful time—was not far off. After some quiet months of married life, as the summer was ending, and the year was getting on towards the month of his birthday, Isaac found his wife altering towards him. She grew sullen and contemptuous—she formed acquaintances of the most dangerous kind, in defiance of his objections, his entreaties, and his commands,—and, worst of all, she learnt, ere long, after every fresh difference with her husband, to seek the deadly self-oblivion of drink. Little by little, after the first miserable discovery that his wife was keeping company with drunkards, the shocking certainty forced itself on Isaac that she had grown to be a drunkard herself.

He had been in a sadly desponding state for some time before the occurrence of these domestic calamities. His mother's health, as he could but too plainly discern every time he went to see her at the cottage, was failing fast; and he upbraided himself in secret as the cause of the bodily and mental suffering she endured. When, to his remorse on his mother's account, was added the shame and misery occasioned by the discovery of his wife's degradation, he sank under the double trial—his face began to alter fast, and he looked what he was, a spirit-broken man. His mother, still struggling bravely against the illness that was hurrying her to the grave, was the first to notice the sad alteration in him, and the first to hear of his last bitterest trouble with his wife. She could only weep bitterly, on the day when he made his humiliating confession; but on the next occasion when he went to see her, she had taken a resolution, in reference to his domestic afflictions, which astonished, and even alarmed him. He found her dressed to go out, and on asking the reason, received this answer:

"I am not long for this world, Isaac," said she; "and I shall not feel easy on my death-bed, unless I have done my best to the last, to make my son happy. I mean to put my own fears and my own feelings out of the question, and to go with you to your wife, and try what I can do to reclaim her. Give me your arm, Isaac; and let me do the last thing I can in this world to help my son before it is too late."

He could not disobey her: and they walked together slowly towards his miserable home. It was only one o'clock in the afternoon when they reached the cottage where he lived. It was their dinner hour, and Rebecca was in the kitchen. He was thus able to take his mother quietly into the parlour, and then prepare his wife for the interview. She had fortunately drank but little at that early hour, and she was less sullen and capricious than usual. He returned to his mother, with his mind tolerably at ease. His wife soon followed him into the parlour, and the meeting between her and Mrs. Scatchard passed off better than he had ventured to anticipate: though he observed, with secret apprehension, that his mother, resolutely as she controlled herself in other respects, could not look his wife in the face when she spoke to her. It was a relief to him, therefore, when Rebecca began to lay the cloth.

She laid the cloth—brought in the bread-tray, and cut a slice from the loaf for her husband—then returned to the kitchen. At that moment, Isaac, still anxiously watching his mother, was startled by seeing the same ghastly change pass over her face, which had altered it so awfully on the morning when Rebecca and she first met. Before he could say a word she whispered with a look of horror:—

"Take me back!—home, home, again, Isaac! Come with me, and never come back again."

He was afraid to ask for an explanation,—he could only sign to her to be silent, and help her quickly to the door. As they passed the bread-tray on the table she stopped and pointed to it.

"Did you see what your wife cut your bread with?" she asked, in a low, still whisper.

"No, mother,—I was not noticing—what was it?"

"Look!"

He did look. A new clasp-knife, with a buck-horn handle lay with the loaf in the bread-tray. He stretched out his hand, shudderingly, to possess himself of it; but, at the same time, there was a noise in the kitchen, and his mother caught at his arm.

"The knife of the dream!—Isaac, I'm faint with fear—take me away! before she comes back!"

He was hardly able to support her—the visible, tangible reality of the knife struck him with a panic, and utterly destroyed any faint doubts that he might have entertained up to this time, in relation to the mysterious dream-warning of nearly eight years before. By a last desperate effort, he summoned self-possession enough to help his mother quietly out of the house,—so quietly, that the "dream-woman" (he thought of her by that name, now!) did not hear them departing, from the kitchen.

"Don't go back, Isaac,—don't go back!" implored Mrs. Scatchard, as he turned to go away, after seeing her safely seated again in her own room.

"I must get the knife," he answered, under his breath. She tried to stop him again; but he hurried out without another word.

On his return, he found that his wife had discovered their secret departure from the house. She had been drinking, and was in a fury of passion. The dinner in the kitchen was flung under the grate; the cloth was off the parlour-table. Where was the knife? Unwisely, he asked for it. She was only too glad of the opportunity of irritating him, which the request afforded her. "He wanted the knife, did he? Could he give her a reason why?—No!—Then he should not have it,—not if he went down on his knees to ask for it." Further recriminations elicited the fact that she had bought it a bargain—and that she considered it her own especial property. Isaac saw the uselessness of attempting to get the knife by fair means, and determined to search for it, later in the day, in secret. The search was unsuccessful. Night came on, and he left the house to walk about the streets. He was afraid now to sleep in the same room with her.

Three weeks passed. Still sullenly enraged with him, she would not give up the knife; and still that fear of sleeping in the same room with her, possessed him. He walked about at night, or dozed in the parlour, or sat watching by his mother's bedside. Before the expiration of the first week in the new month his mother died. It wanted then but ten days' of her son's birthday. She had longed to live till that anniversary. Isaac was present at her death; and her last words in this world were addressed to him: "Don't go back, my son, don't go back!"

WILKIE COLLINS

He was obliged to go back, if it were only to watch his wife. Exasperated to the last degree by his distrust of her, she had revenge-fully sought to add a sting to his grief, during the last days of his mother's illness, by declaring that she would assert her right to attend the funeral. In spite of all that he could do, or say, she held with wicked pertinacity to her word; and, on the day appointed for the burial, forced herself—inflamed and shameless with drink—into her husband's presence, and declared that she would walk in the funeral procession to his mother's grave.

This last worst outrage, accompanied by all that was most insulting in word and look, maddened him for the moment. He struck her. The instant the blow was dealt, he repented it. She crouched down, silent in a corner of the room, and eyed him steadily; it was a look that cooled his hot blood, and made him tremble. But there was no time now to think of a means of making atonement. Nothing remained, but to risk the worst till the funeral was over. There was but one way of making sure of her. He locked her into her bedroom.

When he came back some hours after, he found her sitting, very much altered in look and bearing, by the bedside, with a bundle on her lap. She rose, and faced him quietly, and spoke with a strange stillness in her voice, a strange repose in her eyes, a strange compo-sure in her manner.

"No man has ever struck me twice," she said, "and my husband shall have no second opportunity. Set the door open and let me go. From this day forth we see each other no more."

Before he could answer she passed him, and left the room. He saw her walk away up the street.

Would she return? All that night he watched and waited; but no footstep came near the house. The next night, overpowered by fatigue, he lay down in bed, in his clothes, with the door locked, the key on the table, and the candle burning. His slumber was not disturbed. The third night, the fourth, the fifth, the sixth, passed, and nothing happened. He lay down on the seventh, still in his clothes, still with the door locked, the key on the table, and the candle burning; but easier in his mind.

Easier in his mind, and in perfect health of body, when he fell off to sleep. But his rest was disturbed. He woke twice, without any sensation of uneasiness. But the third time it was that never-to-be-forgotten shivering of the night at the lonely inn, that dreadful sinking pain at the heart, which once more aroused him in an instant.

His eyes opened towards the left hand side of the bed, and there stood —— The woman of the dream, again?—No! His wife; the living reality, with the dream-spectre's face—in the dream-spectre's attitude; the fair arm up—the knife clasped in the delicate, white hand.

He sprang upon her, almost at the instant of seeing her, and yet not quickly enough to prevent her from hiding the knife. Without a word from him—without a cry from her—he pinioned her in a chair. With one hand he felt up her sleeve—and, there, where the dream-woman had hidden the knife, she had hidden it,—the knife with the buck-horn handle, that looked like new.

In the despair of that fearful moment his brain was steady, his heart was calm. He looked at her fixedly, with the knife in his hand, and said these last words:

"You told me we should see each other no more, and you have come back. It is my turn, now, to go, and to go for ever. *I* say that we shall see each other no more; and *my* word shall not be broken."

He left her, and set forth into the night. There was a bleak wind abroad, and the smell of recent rain was in the air. The distant church-clocks chimed the quarter as he walked rapidly beyond the last houses in the suburb. He asked the first policeman he met, what hour that was, of which the quarter past had just struck.

The man referred sleepily to his watch, and answered: "Two o'clock." Two in the morning. What day of the month was this day that had just begun? He reckoned it up from the date of his mother's funeral. The fatal parallel was complete—it was his birthday!

Had he escaped the mortal peril which his dream foretold? or had he only received a second warning? As that ominous doubt forced itself on his mind, he stopped, reflected, and turned back again towards the city. He was still resolute to hold to his word, and never to let her see him more; but there was a thought now in his mind of having her watched and followed. The knife was in his possession—the world was before him; but a new distrust of her—a vague, unspeakable, superstitious dread—had overcome him.

"I must know where she goes, now she thinks I have left her," he said to himself, as he stole back wearily to the precincts of his house.

It was still dark. He had left the candle burning in the bedchamber: but when he looked up at the window of the room now, there was no light in it. He crept cautiously to the house-door. On going away, he remembered to have closed it: on trying it now, he found it open.

He waited outside, never losing sight of the house, till daylight. Then he ventured indoors—listened, and heard nothing—looked into kitchen, scullery, parlour; and found nothing: went up, at last, into the bedroom—it was empty. A pick-lock lay on the floor, betraying how she had gained entrance in the night; and that was the only trace of her.

Whither had she gone? That no mortal tongue could tell him. The darkness had covered her flight; and when the day broke, no man could say where the light found her.

Before leaving the house and the town for ever, he gave instructions to a friend and neighbour to sell his furniture for anything that it would fetch, and apply the proceeds to employing the police to trace her. The directions were honestly followed, and the money was all spent; but the enquiries led to nothing. The pick-lock on the bedroom floor remained the one last useless trace of her.

At this point of the narrative the landlord paused, and looked towards the stable-door.

"So far," he said, "I tell you what was told to me. The little that remains to be added lies within my own experience. Between two and three months after the events I have just been relating, Isaac Scatchard came to me, withered and old-looking before his time, just as you saw him to-day. He had his testimonials to character with him, and he asked for employment here. I gave him a trial, and liked him in spite of his queer habits. He is as sober, honest, and willing a man as there is in England. As for his restlessness at night, and his sleeping away his leisure time in the day, who can wonder at it after hearing his story? Besides, he never objects to being roused up, when he's wanted, so there's not much inconvenience to complain of, after all."

"I suppose he is afraid of waking out of that dreadful dream in the dark?" said I.

"No," returned the landlord. "The dream comes back to him so often, that he has got to bear with it by this time resignedly enough. It's his wife keeps him waking at night, as he has often told me."

"What! Has she never been heard of yet?"

"Never. Isaac himself has the one perpetual thought about her, that she is alive and looking for him. I believe he wouldn't let himself drop off to sleep towards two in the morning for a king's ransom. Two in the morning, he says, is the time when she will find him, one of these days. Two in the morning is the time all the year round, when he likes to be most certain that he has got that clasp-knife safe about him. He does not mind being alone, as long as he is awake, except on the night before his birthday, when he firmly believes himself to be in peril of his life. The birthday has only come round once since he has been here; and then he sat up, along with the night-porter. 'She's looking for me,' he always says, when I speak to him on the one theme of his life; 'she's looking for me.' He may be right. She *may* be looking for him. Who can tell?"

"Who can tell!" said I.

AN ENGINEER'S STORY

Amelia B. Edwards

Amelia B. Edwards (1831–1892) was a journalist, author, and Egyptologist. She is rarely read these days, but her novels were popular and received good reviews from the critics in her lifetime. Her most popular novels were *My Brother's Wife* (1855) and *Lord Brackenbury* (1880).[*] Like Collins's "The Ostler", "An Engineer's Story" was also a Christmas story for one of Dickens's publications, in this case the later periodical *All the Year Round*. The issue, entitled "Mugby Junction" brought together stories about railways and featured one of Dickens's most famous ghost stories: "The Signalman".

Originally published as "No. 5 Branch Line: The Engineer", "An Engineer's Story" reflects Edwards's adventurous love of travel as the two protagonists journey from England to Italy and on to Austria in the course of the short story while working on the railways. As Nick Freeman argues, the story places "male friendship at its centre".[†] The place of alcohol in this story is more straightforward than others, the frequent drunkenness of the two men in the middle of the story

---

[*] For more information on the author and her writing go to "Celebration of Women's Writing" on the University of Pennsylvania website (<https://digital.library.upenn.edu/women/edwards/edwards.html>). This is also an excellent place to find free copies of writing by women, often rare or forgotten.

[†] Nick Freeman, "Sensational Ghosts, Ghostly Sensations", *Women's Writing* (2013).

results in the unhappy jealousy and misunderstandings between them that escalate the plot towards its finale featuring another supernatural manifestation but this time, not witnessed under the influence of drink but rather, passion.

His name, sir, was Matthew Price; mine is Benjamin Hardy. We were born within a few days of each other; bred up in the same village; taught at the same school. I cannot remember the time when we were not close friends. Even as boys, we never knew what it was to quarrel. We had not a thought, we had not a possession, that was not in common. We would have stood by each other, fearlessly, to the death. It was such a friendship as one reads about sometimes in books: fast and firm as the great Tors upon our native moorlands, true as the sun in the heavens.

The name of our village was Chadleigh. Lifted high above the pasture flats which stretched away at our feet like a measureless green lake and melted into mist on the furthest horizon, it nestled, a tiny stone-built hamlet, in a sheltered hollow about midway between the plain and the plateau. Above us, rising ridge beyond ridge, slope beyond slope, spread the mountainous moor-country, bare and bleak for the most part, with here and there a patch of cultivated field or hardy plantation, and crowned highest of all with masses of huge grey crag, abrupt, isolated, hoary, and older than the deluge. These were the Tors—Druids' Tor, King's Tor, Castle Tor, and the like; sacred places, as I have heard, in the ancient time, where crownings, burnings, human sacrifices, and all kinds of bloody heathen rites were performed. Bones, too, had been found there, and arrow-heads, and ornaments of gold and glass. I had a vague awe of the Tors in those days, and would not have gone near them after dark for the heaviest bribe.

I have said that we were born in the same village. He was the son of a small farmer, named William Price, and the eldest of a family of seven; I was the only child of Ephraim Hardy, the Chadleigh blacksmith—a well-known man in those parts, whose memory is not forgotten to this day. Just so far as a farmer is supposed to be a bigger man than a blacksmith, Mat's father might be said to have a better standing than mine; but William Price with his small holding and his seven boys, was, in fact, as poor as many a day-labourer; whilst, the blacksmith, well-to-do, bustling, popular, and open-handed, was a person of some importance in the place. All this, however, had nothing to do with Mat and myself. It never occurred to either of us that his jacket was out at elbows, or that our mutual funds came alto-gether from my pocket. It was enough for us that we sat on the same school-bench, conned our tasks from the same primer, fought each other's battles, screened each other's faults, fished, nutted, played truant, robbed orchards and birds' nests together, and spent every half-hour, authorised or stolen, in each other's society. It was a happy time; but it could not go on for ever. My father, being prosperous, resolved to put me forward in the world. I must know more, and do better, than himself. The forge was not good enough, the little world of Chadleigh not wide enough, for me. Thus it happened that I was still swinging the satchel when Mat was whistling at the plough, and that at last, when my future course was shaped out, we were separated, as it then seemed to us, for life. For, blacksmith's son as I was, furnace and forge, in some form or other, pleased me best, and I chose to be a working engineer. So my father by-and-by apprenticed me to a Birmingham iron-master; and, having bidden farewell to Mat, and Chadleigh, and the grey old Tors in the shadow of which I had spent all the days of my life, I turned my face northward, and went over into "the Black country."

I am not going to dwell on this part of my story. How I worked out the term of my apprenticeship; how, when I had served my full time and become a skilled workman, I took Mat from the plough and brought him over to the Black Country, sharing with him lodging, wages, experience—all, in short, that I had to give; how he, naturally quick to learn and brimful of quiet energy, worked his way up a step at a time, and came by-and-by to be a "first hand" in his own department; how, during all these years of change, and trial, and effort, the old boyish affection never wavered or weakened, but went on, growing with our growth and strengthening with our strength—are facts which I need do no more than outline in this place.

About this time—it will be remembered that I speak of the days when Mat and I were on the bright side of thirty—it happened that our firm contracted to supply six first-class locomotives to run on the new line, then in process of construction, between Turin and Genoa. It was the first Italian order we had taken. We had had dealings with France, Holland, Belgium, Germany; but never with Italy. The connexion, therefore, was new and valuable—all the more valuable because our Transalpine neighbours had but lately begun to lay down the iron roads, and would be safe to need more of our good English work as they went on. So the Birmingham firm set themselves to the contract with a will, lengthened our working hours, increased our wages, took on fresh hands, and determined, if energy and promptitude could do it, to place themselves at the head of the Italian labour-market, and stay there. They deserved and achieved success. The six locomotives were not only turned out to time, but were shipped, despatched, and delivered with a promptitude that fairly amazed our Piedmontese consignee. I was not a little proud, you may be sure, when I found myself appointed to superintend the transport of the engines. Being allowed a couple of assistants, I contrived that

Mat should be one of them; and thus we enjoyed together the first great holiday of our lives.

It was a wonderful change for two Birmingham operatives fresh from the Black Country. The fairy city, with its crescent background of Alps; the port crowded with strange shipping; the marvellous blue sky and bluer sea; the painted houses on the quays; the quaint cathedral, faced with black and white marble; the street of jewellers, like an Arabian Nights' bazaar; the street of palaces, with its Moorish court-yards, its fountains and orange-trees; the women veiled like brides; the galley-slaves chained two and two; the processions of priests and friars; the everlasting clangour of bells; the babble of a strange tongue; the singular lightness and brightness of the climate—made, altogether, such a combination of wonders that we wandered about, the first day, in a kind of bewildered dream, like children at a fair. Before that week was ended, being tempted by the beauty of the place and the liberality of the pay, we had agreed to take service with the Turin and Genoa Railway Company, and to turn our backs upon Birmingham for ever.

Then began a new life—a life so active and healthy, so steeped in fresh air and sunshine, that we sometimes marvelled how we could have endured the gloom of the Black Country. We were constantly up and down the line: now at Genoa, now at Turin, taking trial trips with the locomotives, and placing our old experiences at the service of our new employers.

In the mean while we made Genoa our headquarters, and hired a couple of rooms over a small shop in a by-street sloping down to the quays. Such a busy little street—so steep and winding that no vehicles could pass through it, and so narrow that the sky looked like a mere strip of deep-blue ribbon overhead! Every house in it, however, was a shop, where the goods encroached on the footway, or were piled about the door, or hung like tapestry from the balconies; and all day long, from dawn to dusk, an incessant stream of passers-by poured up and down between the port and the upper quarter of the city.

Our landlady was the widow of a silver-worker, and lived by the sale of filigree ornaments, cheap jewellery, combs, fans, and toys in ivory and jet. She had an only daughter named Gianetta, who served in the shop, and was simply the most beautiful woman I ever beheld. Looking back across this weary chasm of years, and bringing her image before me (as I can and do) with all the vividness of life, I am unable, even now, to detect a flaw in her beauty. I do not attempt to describe her. I do not believe there is a poet living who could find the words to do it; but I once saw a picture that was somewhat like her (not half so lovely, but still like her), and, for aught I know, that picture is still hanging where I last looked at it—upon the walls of the Louvre. It represented a woman with brown eyes and golden hair, looking over her shoulder into a circular mirror held by a bearded man in the background. In this man, as I then understood, the artist had painted his own portrait; in her, the portrait of the woman he loved. No picture that I ever saw was half so beautiful, and yet it was not worthy to be named in the same breath with Gianetta Coneglia.

You may be certain the widow's shop did not want for customers. All Genoa knew how fair a face was to be seen behind that dingy little counter; and Gianetta, flirt as she was, had more lovers than she cared to remember, even by name. Gentle and simple, rich and poor, from the red-capped sailor buying his earrings or his amulet, to the nobleman carelessly purchasing half the filigrees in the window, she treated them all alike—encouraged them, laughed at them, led them on and turned them off at her pleasure. She had no more heart than a marble statue; as Mat and I discovered by-and-by, to our bitter cost.

I cannot tell to this day how it came about, or what first led me to suspect how things were going with us both; but long before the waning of that autumn a coldness had sprung up between my friend and myself. It was nothing that could have been put into words. It was nothing that either of us could have explained or justified, to save his life. We lodged together, ate together, worked together, exactly as before; we even took our long evening's walk together, when the day's labour was ended; and except, perhaps, that we were more silent than of old, no mere looker-on could have detected a shadow of change. Yet there it was, silent and subtle, widening the gulf between us every day.

It was not his fault. He was too true and gentle-hearted to have willingly brought about such a state of things between us. Neither do I believe—fiery as my nature is—that it was mine. It was all hers—hers from first to last—the sin, and the shame, and the sorrow.

If she had shown a fair and open preference for either of us, no real harm could have come of it. I would have put any constraint upon myself, and, Heaven knows! have borne any suffering, to see Mat really happy. I know that he would have done the same, and more if he could, for me. But Gianetta cared not one sou for either. She never meant to choose between us. It gratified her vanity to divide us; it amused her to play with us. It would pass my power to tell how, by a thousand imperceptible shades of coquetry—by the lingering of a glance, the substitution of a word, the flitting of a smile—she contrived to turn our heads, and torture our hearts, and lead us on to love her. She deceived us both. She buoyed us both up with hope; she maddened us with jealousy; she crushed us with despair. For my part, when I seemed to wake to a sudden sense of the ruin that was about our path and I saw how the truest friendship that ever bound two lives together was drifting on to wreck and ruin, I asked myself whether any woman in the world was worth what Mat had been to me and I to him. But this was not often. I was readier to shut my eyes upon the truth than to face it; and so lived on, wilfully, in a dream.

Thus the autumn passed away, and winter came—the strange, treacherous Genoese winter, green with olive and ilex, brilliant with sunshine, and bitter with storm. Still, rivals at heart and friends on the surface, Mat and I lingered on in our lodging in the Vicolo Balba. Still Gianetta held us, with her fatal wiles and her still more fatal beauty. At length there came a day when I felt I could bear the horrible misery and suspense of it no longer. The sun, I vowed, should not go down before I knew my sentence. She must choose between us. She must either take me or let me go. I was reckless. I was desperate. I was determined to know the worst, or the best. If the worst, I would at once turn my back upon Genoa, upon her, upon all the pursuits and purposes of my past life, and begin the world anew. This I told her, passionately and sternly, standing before her in the little parlour at the back of the shop, one bleak December morning.

"If it's Mat whom you care for most," I said, "tell me so in one word, and I will never trouble you again. He is better worth your love. I am jealous and exacting; he is as trusting and unselfish as a woman. Speak, Gianetta; am I to bid you good-bye for ever and ever, or am I to write home to my mother in England, bidding her pray to God to bless the woman who has promised to be my wife?"

"You plead your friend's cause well," she replied, haughtily. "Matteo ought to be grateful. This is more than he ever did for you."

"Give me my answer, for pity's sake," I exclaimed, "and let me go!"

"You are free to go or stay, Signor Inglese," she replied. "I am not your jailor."

"Do you bid me leave you?"

"Beata Madre! not I."

"Will you marry me, if I stay?"

She laughed aloud—such a merry, mocking, musical laugh, like a chime of silver bells!

"You ask too much," she said.

"Only what you have led me to hope these five or six months past!"

"That is just what Matteo says. How tiresome you both are!"

"O, Gianetta," I said, passionately, "be serious for one moment! I am a rough fellow, it is true—not half good enough or clever enough for you; but I love you with my whole heart, and an Emperor could do no more."

"I am glad of it," she replied; "I do not want you to love me less."

"Then you cannot wish to make me wretched! Will you promise me?"

"I promise nothing," said she, with another burst of laughter; "except that I will not marry Matteo!"

Except that she would not marry Matteo! Only that. Not a word of hope for myself. Nothing but my friend's condemnation. I might get comfort, and selfish triumph, and some sort of base assurance out of that, if I could. And so, to my shame, I did. I grasped at the vain encouragement, and, fool that I was! let her put me off again unanswered. From that day, I gave up all effort at self-control, and let myself drift blindly on—to destruction.

At length things became so bad between Mat and myself that it seemed as if an open rupture must be at hand. We avoided each other, scarcely exchanged a dozen sentences in a day, and fell away from all our old familiar habits. At this time—I shudder to remember it!—there were moments when I felt that I hated him.

Thus, with the trouble deepening and widening between us day by day, another month or five weeks went by; and February came; and, with February, the Carnival. They said in Genoa that it was a particularly dull carnival; and so it must have been; for, save a flag or two hung out in some of the principal streets, and a sort of festa look about the women, there were no special indications of the season. It was, I think, the second day when, having been on the line all the morning, I returned to Genoa at dusk, and, to my surprise, found Mat Price on the platform. He came up to me, and laid his hand on my arm.

"You are in late," he said. "I have been waiting for you three-quarters of an hour. Shall we dine together to-day?"

Impulsive as I am, this evidence of returning good will at once called up my better feelings.

"With all my heart, Mat," I replied; "shall we go to Gozzoli's?"

"No, no," he said, hurriedly. "Some quieter place—some place where we can talk. I have something to say to you."

I noticed now that he looked pale and agitated, and an uneasy sense of apprehension stole upon me. We decided on the "Pescatore," a little out-of-the-way trattoria, down near the Molo Vecchio. There, in a dingy salon, frequented chiefly by seamen, and redolent of tobacco, we ordered our simple dinner. Mat scarcely swallowed a morsel; but, calling presently for a bottle of Sicilian wine, drank eagerly.

"Well, Mat," I said, as the last dish was placed on the table, "what news have you?"

"Bad."

"I guessed that from your face."

"Bad for you—bad for me. Gianetta."

"What of Gianetta?"

He passed his hand nervously across his lips. "Gianetta is false—worse than false," he said, in a hoarse voice. "She values an honest man's heart just as she values a flower for her hair—wears it for a day, then throws it aside for ever. She has cruelly wronged us both."

"In what way? Good Heavens, speak out!"

"In the worst way that a woman can wrong those who love her. She has sold herself to the Marchese Loredano."

The blood rushed to my head and face in a burning torrent. I could scarcely see, and dared not trust myself to speak.

"I saw her going towards the cathedral," he went on, hurriedly. "It was about three hours ago. I thought she might be going to confession, so I hung back and followed her at a distance. When she got inside, however, she went straight to the back of the pulpit, where this man was waiting for her. You remember him—an old man who used to haunt the shop a month or two back. Well, seeing how deep in conversation they were, and how they stood close under the pulpit with their backs towards the church, I fell into a passion of anger and went straight up the aisle, intending to say or do something: I scarcely knew what; but, at all events, to draw her arm through mine, and take her home. When I came within a few feet, however, and found only a big pillar between myself and them, I paused. They could not see me, nor I them; but I could hear their voices distinctly, and—and I listened."

"Well, and you heard—"

"The terms of a shameful bargain—beauty on the one side, gold on the other; so many thousand francs a year; a villa near Naples—Pah! it makes me sick to repeat it."

And, with a shudder, he poured out another glass of wine and drank it at a draught.

"After that," he said, presently, "I made no effort to bring her away. The whole thing was so cold-blooded, so deliberate, so shameful, that I felt I had only to wipe her out of my memory, and leave her to her fate. I stole out of the cathedral, and walked about here by the sea for ever so long, trying to get my thoughts straight. Then I remembered you, Ben; and the recollection of how this wanton had come between us and broken up our lives drove me wild. So I went up to the station and waited for you. I felt you ought to know it all; and—and I thought, perhaps, that we might go back to England together."

"The Marchese Loredano!"

It was all that I could say; all that I could think. As Mat had just said of himself, I felt "like one stunned."

"There is one other thing I may as well tell you," he added, reluctantly, "if only to show you how false a woman can be. We—we were to have been married next month."

"*We?* Who? What do you mean?"

"I mean that we were to have been married—Gianetta and I."

A sudden storm of rage, of scorn, of incredulity, swept over me at this, and seemed to carry my senses away.

"*You!*" I cried. "Gianetta marry you! I don't believe it."

"I wish I had not believed it," he replied, looking up as if puzzled by my vehemence. "But she promised me; and I thought, when she promised it, she meant it."

"She told me, weeks ago, that she would never be your wife!"

His colour rose, his brow darkened; but when his answer came, it was as calm as the last.

"Indeed!" he said. "Then it is only one baseness more. She told me that she had refused you; and that was why we kept our engagement secret."

"Tell the truth, Mat Price," I said, well-nigh beside myself with suspicion. "Confess that every word of this is false! Confess that Gianetta will not listen to you, and that you are afraid I may succeed where you have failed. As perhaps I shall—as perhaps I shall, after all!"

"Are you mad?" he exclaimed. "What do you mean?"

"That I believe it's just a trick to get me away to England—that I don't credit a syllable of your story. You're a liar, and I hate you!"

He rose, and, laying one hand on the back of his chair, looked me sternly in the face.

"If you were not Benjamin Hardy," he said, deliberately, "I would thrash you within an inch of your life."

The words had no sooner passed his lips than I sprang at him. I have never been able distinctly to remember what followed. A curse—a blow—a struggle—a moment of blind fury—a cry—a confusion of tongues—a circle of strange faces. Then I see Mat lying back in the arms of a bystander; myself trembling and bewildered—the knife dropping from my grasp; blood upon the floor; blood upon my hands; blood upon his shirt. And then I hear those dreadful words:

"O, Ben, you have murdered me!"

He did not die—at least, not there and then. He was carried to the nearest hospital, and lay for some weeks between life and death. His case, they said, was difficult and dangerous. The knife had gone in just below the collarbone, and pierced down into the lungs. He was not allowed to speak or turn—scarcely to breathe with freedom. He might not even lift his head to drink. I sat by him day and night all through that sorrowful time. I gave up my situation on the railway; I quitted my lodging in the Vicolo Balba; I tried to forget that such a woman as Gianetta Coneglia had ever drawn breath. I lived only for Mat; and he tried to live more, I believe, for my sake than his own. Thus, in the bitter silent hours of pain and penitence, when no hand but mine approached his lips or smoothed his pillow, the old friendship came back with even more than its old trust and faithfulness. He forgave me, fully and freely; and I would thankfully have given my life for him.

At length there came one bright spring morning, when, dismissed as convalescent, he tottered out through the hospital gates, leaning on my arm, and feeble as an infant. He was not cured; neither, as I then learned to my horror and anguish, was it possible that he ever could be cured. He might live, with care, for some years; but the lungs were injured beyond hope of remedy, and a strong or healthy man he could never be again. These, spoken aside to me, were the parting words of the chief physician, who advised me to take him further south without delay.

I took him to a little coast-town called Rocca, some thirty miles beyond Genoa—a sheltered lonely place along the Riviera, where the sea was even bluer than the sky, and the cliffs were green with strange tropical plants, cacti, and aloes, and Egyptian palms. Here we lodged in the house of a small tradesman; and Mat, to use his own words, "set to work at getting well in good earnest." But, alas! it was a work which no earnestness could forward. Day after day he went down to the beach, and sat for hours drinking the sea air and watching the sails that came and went in the offing. By-and-by he could go no further than the garden of the house in which we lived. A little later, and he spent his days on a couch beside the open window, waiting patiently for the end. Ay, for the end! It had come to that. He was fading fast, waning with the waning summer, and conscious that the Reaper was at hand. His whole aim now was to soften the agony of my remorse, and prepare me for what must shortly come.

"I would not live longer, if I could," he said, lying on his couch one summer evening, and looking up to the stars. "If I had my choice at this moment, I would ask to go. I should like Gianetta to know that I forgave her."

"She shall know it," I said, trembling suddenly from head to foot. He pressed my hand.

"And you'll write to father?"

"I will."

I had drawn a little back, that he might not see the tears raining down my cheeks; but he raised himself on his elbow, and looked round.

"Don't fret, Ben," he whispered; laid his head back wearily upon the pillow—and so died.

And this was the end of it. This was the end of all that made life life to me. I buried him there, in hearing of the wash of a strange sea on a strange shore. I stayed by the grave till the priest and the bystanders were gone. I saw the earth filled in to the last sod, and the gravedigger stamp it down with his feet. Then, and not till then, I felt that I had lost him for ever—the friend I had loved, and hated, and slain. Then, and not till then, I knew that all rest, and joy, and hope were over for me. From that moment my heart hardened within me, and my life was filled with loathing. Day and night, land and sea, labour and rest, food and sleep, were alike hateful to me. It was the curse of Cain, and that my brother had pardoned me made it lie none the lighter. Peace on earth was for me no more, and goodwill towards men was dead in my heart for ever. Remorse softens some natures; but it poisoned mine. I hated all mankind but above all mankind I hated the woman who had come between us two, and ruined both our lives.

He had bidden me seek her out, and be the messenger of his forgiveness. I had sooner have gone down to the port of Genoa and taken upon me the serge cap and shotted chain of any galley-slave at his toil in the public works; but for all that I did my best to obey him. I went back, alone and on foot. I went back, intending to say to her, "Gianetta Coneglia, he forgave you; but God never will."

But she was gone. The little shop was let to a fresh occupant; and the neighbours only knew that mother and daughter had left the place quite suddenly, and that Gianetta was supposed to be under the "protection" of the Marchese Loredano. How I made inquiries here and there—how I heard that they had gone to Naples—and how, being restless and reckless of my time, I worked my passage in a French steamer, and followed her—how, having found the sumptuous villa that was now hers, I learned that she had left there some ten days and gone to Paris, where the Marchese was ambassador for the Two Sicilies—how, working my passage back again to Marseilles, and thence, in part by the river and in part by the rail, I made my way to Paris—how, day after day, I paced the streets and the parks, watched at the ambassador's gates, followed his carriage, and at last, after weeks of waiting, discovered her address—how, having written to request an interview, her servants spurned me from her door and flung my letter in my face—how, looking up at her windows, I then, instead of forgiving, solemnly cursed her with the bitterest curses my tongue could devise—and how, this done, I shook the dust of Paris from my feet, and became a wanderer upon the face of the earth, are facts which I have now no space to tell.

The next six or eight years of my life were shifting and unsettled enough. A morose and restless man, I took employment here and there, as opportunity offered, turning my hand to many things, and caring little what I earned, so long as the work was hard and the change incessant. First of all I engaged myself as chief engineer in one of the French steamers plying between Marseilles and Constantinople. At Constantinople I changed to one of the Austrian Lloyd's boats, and worked for some time to and from Alexandria, Jaffa, and those parts. After that, I fell in with a party of Mr. Layard's men at Cairo, and so went up the Nile and took a turn at the excavations of the mound of Nimroud. Then I became a working engineer on the new desert line between Alexandria and Suez; and by-and-by I worked my passage out to Bombay, and took service as an engine fitter on one of the great Indian railways. I stayed a long time in India; that is to say, I stayed nearly two years, which was a long time for me; and I might not even have left so soon, but for the war that was declared just then with Russia. That tempted me. For I loved danger and hardship as other men love safety and ease; and as for my life, I had sooner have parted from it than kept it, any day. So I came straight back to England; betook myself to Portsmouth, where my testimonials at once procured me the sort of berth I wanted. I went out to the Crimea in the engine-room of one of her Majesty's warsteamers.

I served with the fleet; of course, while the war lasted; and when it was over, went wandering off again, rejoicing in my liberty. This time I went to Canada, and after working on a railway then in progress near the American frontier, I presently passed over into the States; journeyed from north to south; crossed the Rocky Mountains; tried a month or two of life in the gold country; and then, being seized with a sudden, aching, unaccountable longing to revisit that solitary grave so far away on the Italian coast, I turned my face once more towards Europe.

Poor little grave! I found it rank with weeds, the cross half shattered, the inscription half effaced. It was as if no one had loved him, or remembered him. I went back to the house in which we had lodged together. The same people were still living there, and made me kindly welcome. I stayed with them for some weeks. I weeded, and planted, and trimmed the grave with my own hands, and set up a fresh cross in pure white marble. It was the first season of rest that I had known since I laid him there; and when at last I shouldered my knapsack and set forth again to battle with the world, I promised myself that,

God willing, I would creep back to Rocca, when my days drew near to ending, and be buried by his side.

From hence, being, perhaps, a little less inclined than formerly for very distant parts, and willing to keep within reach of that grave, I went no further than Mantua, where I engaged myself as an engine-driver on the line, then not long completed, between that city and Venice. Somehow, although I had been trained to the working engineering, I preferred in these days to earn my bread by driving. I liked the excitement of it, the sense of power, the rush of the air, the roar of the fire, the flitting of the landscape. Above all, I enjoyed to drive a night express. The worse the weather, the better it suited with my sullen temper. For I was as hard, and harder than ever. The years had done nothing to soften me. They had only confirmed all that was blackest and bitterest in my heart.

I continued pretty faithful to the Mantua line, and had been working on it steadily for more than seven months when that which I am now about to relate took place.

It was in the month of March. The weather had been unsettled for some days past, and the nights stormy; and at one point along the line, near Ponte di Brenta, the waters had risen and swept away some seventy yards of embankment. Since this accident, the trains had all been obliged to stop at a certain spot between Padua and Ponte di Brenta, and the passengers, with their luggage, had thence to be transported in all kinds of vehicles, by a circuitous country road, to the nearest station on the other side of the gap, where another train and engine awaited them. This, of course, caused great confusion and annoyance, put all our time-tables wrong, and subjected the public to a large amount of inconvenience. In the mean while an army of navvies was drafted to the spot, and worked day and night to repair the damage. At this time I was driving two through trains each day;

namely, one from Mantua to Venice in the early morning, and a return train from Venice to Mantua in the afternoon—a tolerably full day's work, covering about one hundred and ninety miles of ground, and occupying between ten and eleven hours. I was therefore not best pleased when, on the third or fourth day after the accident, I was informed that, in addition to my regular allowance of work, I should that evening be required to drive a special train to Venice. This special train, consisting of an engine, a single carriage, and a break-van, was to leave the Mantua platform at eleven; at Padua the passengers were to alight and find post-chaises waiting to convey them to Ponte di Brenta; at Ponte di Brenta another engine, carriage, and break-van were to be in readiness. I was charged to accompany them throughout.

"Corpo di Bacco," said the clerk who gave me my orders, "you need not look so black, man. You are certain of a handsome gratuity. Do you know who goes with you?"

"Not I."

"Not you, indeed! Why, it's the Duca Loredano, the Neapolitan ambassador."

"Loredano!" I stammered. "What Loredano? There was a Marchese—"

"Certo. He was the Marchese Loredano some years ago; but he has come into his dukedom since then."

"He must be a very old man by this time."

"Yes, he is old; but what of that? He is as hale, and bright, and stately as ever. You have seen him before?"

"Yes," I said, turning away; "I have seen him—years ago."

"You have heard of his marriage?"

I shook my head.

The clerk chuckled, rubbed his hands, and shrugged his shoulders.

"An extraordinary affair," he said. "Made a tremendous esclandre at the time. He married his mistress—quite a common, vulgar girl—a Genoese—very handsome; but not received, of course. Nobody visits her."

"Married her!" I exclaimed. "Impossible."

"True, I assure you."

I put my hand to my head. I felt as if I had had a fall or a blow.

"Does she—does she go to-night?" I faltered.

"O dear, yes—goes everywhere with him—never lets him out of her sight. You'll see her—la bella Duchessa!"

With this my informant laughed, and rubbed his hands again, and went back to his office.

The day went by, I scarcely know how, except that my whole soul was in a tumult of rage and bitterness. I returned from my afternoon's work about 7.25, and at 10.30 I was once again at the station. I had examined the engine; given instructions to the Fochista, or stoker, about the fire; seen to the supply of oil; and got all in readiness, when, just as I was about to compare my watch with the clock in the ticket-office, a hand was laid upon my arm, and a voice in my ear said:

"Are you the engine-driver who is going on with this special train?"

I had never seen the speaker before. He was a small, dark man, muffled up about the throat, with blue glasses, a large black beard, and his hat drawn low upon his eyes.

"You are a poor man, I suppose," he said, in a quick, eager whisper, "and, like other poor men, would not object to be better off. Would you like to earn a couple of thousand florins?"

"In what way?"

"Hush! You are to stop at Padua, are you not, and to go on again at Ponte di Brenta?"

I nodded.

"Suppose you did nothing of the kind. Suppose, instead of turning off the steam, you jump off the engine, and let the train run on?"

"Impossible. There are seventy yards of embankment gone, and—"

"Basta! I know that. Save yourself, and let the train run on. It would be nothing but an accident."

I turned hot and cold; I trembled; my heart beat fast, and my breath failed.

"Why do you tempt me?" I faltered.

"For Italy's sake," he whispered; "for liberty's sake. I know you are no Italian; but, for all that, you may be a friend. This Loredano is one of his country's bitterest enemies. Stay, here are the two thousand florins."

I thrust his hand back fiercely.

"No—no," I said. "No blood-money. If I do it, I do it neither for Italy nor for money; but for vengeance."

"For vengeance!" he repeated.

At this moment the signal was given for backing up to the platform. I sprang to my place upon the engine without another word. When I again looked towards the spot where he had been standing, the stranger was gone.

I saw them take their places—Duke and Duchess, secretary and priest, valet and maid. I saw the station-master bow them into the carriage, and stand, bareheaded, beside the door. I could not distinguish their faces; the platform was too dusk, and the glare from the engine fire too strong; but I recognised her stately figure, and the poise of her head. Had I not been told who she was, I should have known her by those traits alone. Then the guard's whistle shrilled out, and the station-master made his last bow; I turned the steam on; and we started.

My blood was on fire. I no longer trembled or hesitated. I felt as if every nerve was iron, and every pulse instinct with deadly purpose. She was in my power, and I would be revenged. She should die—she, for whom I had stained my soul with my friend's blood! She should die, in the plenitude of her wealth and her beauty, and no power upon earth should save her!

The stations flew past. I put on more steam; I bade the fireman heap in the coke, and stir the blazing mass. I would have outstripped the wind, had it been possible. Faster and faster—hedges and trees, bridges and stations, flashing past—villages no sooner seen than gone—telegraph wires twisting, and dipping, and twining themselves in one, with the awful swiftness of our pace! Faster and faster, till the fireman at my side looks white and scared, and refuses to add more fuel to the furnace. Faster and faster, till the wind rushes in our faces and drives the breath back upon our lips.

I would have scorned to save myself. I meant to die with the rest. Mad as I was—and I believe from my very soul that I was utterly mad for the time—I felt a passing pang of pity for the old man and his suite. I would have spared the poor fellow at my side, too, if I could; but the pace at which we were going made escape impossible.

Vicenza was passed—a mere confused vision of lights. Pojana flew by. At Padua, but nine miles distant, our passengers were to alight. I saw the fireman's face turned upon me in remonstrance; I saw his lips move, though I could not hear a word; I saw his expression change suddenly from remonstrance to a deadly terror, and then—merciful Heaven! then, for the first time, I saw that he and I were no longer alone upon the engine.

There was a third man—a third man standing on my right hand, as the fireman was standing on my left—a tall, stalwart man, with short curling hair, and a flat Scotch cap upon his head. As I fell back in the first shock of surprise, he stepped nearer; took my place at the engine, and turned the steam off. I opened my lips to speak to him; he turned his head slowly, and looked me in the face.

Matthew Price!

I uttered one long wild cry, flung my arms wildly up above my head, and fell as if I had been smitten with an axe.

I am prepared for the objections that may be made to my story. I expect, as a matter of course, to be told that this was an optical illusion, or that I was suffering from pressure on the brain, or even that I laboured under an attack of temporary insanity. I have heard all these arguments before, and, if I may be forgiven for saying so, I have no desire to hear them again. My own mind has been made up upon this subject for many a year. All that I can say—all that I *know* is—that Matthew Price came back from the dead to save my soul and the lives of those whom I, in my guilty rage, would have hurried to destruction. I believe this as I believe in the mercy of Heaven and the forgiveness of repentant sinners.

UNDER THE CLOAK

Rhoda Broughton

Another story set on the railways but in this case featuring the passengers and their misdeeds. Rhoda Broughton (1840–1920) was a prolific and popular author whose novels have fallen out of fashion but who sold incredibly well in her lifetime. Welsh-born Broughton was educated on her father's instructions and her uncle, Sheridan Le Fanu, was a very famous author of the period.[*] Le Fanu, well-known for his weird writings, edited the magazine *Dublin University Magazine*, which serialised Broughton's first novel, *Not Wisely but Too Well* (1867). Her novels are often described as featuring strong and sometimes transgressive women who went against some of the more conservative social norms of the time.

"Under the Cloak" features a female narrator who is quick-witted. She confidently narrates the story with a very dry sense of humour. This is an unusual story for a collection of this kind because the narrator specifies that the intoxicating liquid involved is not alcoholic. She says it is "not sherry or spirit of any kind, for it has diffused no odour through the carriage". Yet, I would argue that this story is a warning against accepting drinks from strangers and of the resulting vulnerability of women after drinking. This comes at a time when

---

[*] For some more information on Rhoda Broughton, go to the Victorian Secrets page: <https://victoriansecrets.co.uk/authors/rhoda-broughton/>.

women were regularly told that they could lose their dignity or their virginity under the influence of strong drink shared with an unsuitable man.* There is symbolism in the robbery of the lady's "jewels" from the box secured under her feet as "jewel" was often used as a euphemism for virginity at this time.

---

* See for example the moving interviews with prostitutes in Henry Mayhew's *London Labour and the London Poor* (1851).

If there be a thing in the world that my soul hateth it is a long night journey by rail. In the old coaching days I do not think that I should have minded it, passing swiftly through a summer night on the top of a speedy coach, with the star arch black-blue above one's head, the sweet smell of earth, and her numberless flowers and grasses, in one's nostrils, and the pleasant trot, trot, trot, trot, of the four strong horses in one's ears. But by railway!—in a little stuffy compartment, with nothing to amuse you if you keep awake; with a dim lamp hanging above you, tantalising you with the idea that you can read by its light, and when you try, satisfactorily proving to you that you cannot, and, if you sleep, breaking your neck, or at least stiffening it, by the brutal arrangement of the hard cushions. These thoughts pass sulkily and rebelliously through my head as I sit in my *salon* in the *Écu*, at Geneva, on the afternoon of the fine autumn day on which, in an evil hour, I have settled to take my place in the night train for Paris. I have put off going as long as I can.

I like Geneva, and am leaving some pleasant and congenial friends, but now go I must. My husband is to meet me at the station in Paris at six o'clock to-morrow morning. Six o'clock! what a barbarous hour at which to arrive! I am putting on my bonnet and cloak; I look at myself in the glass with an air of anticipative disgust. Yes, I look trim and spruce enough now—a not disagreeable object perhaps—with sleek hair, quick and alert eyes, and pink-tinted cheeks Alas! at six o'clock to-morrow morning what a different tale there will be to tell!

Dishevelled, dusty locks, half-open weary eyes, a disordered dress, and a green-coloured countenance.

I turn away with a pettish gesture, and reflecting that at least there is no wisdom in living my miseries twice over, I go downstairs, and get into the hired open carriage which awaits me. My maid and man follow with the luggage. I give stricter injunctions than ordinary to my maid never for one moment to lose her hold of the dressing-case which contains, as it happens, a great many more valuable jewels than people are wont to travel in foreign parts with, nor of a certain costly and beautiful Dresden china and gold Louis-Quatorze clock, which I am carrying home as a present to my people. We reach the station, and I straightway betake myself to the first class *salle d'attente*, there to remain penned up till the officials undo the gates of purgatory and release us—an arrangement whose wisdom I have yet to learn. There are ten minutes to spare, and the *salle* is filling fuller and fuller every moment. Chiefly my countrymen, countrywomen, and country children, beginning to troop home to their partridges. I look curiously round at them, speculating as to which of them will be my companion or companions through the night.

There are no very unusual types: girls in sailor hats and blonde hair-fringes; strong-minded old maids in painstakingly ugly waterproofs; baldish fathers; fattish mothers; a German or two, with prominent pale eyes and spectacles. I have just decided on the companions I should prefer; a large young man, who belongs to nobody, and looks as if he spent most of his life in laughing—alas! he is not likely! he is sure to want to smoke!—and a handsome and prosperous-looking young couple. They are more likely, as very probably, in the man's case, the bride-love will overcome the cigar-love. The porter comes up. The key turns in the lock; the doors open. At first I am standing close to them, flattening my nose against the glass, and looking out on the pavement; but as the passengers become more numerous, I withdraw from my prominent position, anticipating a rush for carriages. I hate and dread exceedingly a crowd, and would much prefer at any time to miss my train rather than be squeezed and jostled by one. In consequence, my maid and I are almost the last people to emerge and have the last and worst choice of seats. We run along the train looking in; the footman, my maid, and I. Full—full everywhere!

"*Dames seules?*" asks the guard.

"Certainly not! Neither '*Dames seules*' nor '*Fumeurs;*' but if it must be one or the other, certainly '*Fumeurs.*'"

I am growing nervous, when I see the footman, who is a little ahead of us, standing with an open carriage door in his hand, and signing to us to make haste. Ah! it is all right! it always comes right when one does not fuss oneself.

"Plenty of room here, 'm; only two gentlemen."

I put my foot on the high step and climb in. Rather uncivil of the two gentlemen!—neither of them offers to help me; but they are not looking this way, I suppose. "Mind the dressing-case!" I cry nervously, as I stretch out my hand to help the maid Watson up. The man pushes her from behind; in she comes—dressing-case, clock and all. Here we are for the night!

I am so busy and amused looking out of the window, seeing the different parties bidding their friends good-bye, and watching with indignation the barbaric and malicious manner in which the porters hurl the luckless luggage about, that we have steamed out of the station, and are fairly off for Paris, before I have the curiosity to glance at my fellow passengers. Well! when I do take a look at them, I do not make much of it. Watson and I occupy the two seats by one window, facing one another, our fellow-travellers have not taken the other two window seats; they occupy the middle ones, next us.

They are both reading, behind newspapers. Well! we shall not get much amusement out of them. I give them up as a bad job. Ah! if I could have had my wish, and had the laughing young man, and the pretty young couple, for company, the night would not perhaps have seemed so long. However, I should have been mortified for them to have seen how *green* I looked when the dawn came; and, as to these *commis-voyageurs* I do not care if I look as green as grass in their eyes. Thus, all no doubt is for the best; and at all events it is a good trite copy-book maxim to say so. So I forget all about them, fix my eyes on the landscape racing by, and fall into a variety of thoughts. "Will my husband really get up in time to come and meet me at the station to-morrow morning?" He does so cordially hate getting up. My only chance is his not having gone to bed at all. How will he be looking? I have not seen him for four months. Will he have succeeded in curbing his tendency to fat, during his Norway fishing? Probably not. Fishing, on the contrary, is rather a *fat-making* occupation; sluggish and sedentary. Shall we have a pleasant party at the house we are going to, for shooting? To whom in Paris shall I go for my gown? Worth? No, Worth is beyond me. There I leave the future, and go back into past enjoyments; excursions to Lansmere; trips down the lake to Chilton; a hundred and one pleasantnesses. The time slips by; the afternoon is drawing towards evening; a beginning of dusk is coming over the landscape.

I look round. God heavens! what can those men find so interesting in the papers? I thought them hideously dull, when I looked over them this morning; and yet they are still persistently reading. What can they have got hold of? I cannot well see what the man beside me has; his *vis-à-vis* is buried in an English *Times*. Just as I am thinking about him he puts down his paper and I see his face. Nothing very remarkable; a long black beard, and a hat tilted somewhat low over his forehead. I turn away my eyes hastily, for fear of being caught inquisitively scanning; but still, out of their corners I see that he has taken a little bottle out of his travelling bag, has poured some of its contents into a glass, and is putting it to its lips. It appeals as if—and, at the time it happens, I have no manner of doubt that he is drinking. Then I feel that he is addressing me. I look up and towards him; he is holding out the phial to me and saying,

"May I take the liberty of offering madame some?"

"No thank you, monsieur!" I answer, shaking my head hastily and speaking rather abruptly. There is nothing that I dislike more than being offered strange eatables or drinkables in a train or a strange hymn book in church.

He smiles politely, and then adds,

"Perhaps the *other* lady might be persuaded to take a little?"

"No thank you, sir, I'm much obliged to you," replies Watson briskly, in almost as ungrateful a tone as mine.

Again he smiles, bows, and re-buries himself in his newspaper. The thread of my thoughts is broken, I feel an odd curiosity as to the nature of the contents of that bottle. Certainly it is not sherry or spirit of any kind, for it has diffused no odour through the carriage. All this time the man beside me has said and done nothing. I wish he would move or speak, or do something. I peep covertly at him. Well! at all events, he is well defended against the night chill. What a voluminous cloak he is wrapped in; how entirely it shrouds his figure!—trimmed with *fur* too! Why it might be January instead of September. I do not know why, but that cloak makes me feel rather uncomfortable. I wish they would both move to the window, instead of sitting next us. Bah! am *I* setting up to be a timid dove? I who rather pique myself on my bravery—on my indifference to tramps, bulls, ghosts? The clock has been deposited with the umbrellas, parasols, spare shawls, rugs, etc., in the netting above Watson's head. The dressing-case—a very large and heavy one—is sitting on her lap. I lean forward and say to her,

"That box must rest very heavily on your knee, and I want a footstool—I should to more comfortable if I had one—let me put my feet on it."

I have an idea that somehow my sapphire will be safer if I have them where I can always feel that they are *there*. We make the desired change in our arrangements. Yes, both my feet are on it.

The landscape outside is darkening quickly now; our dim lamp is beginning to assert its importance. Still the men read. I feel a sensation of irritation. What can they mean by it? It is utterly impossible that they can decipher the small print of the *Times* by this feeble shaky glimmer.

As I am so thinking, the one who had before spoken lays down his paper, folds it up and deposes it on the seat beside him. Then drawing his little bottle out of his bag a second time, drinks, or seems to drink, from it. Then he again turns to me:

"Madame will pardon me; but if madame *could* be induced to try a little of this; it is a cordial of a most refreshing and invigorating description; and if she will have the amiability to allow me to say so, madame looks faint."

What *can* he mean by his urgency? *Is* it pure politeness? I wish it were not growing so dark. These thoughts run through my head as I hesitate for an instant what answer to make. Then an idea occurs to me, and I manufacture a civil smile and say, "Thank you very much, monsieur! I am a little faint, as you observe. I think I will avail myself of your obliging offer." So saying, I take the glass and touch it with my lips. I give you my word of honour that I do not think I did more; I did not mean to swallow a drop, but I suppose I must have done. He smiles with a gratified air.

"The other lady will now, perhaps, follow your example?"

By this time I am beginning to feel thoroughly uncomfortable; *why*, I should be puzzled to explain. What *is* this cordial that he is so eager to urge upon us? Though determined not to subject *myself* to its influence, I *must* see its effects upon another person. Rather brutal of me perhaps; rather in the spirit of the anatomist, who, in the interest of science, tortures live dogs and cats; but I am telling you *facts*—not what I ought to have done, but what I *did*. I make a sign to Watson to drink some. She obeys, nothing loath. She has been working hard all day packing and getting under way, and she is tired. There is no feigning about her! She has emptied the glass. Now to see what comes of it—what happens to my live dog! The bottle is replaced in the bag; still we are racing on, racing on, past the hills and fields and villages. How indistinct they are all growing! I turn back from the contemplation of the outside view to the inside one. Why, the woman is asleep already!—her chin buried in her chest, her mouth half open, looking exceedingly imbecile and very plain, as most people, when asleep out of bed, do look. A nice invigorating potion, indeed! I wish to heaven that I had gone *aux fumeurs*, or even with that cavalcade of nursery-maids and unwholesome-looking babies, *aux dames seules*, next door. At all events, I am not at all sleepy myself—that is a blessing. I shall see what happens. Yes, by-the-by, I must see what he meant to happen; I must affect to fall asleep too. I close my eyes, and gradually sinking my chin on my chest, try to droop my jaws and hang my cheeks, with a semblance of *bonâ fide* slumber. Apparently I succeed pretty well. After the lapse of some minutes I distinctly feel two hands very cautiously and carefully lifting and removing my feet from the dressing-box.

A cold chill creeps over me, and then the blood rushes to my head and ears. What am I to do? what am I to do? I have always thought the better of myself ever since for it; but, strange to say, I keep my presence of mind. Still affecting to sleep, I give a sort of kick, and instantly the hands are withdrawn and all is perfectly quiet again. I now feign to wake gradually, with a yawn and a stretch; and on moving about my feet a little, find that, despite my kick, they have been too clever for me, and have dexterously removed my box and substituted another. The way in which I make this pleasant discovery is, that whereas mine was perfectly flat at the top, on the surface of the object that is now beneath my feet there is some sort of excrescence—a handle of some sort or other. There is no denying it—brave I *may* be—I may laugh at people for running from bulls, for disliking to sleep in a room by themselves for fear of ghosts, for hurrying past tramps, but now I am most thoroughly frightened. I look cautiously, in a sideway manner, at the man beside me. How very still he is! Were they *his* hands, or the hands of the man opposite him? I take a fuller look than I have yet ventured to do, turning slightly round for the purpose. He is still reading, or at least still holding the paper, for the reading must be a farce. I look at his hands; they are in precisely the same position as they were when I affected to go to sleep although the *pose* of the rest of his body is slightly altered. Suddenly I turn extremely cold, for it has dawned on me that they are not real hands—they are certainly false ones. Yes, though the carriage is shaking very much with our rapid motion, and the light is shaking too, yet there is no mistake. I look indeed more closely, so as to be quite sure. The one nearest me is ungloved, the other gloved. I look at the nearest one. Yes, it is of an opaque waxen whiteness. I can plainly see the rouge put under the finger-nails to represent the colouring of life. I try to give one glance at his face. The paper still partially hides it, and as he is leaning his head back against the cushion, where the light hardly penetrates, I am completely baffled in my efforts.

Great heavens! What is going to happen to me? what shall I do? how much of him is *real*? where are his *real* hands? what is going on under that awful cloak? The fur border touches me as I sit by him. I draw convulsively and shrinkingly away, and try to squeeze myself up as close as possible to the window. But alas! to what good? How absolutely and utterly powerless I am! How entirely at their mercy! And there is Watson still sleeping swinishly—breathing heavily, opposite me. Shall I try to wake her? But to what end? She being under the influence of that vile drug, my efforts will certainly be useless, and will probably arouse the man to employ violence against me. Sooner or later in the course of the night I suppose they are pretty sure to murder me, but I had rather that it should be later than sooner.

While I think these things, I am lying back quite still, for, as I philosophically reflect, not all the screaming in the world will help me: if I had twenty-lung power I could not drown the rush of an express train. Oh, if my dear boy were but here—my husband I mean—fat or lean, how thankful I should be to see him! Oh, that cloak, and those horrid waxy hands! Of course—I see it now!—they remained stuck out, while the man's red ones were fumbling about my feet. In the midst of my agony of fright a thought of Madame Tussaud flashes ludicrously across me. Then they begin to talk of me. It is plain that they are not taken in by my feint of sleep; they speak in a clear loud voice evidently for my benefit. One of them begins by saying, "What a good-looking woman she is! Evidently in her *première jeunesse* too"—reader, I struck thirty last May—"and also there can be no doubt as to her being of exalted rank—a duchess probably."—(A dead duchess by morning, think I grimly.) They go on to say how odd it is that people in my class of life never travel with their own jewels, but always with paste ones, the real ones being meanwhile deposited at the banker's. My poor, poor sapphires! good-bye—a long good-bye to you. But indeed I will willingly compound for the loss of you and the rest of my ornaments—will go bare-necked, and bare-armed, or clad in Salviati beads for the rest of my life—so that I do but attain the next stopping place alive.

As I am so thinking one of the men looks, or I imagine that he looks, rather curiously towards me. In a paroxysm of fear lest they should read on my face the signs of the agony of terror I am enduring, I throw my pocket handkerchief—a very fine cambric one—over my face.

And now, oh reader! I am going to tell you something which I am sure you will not believe; I can hardly believe it myself; but, as I so lie, despite the tumult of my mind—despite the chilly terror which seems to be numbing my feelings—in the midst of it all a drowsiness keeps stealing over me. I am now convinced either that vile potion must have been of extraordinary strength, or that I, through the shaking of the carriage or the unsteadiness of my hand, carried more to my mouth and swallowed more—I did not *mean* to swallow any—than I intended, for—you will hardly credit it, but—I *fell asleep!*

When I awake—awake with a bewildered mixed sense of having been a long time asleep—of not knowing where I am—and of having some great dread and horror on my mind—awake and look round the dawn is breaking. I shiver, with the chilly sensation that the coming of even a warm day brings, and look round, still half unconsciously, in a misty way. But what has happened? How empty the carriage is! The dressing-case is gone! the clock is gone! the man who sat nearly opposite me is gone! *Watson is gone!* But the man in the cloak and the wax hands still sits beside me; still the hands are holding the paper; still the fur is touching me. Good God! I am *tête-à-tête* with him! A feeling of the most appalling desolation and despair comes over me—vanquishes me utterly. I clasp my hands together frantically, and, still looking at the dim form beside me, groan out, "Well! I did not think that Watson would have forsaken me!" Instantly, a sort of movement and shiver runs through the figure; the newspaper drops from the hands, which, however, continue to be still held out in the same position, as if still grasping it; and behind the newspaper, I see, by the dim morning light and the dim lamp-gleams, that there is no real face, but a mask. A sort of choked sound is coming from behind the mask. Shivers of cold fear are running over me. Never to this day shall I know what gave me the despairing courage to do it, but before I know what I am doing, I find myself tearing at the cloak—tearing away the mask—tearing away the hands. It would be better to find *anything* underneath—Satan himself—a horrible dead body—anything, sooner than submit any longer to this hideous mystery. And I am rewarded. When the cloak lies at the bottom of the carriage—when the mask, and the false hands and false feet—there are false *feet* too—are also cast away, in different direction, what do you think I find underneath?

Watson! Yes: it appears that while I slept—I feel sure that they must have rubbed some more of the drug on my lips while I was unconscious, or I never could have slept so heavily or so long—they dressed up Watson in the mask, feet, hands, and cloak; set the hat on her head, gagged her, and placed her beside me in the attitude occupied by the man. They had then, at the next station, got out, taking with them dressing-case and clock, and had made off in all security. When I arrive in Paris, you will not be surprised to hear that it does not once occur to me whether I am looking green or no.

And this is the true history of my night journey to Paris! You will be glad, I daresay, to hear that I ultimately recovered my sapphires, and a good many of my other ornaments. The police being promptly set on, the robbers were, after much trouble and time, at length secured; and it turned out that the man in the cloak was an ex-valet of my husband's, who was acquainted with my bad habit of travelling in company with my trinkets—a bad habit which I have since seen fit to abandon.

What I have written is literally true, though it did not happen to myself.

HOW WE GOT UP THE GLENMUTCHKIN RAILWAY

William Aytoun

Scottish author, William Aytoun, was a lawyer until he joined the staff of the famous *Blackwood's Edinburgh Magazine*. The following year, he was appointed a Professor of Rhetoric and Belles Lettres at Edinburgh University. He was a writer of both poetry and prose but best known for his ballads, and the parodies he wrote of traditional Scottish ballads.

First published in *Blackwood's Edinburgh Magazine* in 1845, "How We Got Up the Glenmutchkin Railway" is the silliest story of this collection. It only just counts as a "Tale of the Weird", mostly because of the strange and often dark sense of humour with which it is written. The story satirises the great railway boom of the mid-1840s, a popular topic at the time. Two chancers, Bob McCorkindale and the narrator, Augustus Dunshunner, short on money and unwilling to work for a living cook up a scheme over drinks to create a sham railway project. These "Ponzi" schemes were common and much-reported frauds at the time (a much longer and more complicated one makes the bulk of the plot in Anthony Trollope's *The Way We Live Now*, based on the real-life cases of John Sadleir and Charles Lefevre). Andrew Odlyzko argues that the story was a warning, citing the final lines as evidence:

"[i]t contains a deep moral, if anybody has sense enough to see it; if not, I have a new project in my eye for next session, of which timely notice shall be given."*

The phrase "next session" refers to the sessions called by the British Parliament to consider proposals for new railway projects at this time.

* See Andrew Odlyzko's useful source materials on the early railroads and the "Railway Mania" here: <www-users.cse.umn.edu/~odlyzko/rrsources/> and his excellent chapter on railway mania here: <www-users.cse.umn.edu/~odlyzko/doc/mania18.pdf>.

I was confoundedly hard up. My patrimony, never of the largest, had been for the last year on the decrease—a herald would have emblazoned it, "ARGENT, a money-bag improper, in detriment"—and though the attenuating process was not excessively rapid, it was, nevertheless, proceeding at a steady ratio. As for the ordinary means and appliances by which men contrive to recruit their exhausted exchequers, I knew none of them. Work I abhorred with a detestation worthy of a scion of nobility; and, I believe, you could just as soon have persuaded the lineal representative of the Howards or Percys to exhibit himself in the character of a mountebank, as have got me to trust my person on the pinnacle of a three-legged stool. The rule of three is all very well for base mechanical souls; but I flatter myself I have an intellect too large to be limited to a ledger. "Augustus," said my poor mother to me, while stroking my hyacinthine tresses, one fine morning, in the very dawn and budding-time of my existence— "Augustus, my dear boy, whatever you do, never forget that you are a gentleman." The maternal maxim sunk deeply into my heart, and I never for a moment have forgotten it.

Notwithstanding this aristocratic resolution, the great practical question, "How am I to live?" began to thrust itself unpleasantly before me. I am one of that unfortunate class who have neither uncles nor aunts. For me, no yellow liverless individual, with characteristic bamboo and pigtail—emblems of half-a-million—returned to his native shores from Ceylon or remote Penang. For me, no venerable spinster hoarded in the Trongate, permitting herself few luxuries during a long-protracted life, save a lass and a lanthorn, a parrot, and the invariable baudrons of antiquity. No such luck was mine. Had all Glasgow perished by some vast epidemic, I should not have found myself one farthing the richer. There would have been no golden balsam for me in the accumulated woes of Tradestown, Shettleston, and Camlachie. The time has been when—according to Washington Irving and other veracious historians—a young man had no sooner got into difficulties than a guardian angel appeared to him in a dream, with the information that at such and such a bridge, or under such and such a tree, he might find, at a slight expenditure of labour, a gallipot secured with bladder, and filled with glittering tomauns; or in the extremity of despair, the youth had only to append himself to a cord, and straightway the other end thereof, forsaking its staple in the roof, would disclose amidst the fractured ceiling the glories of a profitable pose. These blessed days have long since gone by—at any rate, no such luck was mine. My guardian angel was either woefully ignorant of metallurgy or the stores had been surreptitiously ransacked; and as to the other expedient, I frankly confess I should have liked some better security for its result, than the precedent of the "Heir of Lynn."

It is a great consolation amidst all the evils of life, to know that, however bad your circumstances may be, there is always somebody else in nearly the same predicament. My chosen friend and ally, Bob M'Corkindale, was equally hard up with myself, and, if possible, more averse to exertion. Bob was essentially a speculative man—that is, in a philosophical sense. He had once got hold of a stray volume of Adam Smith, and muddled his brains for a whole week over the intricacies of the *Wealth of Nations*. The result was a crude farrago of notions regarding the true nature of money, the soundness of currency, and relative value of capital, with which he nightly favoured an admiring audience at "The Crow;" for Bob was by no means—in the literal acceptation of the word—a dry philosopher. On the contrary, he perfectly appreciated the merits of each distinct distillery; and was understood to be the compiler of a statistical work, entitled, *A Tour through the Alcoholic Districts of Scotland*. It had very early occurred to me, who knew as much of political economy as of the bagpipes, that a gentleman so well versed in the art of accumulating national wealth, must have some remote ideas of applying his principles profitably on a smaller scale. Accordingly, I gave M'Corkindale an unlimited invitation to my lodgings; and, like a good hearty fellow as he was, he availed himself every evening of the license; for I had laid in a fourteen-gallon cask of Oban whisky, and the quality of the malt was undeniable.

These were the first glorious days of general speculation. Railroads were emerging from the hands of the greater into the fingers of the lesser capitalists. Two successful harvests had given a fearful stimulus to the national energy; and it appeared perfectly certain that all the populous towns would be united, and the rich agricultural districts intersected, by the magical bands of iron. The columns of the newspapers teemed every week with the parturition of novel schemes; and the shares were no sooner announced than they were rapidly subscribed for. But what is the use of my saying anything more about the history of last year? Every one of us remembers it perfectly well. It was a capital year on the whole, and put money into many a pocket. About that time, Bob and I commenced operations. Our available capital, or negotiable bullion, in the language of my friend, amounted to about three hundred pounds, which we set aside as a joint fund for speculation. Bob, in a series of learned discourses, had convinced me that it was not only folly, but a positive sin, to leave this sum lying in the bank at a pitiful rate of interest, and otherwise unemployed, whilst every one else in the kingdom was having a pluck at the public pigeon. Somehow or other, we were unlucky in our first attempts. Speculators are like wasps; for when they have once got hold of a ripening and peach-like project, they keep it rigidly for their own swarm, and repel the approach of interlopers. Notwithstanding all our efforts, and very ingenious ones they were, we never, in a single instance, succeeded in procuring an allocation of original shares; and though we did now and then make a hit by purchase, we more frequently bought at a premium, and parted with our scrip at a discount. At the end of six months, we were not twenty pounds richer than before.

"This will never do," said Bob, as he sat one evening in my rooms compounding his second tumbler. "I thought we were living in an enlightened age; but I find I was mistaken. That brutal spirit of monopoly is still abroad and uncurbed. The principles of free-trade are utterly forgotten, or misunderstood. Else how comes it that David Spreul received but yesterday an allocation of two hundred shares in the Westermidden Junction; whilst your application and mine, for a thousand each, were overlooked? Is this a state of things to be tolerated? Why should he, with his fifty thousand pounds, receive a slapping premium, whilst our three hundred of available capital remains unrepresented? The fact is monstrous, and demands the immediate and serious interference of the legislature."

"It is a burning shame," said I, fully alive to the manifold advantages of a premium.

"I'll tell you what, Dunshunner," rejoined M'Corkindale, "it's no use going on in this way. We haven't shown half pluck enough. These fellows consider us as snobs, because we don't take the bull by the horns. Now's the time for a bold stroke. The public are quite ready to subscribe for anything—and we'll start a railway for ourselves."

"Start a railway with three hundred pounds of capital!"

"Pshaw, man! you don't know what you're talking about—we've a great deal more capital than that. Have not I told you seventy times over, that everything a man has—his coat, his hat, the tumblers he drinks from, nay, his very corporeal existence—is absolute marketable capital? What do you call that fourteen-gallon cask, I should like to know?"

"A compound of hoops and staves, containing about a quart and a half of spirits—you have effectually accounted for the rest."

"Then it has gone to the fund of profit and loss, that's all. Never let me hear you sport those old theories again. Capital is indestructible, as I am ready to prove to you any day, in half an hour. But let us sit down seriously to business. We are rich enough to pay for the advertisements, and that is all we need care for in the mean time. The public is sure to step in, and bear us out handsomely with the rest."

"But where in the face of the habitable globe shall the railway be? England is out of the question, and I hardly know a spot in the Lowlands that is not occupied already."

"What do you say to a Spanish scheme—the Alcantara Union? Hang me if I know whether Alcantara is in Spain or Portugal; but nobody else does, and the one is quite as good as the other. Or what would you think of the Palermo Railway, with a branch to the sulphur mines?—that would be popular in the North—or the Pyrenees Direct? They would all go to a premium."

"I must confess I should prefer a line at home."

"Well, then, why not try the Highlands? There must be lots of traffic there in the shape of sheep, grouse, and Cockney tourists, not to mention salmon and other et-ceteras. Couldn't we tip them a railway somewhere in the west?"

"There's Glenmutchkin, for instance—"

"Capital, my dear fellow! Glorious! By Jove, first-rate!" shouted Bob in an ecstasy of delight. "There's a distillery there, you know, and a fishing-village at the foot—at least there used to be six years ago, when I was living with the exciseman. There may be some bother about the population, though. The last laird shipped every mother's son of the aboriginal Celts to America; but, after all, that's not of much consequence. I see the whole thing! Unrivalled scenery—stupendous waterfalls—herds of black cattle—spot where Prince Charles Edward met Macgrugar of Glengrugar and his clan! We could not possibly have lighted on a more promising place. Hand us over that sheet of paper, like a good fellow, and a pen. There is no time to be lost, and the sooner we get out the prospectus the better."

"But, heaven bless you, Bob, there's a great deal to be thought of first. Who are we to get for a Provisional Committee?"

"That's very true," said Bob, musingly. "We *must* treat them to some respectable names, that is, good sounding ones. I'm afraid there is little chance of our producing a Peer to begin with?"

"None whatever—unless we could invent one, and that's hardly safe—*Burke's Peerage* has gone through too many editions. Couldn't we try the Dormants?"

"That would be rather dangerous in the teeth of the standing orders. But what do you say to a baronet? There's Sir Polloxfen Tremens. He got himself served the other day to a Nova Scotia baronetcy, with just as much title as you or I have; and he has sported the riband, and dined out on the strength of it ever since. He'll join us at once, for he has not a sixpence to lose."

"Down with him, then," and we headed the Provisional list with the pseudo Orange-tawny.

"Now," said Bob, "it's quite indispensable, as this is a Highland line, that we should put forward a Chief or two. That has always a great effect upon the English, whose feudal notions are rather of the mistiest, and principally derived from Waverley."

"Why not write yourself down as the Laird of M'Corkindale?" said I. "I daresay you would not be negatived by a counter-claim."

"That would hardly do," replied Bob, "as I intend to be Secretary. After all, what's the use of thinking about it? Here goes for an extempore Chief;" and the villain wrote down the name of Tavish M'Tavish of Invertavish.

"I say, though," said I, "we must have a real Highlander on the list. If we go on this way, it will become a Justiciary matter."

"You're devilish scrupulous, Gus," said Bob, who, if left to himself, would have stuck in the names of the heathen gods and goddesses, or borrowed his directors from the Ossianic chronicles, rather than have delayed the prospectus. "Where the mischief are we to find the men? I can think of no others likely to go the whole hog; can you?"

"I don't know a single Celt in Glasgow except old M'Closkie, the drunken porter at the corner of Jamaica Street."

"He's the very man! I suppose, after the manner of his tribe, he will do anything for a pint of whisky. But what shall we call him? Jamaica Street, I fear, will hardly do for a designation."

"Call him THE M'CLOSKIE. It will be sonorous in the ears of the Saxon!"

"Bravo!" and another Chief was added to the roll of the clans.

"Now," said Bob, "we must put you down. Recollect, all the management—that is, the allocation—will be intrusted to you. Augustus— you haven't a middle name, I think?—well, then, suppose we interpolate 'Reginald;' it has a smack of the Crusades. Augustus Reginald Dunshunner, Esq. of—where, in the name of Munchausen!"

"I'm sure I don't know. I never had any land beyond the contents of a flower-pot. Stay—I rather think I have a superiority somewhere about Paisley."

"Just the thing," cried Bob. "It's heritable property, and therefore titular. What's the denomination?"

"St. Mirrens."

"Beautiful! Dunshunner of St. Mirrens, I give you joy! Had you discovered that a little sooner—and I wonder you did not think of it—we might both of us have had lots of allocations. These are not the times to conceal hereditary distinctions. But now comes the serious work. We must have one or two men of known wealth upon the list. The chaff is nothing without a decoy-bird. Now, can't you help me with a name?"

"In that case," said I, "the game is up, and the whole scheme exploded. I would as soon undertake to evoke the Ghost of Crœsus."

"Dunshunner," said Bob very seriously, "to be a man of information, you are possessed of marvellous few resources. I am quite ashamed of you. Now listen to me. I have thought deeply upon this subject, and am quite convinced that, with some little trouble, we may secure the co-operation of a most wealthy and influential body—one, too, that is generally supposed to have stood aloof from all speculation of the kind, and whose name would be a tower of strength in the moneyed quarters. I allude," continued Bob, reaching across for the kettle, "to the great Dissenting Interest."

"The what?" cried I, aghast.

"The great Dissenting Interest. You can't have failed to observe the row they have lately been making about Sunday travelling and education. Old Sam Sawley, the coffin-maker, is their principal spokesman here; and wherever he goes the rest will follow, like a flock of sheep bounding after a patriarchal ram. I propose, therefore, to wait upon him to-morrow, and request his co-operation in a scheme which is not only to prove profitable, but to make head against the lax principles of the present age. Leave me alone to tickle him. I consider his name, and those of one or two others belonging to the same meeting-house—fellows with bank-stock, and all sorts of tin, as perfectly secure. These dissenters smell a premium from an almost incredible distance. We can fill up the rest of the committee with ciphers, and the whole thing is done."

"But the engineer—we must announce such an officer as a matter of course."

"I never thought of that," said Bob. "Couldn't we hire a fellow from one of the steamboats?"

"I fear that might get us into trouble: You know there are such things as gradients and sections to be prepared. But there's Watty Solder, the gas-fitter, who failed the other day. He's a sort of civil engineer by trade, and will jump at the proposal like a trout at the tail of a May fly."

"Agreed. Now, then, let's fix the number of shares. This is our first experiment, and I think we ought to be moderate. No sound political economist is avaricious. Let us say twelve thousand, at twenty pounds a-piece."

"So be it."

"Well, then, that's arranged. I'll see Sawley and the rest to-morrow; settle with Solder, and then write out the prospectus. You look in upon me in the evening, and we'll revise it together. Now, by your leave, let's have in the Welsh rabbit and another tumbler to drink success and prosperity to the Glenmutchkin Railway."

I confess that, when I rose on the morrow, with a slight head-ache and a tongue indifferently parched, I recalled to memory, not without perturbation of conscience, and some internal qualms, the conversation of the previous evening. I felt relieved, however, after two spoonfuls of carbonate of soda, and a glance at the newspaper, wherein I perceived the announcement of no less than four other schemes equally preposterous with our own. But, after all, what right had I to assume that the Glenmutchkin project would prove an ultimate failure? I had not a scrap of statistical information that might entitle me to form such an opinion. At any rate, Parliament, by substituting the Board of Trade as an initiating body of inquiry, had created a responsible tribunal, and freed us from the chance of obloquy. I saw before me a vision of six months' steady gambling, at manifest advantage, in the shares, before a report could possibly be pronounced, or our proceedings be in any way overhauled. Of course I attended that evening punctually at my friend M'Corkindale's. Bob was in high feather; for Sawley no sooner heard of the principles upon which the railway was to be conducted, and his own nomination as a director, than he gave in his adhesion, and promised his unflinching support to the uttermost. The Prospectus ran as follows:—

"DIRECT GLENMUTCHKIN RAILWAY.

IN 12,000 SHARES OF £20 EACH. DEPOSIT £1 PER SHARE

Provisional Committee.

SIR POLLOXFEN TREMENS, Bart. of Toddymains.

TAVISH M'TAVISH of Invertavish.

THE M'CLOSKIE.

AUGUSTUS REGINALD DUNSHUNNER, Esq. of St. Mirrens.

SAMUEL SAWLEY, Esq., Merchant.

MHIC-MHAC-VICH-INDUIBH.

PHELIM O'FINLAN, Esq. of Castle-rook, Ireland.

THE CAPTAIN OF M'ALCOHOL.

FACTOR FOR GLENTUMBLERS.

JOHN JOB JOBSON, Esq., Manufacturer.
EVAN M'CLAW of Glenscart and Inveryewky.
JOSEPH HECKLES, Esq.
HABBAKUK GRABBIE, Portioner in Ramoth-Drumclog.

Engineer—WALTER SOLDER, Esq.
Interim-Secretary—ROBERT M'CORKINDALE, Esq.

"The necessity of a direct line of Railway communication through the fertile and populous district known as the VALLEY of GLENMUTCHKIN, has been long felt and universally acknowledged. Independently of the surpassing grandeur of its mountain scenery, which shall immediately be referred to, and other considerations of even greater importance, GLENMUTCHKIN is known to the capitalist as the most important BREEDING STATION in the Highlands of Scotland, and indeed as the great emporium from which the southern markets are supplied. It has been calculated by a most eminent authority, that every acre in the strath is capable of rearing twenty head of cattle; and, as has been ascertained after a careful admeasurement, that there are not less than TWO HUNDRED THOUSAND improvable acres immediately contiguous to the proposed line of Railway, it may confidently be assumed that the number of cattle to be conveyed along the line will amount to FOUR MILLIONS annually, which, at the lowest estimate, would yield a revenue larger, in proportion to the capital subscribed, than that of any Railway as yet completed within the United Kingdom. From this estimate the traffic in Sheep and Goats, with which the mountains are literally covered, has been carefully excluded, it having been found quite impossible (from its extent) to compute the actual revenue to be drawn from that most important branch. It may, however, be roughly assumed as from seventeen to nineteen per cent upon the whole, after deduction of the working expenses.

"The population of Glenmutchkin is extremely dense. Its situation on the west coast has afforded it the means of direct communication with America, of which for many years the inhabitants have actively availed themselves. Indeed, the amount of exportation of live stock from this part of the Highlands to the Western continent, has more than once attracted the attention of Parliament. The Manufactures are large and comprehensive, and include the most famous distilleries in the world. The Minerals are most abundant, and amongst these may be reckoned quartz, porphyry, felspar, malachite, manganese, and basalt.

"At the foot of the valley, and close to the sea, lies the important village known as the CLACHAN of INVERSTARVE. It is supposed by various eminent antiquaries to have been the capital of the Picts, and, amongst the busy inroads of commercial prosperity, it still retains some interesting traces of its former grandeur. There is a large fishing station here, to which vessels from every nation resort, and the demand for foreign produce is daily and steadily increasing.

"As a sporting country Glenmutchkin is unrivalled; but it is by the tourists that its beauties will most greedily be sought. These consist of every combination which plastic nature can afford—cliffs of unusual magnitude and grandeur—waterfalls only second to the sublime cascades of Norway—woods, of which the bark is a remarkable valuable commodity. It need scarcely be added, to rouse the enthusiasm inseparable from this glorious glen, that here, in 1745, Prince Charles Edward Stuart, then in the zenith of his hopes, was joined by the brave Sir Grugar M'Grugar at the head of his devoted clan.

"The Railway will be twelve miles long, and can be completed within six months after the Act of Parliament is obtained. The gradients are easy, and the curves obtuse. There are no viaducts of any importance, and only four tunnels along the whole length of the line. The shortest of these does not exceed a mile and a half.

"In conclusion, the projectors of this Railway beg to state that they have determined, as a principle, to set their face AGAINST ALL SUNDAY TRAVELLING WHATSOEVER, and to oppose EVERY BILL which may hereafter be brought into Parliament, unless it shall contain a clause to that effect. It is also their intention to take up the cause of the poor and neglected STOKER, for whose accommodation, and social, moral, religious, and intellectual improvement, a large stock of evangelical tracts will speedily be required. Tenders of these, in quantities of not less than 12,000, may be sent in to the Interim Secretary. Shares must be applied for within ten days from the present date.

"By order of the Provisional Committee,
"ROBT. M'CORKINDALE, *Secretary*."

"There!" said Bob, slapping down the prospectus on the table, with as much triumph as if it had been the original of Magna Charta—"What do you think of that? If it doesn't do the business effectually, I shall submit to be called a Dutchman. That last touch about the stoker will bring us in the subscriptions of the old ladies by the score."

"Very masterly, indeed," said I. "But who the deuce is Mhic-Mhac-vich-Induibh?"

"A *bona fide* chief, I assure you, though a little reduced: I picked him up upon the Broomielaw. His grandfather had an island somewhere to the west of the Hebrides; but it is not laid down in the maps."

"And the Captain of M'Alcohol?"

"A crack distiller."

"And the Factor for Glentumblers?"

"His principal customer. But, bless you, my dear St. Mirrens! don't bother yourself any more about the committee. They are as respectable a set—on paper at least—as you would wish to see of a summer's morning, and the beauty of it is that they will give us no manner of trouble. Now about the allocation. You and I must restrict ourselves to a couple of thousand shares a-piece. That's only a third of the whole, but it won't do to be greedy."

"But, Bob, consider! Where on earth are we to find the money to pay up the deposits?"

"Can you, the principal director of the Glenmutchkin Railway, ask me, the secretary, such a question? Don't you know that any of the banks will give us tick to the amount 'of half the deposits.' All that is settled already, and you can get your two thousand pounds whenever you please merely for the signing of a bill. Sawley must get a thousand according to stipulation—Jobson, Heckles, and Grabbie, at least five hundred a-piece, and another five hundred, I should think, will exhaust the remaining means of the committee. So that, out of our whole stock, there remain just five thousand shares to be allocated to the speculative and evangelical public. My eyes! won't there be a scramble for them!"

Next day our prospectus appeared in the newspapers. It was read, canvassed, and generally approved of. During the afternoon, I took an opportunity of looking into the Tontine, and whilst under shelter of the *Glasgow Herald*, my ears were solaced with such ejaculations as the following:—

"I say, Jimsy, hae ye seen this grand new prospectus for a railway tae Glenmutchkin?"

"Ay—it looks no that ill. The Hieland lairds are pitting their best fit foremost. Will ye apply for shares?"

"I think I'll tak' twa hundred. Wha's Sir Polloxfen Tremens?"

"He'll be yin o' the Ayrshire folk. He used to rin horses at the Paisley races."

("The devil he did!" thought I.)

"D'ye ken ony o' the directors, Jimsy?"

"I ken Sawley fine. Ye may depend on't, it's a gude thing if he's in't, for he's a howkin' body."

"Then it's sure to gae up. What prem. d'ye think it will bring?"

"Twa pund a share, and maybe mair."

"'Od, I'll apply for three hundred!"

"Heaven bless you, my dear countrymen!" thought I as I sallied forth to refresh myself with a basin of soup, "do but maintain this liberal and patriotic feeling—this thirst for national improvement, internal communication, and premiums—a short while longer, and I know whose fortune will be made."

On the following morning my breakfast-table was covered with shoals of letters, from fellows whom I scarcely ever had spoken to—or who, to use a franker phraseology, had scarcely ever condescended to speak to me—entreating my influence as a director to obtain them shares in the new undertaking. I never bore malice in my life, so I chalked them down, without favouritism, for a certain proportion. Whilst engaged in this charitable work, the door flew open, and M'Corkindale, looking utterly haggard with excitement, rushed in.

"You may buy an estate whenever you please, Dunshunner," cried he, "the world's gone perfectly mad! I have been to Blazes the broker, and he tells me that the whole amount of the stock has been subscribed for four times over already, and he has not yet got in the returns from Edinburgh and Liverpool!"

"Are they good names though, Bob—sure cards—none of your M'Closkies, and M'Alcohols?"

"The first names in the city, I assure you, and most of them holders for investment. I wouldn't take ten millions for their capital."

"Then the sooner we close the list the better."

"I think so too. I suspect a rival company will be out before long. Blazes says the shares are selling already conditionally on allotment, at seven-and-sixpence premium."

"The deuce they are! I say, Bob, since we have the cards in our hands, would it not be wise to favour them with a few hundreds at that rate? A bird in the hand, you know, is worth two in the bush, eh?"

"I know no such maxim in political economy," replied the secretary. "Are you mad, Dunshunner? How are the shares ever to go up, if it gets wind that the directors are selling already? Our business just now, is to *bull* the line, not to *bear* it; and if you will trust me, I shall show them such an operation on the ascending scale, as the Stock Exchange has not witnessed for this long and many a day. Then, to-morrow, I shall advertise in the papers that the committee, having received applications for ten times the amount of stock, have been compelled, unwillingly, to close the lists. That will be a slap in the face to the dilatory gentlemen, and send up the shares like wildfire."

Bob was right. No sooner did the advertisement appear, than a simultaneous groan was uttered by some hundreds of disappointed speculators, who with unwonted and unnecessary caution had been anxious to see their way a little before committing themselves to our splendid enterprise. In consequence, they rushed into the market, with intense anxiety to make what terms they could at the earliest stage, and the seven-and-sixpence of premium was doubled in the course of a forenoon.

The allocation passed over very peaceably. Sawley, Heckles, Jobson, Grabbie, and the Captain of M'Alcohol, besides myself, attended, and took part in the business. We were also threatened with the presence of the M'Closkie and Vich-Induibh; but M'Corkindale, entertaining some reasonable doubts as to the effect which their corporeal appearance might have upon the representatives of the dissenting interest, had taken the precaution to get them snugly housed in a tavern, where an unbounded supply of gratuitous Ferintosh deprived us of the benefit of their experience. We, however, allotted them twenty shares a-piece. Sir Polloxfen Tremens sent a handsome, though rather illegible letter of apology, dated from an island in Lochlomond, where he was said to be detained on particular business.

Mr. Sawley, who officiated as our chairman, was kind enough, before parting, to pass a very flattering eulogium upon the excellence and candour of all the preliminary arrangements. It would now, he said, go forth to the public that this line was not, like some others he could mention, a mere bubble, emanating from the stank of private interest, but a solid, lasting superstructure, based upon the principles of sound return for capital, and serious evangelical truth (hear, hear). The time was fast approaching, when the gravestone, with the words "HIC OBIIT" chiselled upon it, would be placed at the head of all the other lines which rejected the grand opportunity of conveying education to the stoker. The stoker, in his (Mr. Sawley's) opinion, had a right to ask the all-important question, "Am I not a man and a brother?" (Cheers). Much had been said and written lately about a work called *Tracts for the Times*. With the opinions contained in that publication he was not conversant, as it was conducted by persons of another community from that to which he (Mr. Sawley) had the privilege to belong. But he hoped very soon, under the auspices of the Glenmutchkin Railway Company, to see a new periodical established, under the title of *Tracts for the Trains*. He never for a moment would relax his efforts to knock a nail into the coffin, which, he might say, was already made, and measured, and cloth-covered for the reception of all establishments; and with these sentiments, and the conviction that the shares must rise, could it be doubted that he would remain a fast friend to the interests of this Company for ever? (Much cheering.)

After having delivered this address, Mr. Sawley affectionately squeezed the hands of his brother directors, and departed, leaving several of us much overcome. As, however, M'Corkindale had told me that every one of Sawley's shares had been disposed of in the market the day before, I felt less compunction at having refused to allow that excellent man an extra thousand beyond the amount he had applied for, notwithstanding of his broadest hints, and even private entreaties.

"Confound the greedy hypocrite!" said Bob; "does he think we shall let him Burke the line for nothing? No—no! I let him go to the brokers and buy his shares back, if he thinks they are likely to rise. I'll be bound he has made a cool five hundred out of them already."

On the day which succeeded the allocation, the following entry appeared in the Glasgow share-lists. "Direct Glenmutchkin Railway 15s. 15s. 6d. 15s. 6d. 16s. 15s. 6d. 16s. 16s. 6d. 16s. 6d. 16s. 17s. 18s. 18s. 19s. 6d. 21s. 21s. 22s. 6d. 24s. 25s. 6d. 27s. 29s. 29s. 6d. 30s. 31s. p^m."

"They might go higher, and they ought to go higher," said Bob musingly; "but there's not much more stock to come and go upon, and these two share-sharks, Jobson and Grabbie, I know, will be in the market to-morrow. We must not let them have the whip-hand of us. I think upon the whole, Dunshunner, though it's letting them go dog cheap, that we ought to sell half our shares at the present premium, whilst there is a certainty of getting it."

"Why not sell the whole? I'm sure I have no objections to part with every stiver of the scrip on such terms."

"Perhaps," said Bob, "upon general principles you may be right; but then remember that we have a vested interest in the line."

"Vested interest be hanged!"

"That's very well—at the same time it is no use to kill your salmon in a hurry. The bulls have done their work pretty well for us, and we ought to keep something on hand for the bears; they are snuffing at it already. I could almost swear that some of those fellows who have sold to-day are working for a time-bargain."

We accordingly got rid of a couple of thousand shares, the proceeds of which not only enabled us to discharge the deposit loan, but left us a material surplus. Under these circumstances, a two-handed banquet was proposed and unanimously carried, the commencement of which I distinctly remember, but am rather dubious as to the end. So many stories have lately been circulated to the prejudice of railway directors, that I think it my duty to state that this entertainment was scrupulously defrayed by ourselves, and *not* carried to account, either of the preliminary survey, or the expenses of the provisional committee.

Nothing effects so great a metamorphosis in the bearing of the outer man, as a sudden change of fortune. The anemone of the garden differs scarcely more from its unpretending prototype of the woods, than Robert M'Corkindale, Esq., Secretary and Projector of the Glenmutchkin Railway, differed from Bob M'Corkindale, the seedy frequenter of "The Crow." In the days of yore, men eyed the surtout—napless at the velvet collar, and preternaturally white at the seams—which Bob vouchsafed to wear, with looks of dim suspicion, as if some faint reminiscence, similar to that which is said to recall the memory of a former state of existence, suggested to them a notion that the garment had once been their own. Indeed, his whole appearance was then wonderfully second-hand. Now he had cast his slough. A most undeniable Taglioni, with trimmings just bordering upon frogs, gave dignity to his demeanour and twofold amplitude to his chest. The horn eyeglass was exchanged for one of purest gold, the dingy high-lows for well-waxed Wellingtons, the Paisley fogle for the fabric of the China loom. Moreover, he walked with a swagger, and affected in common conversation a peculiar dialect which he opined to be the purest English, but which no one—except a bagman—could be reasonably expected to understand. His pockets were invariably crammed with share-lists; and he quoted, if he did not comprehend, the money article from the *Times*. This sort of assumption, though very ludicrous in itself, goes down wonderfully. Bob gradually became a sort of authority, and his opinions got quoted on 'Change. He was no ass, notwithstanding his peculiarities, and made good use of his opportunity.

For myself, I bore my new dignities with an air of modest meekness. A certain degree of starchness is indispensable for a railway director, if he means to go forward in his high calling and prosper; he must abandon all juvenile eccentricities, and aim at the appearance of a decided enemy to free trade in the article of Wild Oats. Accordingly, as the first step towards respectability, I eschewed coloured waistcoats, and gave out that I was a marrying man. No man under forty, unless he is a positive idiot, will stand forth as a theoretical bachelor. It is all nonsense to say that there is anything unpleasant in being courted. Attention, whether from male or female, tickles the vanity; and although I have a reasonable, and, I hope, not unwholesome regard for the gratification of my other appetites, I confess that this same vanity is by far the most poignant of the whole. I therefore surrendered myself freely to the soft allurements thrown in my way by such matronly denizens of Glasgow as were possessed of stock in the shape of marriageable daughters; and walked the more readily into their toils, because every party, though nominally for the purposes of tea, wound up with a hot supper, and something hotter still by way of assisting the digestion.

I don't know whether it was my determined conduct at the allocation, my territorial title, or a most exaggerated idea of my circumstances, that worked upon the mind of Mr. Sawley. Possibly it was a combination of the three; but sure enough few days had elapsed before I received a formal card of invitation to a tea and serious conversation. Now serious conversation is a sort of thing that I never shone in, possibly because my early studies were framed in a different direction; but as I really was unwilling to offend the respectable coffin-maker, and as I found that the Captain of M'Alcohol—a decided trump in his way—had also received a summons, I notified my acceptance.

M'Alcohol and I went together. The Captain, an enormous brawny Celt, with superhuman whiskers, and a shock of the fieriest hair, had figged himself out, *more majorum*, in the full Highland costume. I never saw Rob Roy on the stage look half so dignified or ferocious. He glittered from head to foot, with dirk, pistol, and skean-dhu, and at least a hundred-weight of cairngorms cast a prismatic glory around his person. I felt quite abashed beside him.

We were ushered into Mr. Sawley's drawing-room. Round the walls, and at considerable distances from each other, were seated about a dozen characters, male and female, all of them dressed in sable, and wearing countenances of woe. Sawley advanced, and wrung me by the hand with so piteous an expression of visage, that I could not help thinking some awful catastrophe had just befallen his family.

"You are welcome, Mr. Dunshunner—welcome to my humble tabernacle. Let me present you to Mrs. Sawley"—and a lady, who seemed to have bathed in the Yellow Sea, rose from her seat, and favoured me with a profound curtsy.

"My daughter—Miss Selina Sawley."

I felt in my brain the scorching glance of the two darkest eyes it ever was my fortune to behold, as the beauteous Selina looked up from the perusal of her handkerchief hem. It was a pity that the other features were not corresponding; for the nose was flat, and the mouth of such dimensions, that a Harlequin might have jumped down it with impunity—but the eyes *were* splendid.

In obedience to a sign from the hostess, I sank into a chair beside Selina; and not knowing exactly what to say, hazarded some observation about the weather.

"Yes, it is indeed a suggestive season. How deeply, Mr. Dunshunner, we ought to feel the pensive progress of autumn towards a soft and premature decay! I always think, about this time of the year, that nature is falling into a consumption!"

"To be sure, ma'am," said I, rather taken aback by this style of colloquy, "the trees are looking devilishly hectic."

"Ah, you have remarked that too! Strange! it was but yesterday that I was wandering through Kelvin Grove, and as the phantom breeze brought down the withered foliage from the spray, I thought how probable it was that they might ere long rustle over young and glowing hearts deposited prematurely in the tomb!"

This, which struck me as a very passable imitation of Dickens's pathetic writings, was a poser. In default of language, I looked Miss Sawley straight in the face, and attempted a substitute for a sigh. I was rewarded with a tender glance.

"Ah!" said she, "I see you are a congenial spirit. How delightful, and yet how rare it is to meet with any one who thinks in unison with yourself! Do you ever walk in the Necropolis, Mr. Dunshunner? It is my favourite haunt of a morning. There we can wean ourselves, as it were, from life, and, beneath the melancholy yew and cypress, anticipate the setting star. How often there have I seen the procession—the funeral of some very, very little child"—

"Selina, my love," said Mrs. Sawley, "have the kindness to ring for the cookies."

I, as in duty bound, started up to save the fair enthusiast the trouble, and was not sorry to observe my seat immediately occupied by a very cadaverous gentleman, who was evidently jealous of the progress I was rapidly making. Sawley, with an air of great mystery, informed me that this was a Mr. Dalgleish of Raxmathrapple, the representative of an ancient Scottish family who claimed an important heritable office. The name, I thought, was familiar to me, but there was something in the appearance of Mr. Dalgleish which, notwithstanding the smiles of Miss Selina, rendered a rivalship in that quarter utterly out of the question.

I hate injustice, so let me do due honour in description to the Sawley banquet. The tea-urn most literally corresponded to its name. The table was decked out with divers platters, containing seed-cakes cut into rhomboids, almond biscuits, and ratafia drops. Also, on the sideboard, there were two salvers, each of which contained a congregation of glasses, filled with port and sherry. The former fluid, as I afterwards ascertained, was of the kind advertised as "curious," and proffered for sale at the reasonable rate of sixteen shillings per dozen. The banquet, on the whole, was rather peculiar than enticing; and, for the life of me, I could not divest myself of the idea that the selfsame viands had figured, not long before, as funeral refreshments at a dirgie. No such suspicion seemed to cross the mind of M'Alcohol, who hitherto had remained uneasily surveying his nails in a corner, but at the first symptom of food started forwards, and was in the act of making a clean sweep of the china, when Sawley proposed the singular preliminary of a hymn.

The hymn was accordingly sung. I am thankful to say it was such a one as I never heard before, or expect to hear again; and unless it was composed by the Reverend Saunders Peden in an hour of paroxysm on the moors, I cannot conjecture the author. After this original symphony, tea was discussed, and after tea, to my amazement, more hot brandy-and-water than I ever remember to have seen circulated at the most convivial party. Of course this effected a radical change in the spirits and conversation of the circle. It was again my lot to be placed by the side of the fascinating Selina, whose sentimentality gradually thawed away beneath the influence of sundry sips, which she accepted with a delicate reluctance. This time Dalgleish of Raxmathrapple had not the remotest chance. M'Alcohol got furious, sang Gaelic songs, and even delivered a sermon in genuine Erse, without incurring a rebuke; whilst, for my own part, I must needs confess that I waxed unnecessarily amorous, and the last thing I recollect was the pressure of Mr. Sawley's hand at the door, as he denominated me his dear boy, and hoped I would soon come back and visit Mrs. Sawley and Selina. The recollection of these passages next morning was the surest antidote to my return.

Three weeks had elapsed, and still the Glenmutchkin Railway shares were at a premium, though rather lower than when we sold. Our engineer, Watty Solder, returned from his first survey of the line, along with an assistant who really appeared to have some remote glimmerings of the science and practice of mensuration. It seemed, from a verbal report, that the line was actually practicable; and the survey would have been completed in a very short time—"If," according to the account of Solder, "there had been ae hoos in the glen. But ever sin' the distillery stoppit—and that was twa year last Martinmas—there wasna a hole whaur a Christian could lay his head, muckle less get white sugar to his toddy, forbye the change-house at the clachan; and the auld luckie that keepit it was sair forfochten wi' the palsy, and maist in the dead-thraws. There was naebody else living within twal miles o' the line, barring a taxman, a lamiter, and a bauldie."

We had some difficulty in preventing Mr. Solder from making this report open and patent to the public, which premature disclosure might have interfered materially with the preparation of our traffic tables, not to mention the marketable value of the shares. We therefore kept him steadily at work out of Glasgow, upon a very liberal allowance, to which, apparently, he did not object.

"Dunshunner," said M'Corkindale to me one day, "I suspect that there is something going on about our railway more than we are aware of. Have you observed that the shares are preternaturally high just now?"

"So much the better. Let's sell."

"I did so this morning—both yours and mine, at two pounds ten shillings premium."

"The deuce you did! Then we're out of the whole concern."

"Not quite. If my suspicions are correct, there's a good deal more money yet to be got from the speculation. Somebody has been bulling the stock without orders; and, as they can have no information which we are not perfectly up to, depend upon it, it is done for a purpose. I suspect Sawley and his friends. They have never been quite happy since the allocation; and I caught him yesterday pumping our broker in the back shop. We'll see in a day or two. If they are beginning a bearing operation, I know how to catch them."

And, in effect, the bearing operation commenced. Next day, heavy sales were effected for delivery in three weeks; and the stock, as if water-logged, began to sink. The same thing continued for the following two days, until the premium became nearly nominal. In the mean time, Bob and I, in conjunction with two leading capitalists whom we let into the secret, bought up steadily every share that was offered; and at the end of a fortnight we found that we had purchased rather more than double the amount of the whole original stock. Sawley and his disciples, who, as M'Corkindale suspected, were at the bottom of the whole transaction, having beared to their heart's content, now came into the market to purchase, in order to redeem their engagements. The following extracts from the weekly share-lists will show the result of their endeavours to regain their lost position:—

GLENMUTCHKIN RAIL., £1 paid,	Sat.	Mon.	Tues.	Wed.	Thurs.	Frid.	Sat.
	1⅛	2¼	4⅜	7½	10¾	15⅝	17

and Monday was the day of delivery.

I have no means of knowing in what frame of mind Mr. Sawley spent the Sunday, or whether he had recourse for mental consolation to Peden; but on Monday morning he presented himself at my door in full funeral costume, with about a quarter of a mile of crape swathed round his hat, black gloves, and a countenance infinitely more doleful than if he had been attending the interment of his beloved wife.

"Walk in, Mr. Sawley," said I cheerfully. "What a long time it is since I have had the pleasure of seeing you—too long indeed for brother directors. How are Mrs. Sawley and Miss Selina—won't you take a cup of coffee?"

"Grass, sir, grass!" said Mr. Sawley, with a sigh like the groan of a furnace-bellows. "We are all flowers of the oven—weak, erring creatures, every one of us. Ah! Mr. Dunshunner! you have been a great stranger at Lykewake Terrace!"

"Take a muffin, Mr. Sawley. Anything new in the railway world?"

"Ah, my dear sir—my good Mr. Augustus Reginald—I wanted to have some serious conversation with you on that very point. I am afraid there is something far wrong indeed in the present state of our stock."

"Why, to be sure it is high; but that, you know, is a token of the public confidence in the line. After all, the rise is nothing compared to that of several English railways; and individually, I suppose, neither of us have any reason to complain."

"I don't like it," said Sawley, watching me over the margin of his coffee-cup. "I don't like it. It savours too much of gambling for a man of my habits. Selina, who is a sensible girl, has serious qualms on the subject."

"Then why not get out of it? I have no objection to run the risk, and if you like to transact with me, I will pay you ready money for every share you have at the present market price."

Sawley writhed uneasily in his chair.

"Will you sell me five hundred, Mr. Sawley? Say the word and it is a bargain."

"A time bargain?" quavered the coffin-maker.

"No. Money down, and scrip handed over."

"I—I can't. The fact is, my dear young friend, I have sold all my stock already!"

"Then permit me to ask, Mr. Sawley, what possible objection you can have to the present aspect of affairs? You do not surely suppose that we are going to issue new shares and bring down the market, simply because you have realised at a handsome premium?"

"A handsome premium! O Lord!" moaned Sawley.

"Why, what did you get for them?"

"Four, three, and two and a half."

"A very considerable profit indeed," said I; "and you ought to be abundantly thankful. We shall talk this matter over at another time, Mr. Sawley, but just now I must beg you to excuse me. I have a particular engagement this morning with my broker—rather a heavy transaction to settle—and so"—

"It's no use beating about the bush any longer," said Mr. Sawley in an excited tone, at the same time dashing down his crape-covered castor on the floor. "Did you ever see a ruined man with a large family? Look at me, Mr. Dunshunner—I'm one, and you've done it!"

"Mr. Sawley! are you in your senses?"

"That depends on circumstances. Haven't you been buying stock lately?"

"I am glad to say I have—two thousand Glenmutchkins, I think, and this is the day of delivery."

"Well, then—can't you see how the matter stands? It was I who sold them!"

"Well!"

"Mother of Moses, sir! don't you see I'm ruined?"

"By no means—but you must not swear. I pay over the money for your scrip, and you pocket a premium. It seems to me a very simple transaction."

"But I tell you I haven't got the scrip!" cried Sawley, gnashing his teeth, whilst the cold beads of perspiration gathered largely on his brow.

"That is very unfortunate! Have you lost it?"

"No!—the devil tempted me, and I oversold!"

There was a very long pause, during which I assumed an aspect of serious and dignified rebuke.

"Is it possible?" said I in a low tone, after the manner of Kean's offended fathers. "What! you, Mr. Sawley—the stoker's friend—the enemy of gambling—the father of Selina—condescend to so equivocal a transaction? You amaze me! But I never was the man to press heavily on a friend"—here Sawley brightened up—"your secret is safe with me, and it shall be your own fault if it reaches the ears of the Session. Pay me over the difference at the present market price, and I release you of your obligation."

"Then I'm in the Gazette, that's all," said Sawley doggedly, "and a wife and nine beautiful babes upon the parish! I had hoped other things from you, Mr. Dunshunner—I thought you and Selina"—

"Nonsense, man! Nobody goes into the Gazette just now—it will be time enough when the general crash comes. Out with your cheque-book, and write me an order for four-and-twenty thousand. Confound fractions! in these days one can afford to be liberal."

"I haven't got it," said Sawley. "You have no idea how bad our trade has been of late, for nobody seems to think of dying. I have not sold a gross of coffins this fortnight. But I'll tell you what—I'll give you five thousand down in cash, and ten thousand in shares—further I can't go."

"Now, Mr. Sawley," said I, "I may be blamed by worldly-minded persons for what I am going to do; but I am a man of principle, and feel deeply for the situation of your amiable wife and family. I bear no malice, though it is quite clear that you intended to make me the sufferer. Pay me fifteen thousand over the counter, and we cry quits for ever."

"Won't you take Camlachie Cemetery shares? They are sure to go up."

"No!"

"Twelve Hundred Cowcaddens' Water, with an issue of new stock next week?"

"Not if they disseminated the Ganges!"

"A thousand Ramshorn Gas—four per cent guaranteed until the act?"

"Not if they promised twenty, and melted down the sun in their retort!"

"Blawweary Iron? Best spec. going."

"No, I tell you once for all! If you don't like my offer—and it is an uncommonly liberal one—say so, and I'll expose you this afternoon upon 'Change."

"Well, then—there's a cheque. But may the"—

"Stop, sir! Any such profane expressions, and I shall insist upon the original bargain. So, then—now we're quits. I wish you a very good-morning, Mr. Sawley, and better luck next time. Pray remember me to your amiable family."

The door had hardly closed upon the discomfited coffin-maker, and I was still in the preliminary steps of an extempore *pas seul*, intended as the outward demonstration of exceeding inward joy, when Bob M'Corkindale entered. I told him the result of the morning's conference.

"You have let him off too easily," said the Political Economist. "Had I been his creditor, I certainly should have sacked the shares into the bargain. There is nothing like rigid dealing between man and man."

"I am contented with moderate profits," said I; "besides, the image of Selina overcame me. How goes it with Jobson and Grabbie?"

"Jobson has paid, and Grabbie compounded. Heckles—may he die an evil death!—has repudiated, become a lame duck, and waddled; but no doubt his estate will pay a dividend."

"So, then, we are clear of the whole Glenmutchkin business, and at a handsome profit."

"A fair interest for the outlay of capital—nothing more. But I'm not quite done with the concern yet."

"How so? not another bearing operation?"

"No; that cock would hardly fight. But you forget that I am secretary to the company, and have a small account against them for services already rendered. I must do what I can to carry the bill through Parliament; and, as you have now sold your whole shares, I advise you to resign from the direction, go down straight to Glenmutchkin, and qualify yourself for a witness. We shall give you five guineas a-day, and pay all your expenses."

"Not a bad notion. But what has become of M'Closkie, and the other fellow with the jaw-breaking name?"

"Vich-Induibh? I have looked after their interests, as in duty bound, sold their shares at a large premium, and despatched them to their native hills on annuities."

"And Sir Polloxfen?"

"Died yesterday of spontaneous combustion."

As the company seemed breaking up, I thought I could not do better than take M'Corkindale's hint, and accordingly betook myself to Glenmutchkin, along with the Captain of M'Alcohol, and we quartered ourselves upon the Factor for Glentumblers. We found Watty Solder very shakey, and his assistant also lapsing into habits of painful inebriety. We saw little of them except of an evening, for we shot and fished the whole day, and made ourselves remarkably comfortable. By singular good-luck, the plans and sections were lodged in time, and the Board of Trade very handsomely reported in our favour, with a recommendation of what they were pleased to call "the Glenmutchkin system," and a hope that it might generally be carried out. What this system was, I never clearly understood; but, of course, none of us had any objections. This circumstance gave an additional impetus to the shares, and they once more went up. I was, however, too cautious to plunge a second time into Charybdis, but M'Corkindale did, and again emerged with plunder.

When the time came for the parliamentary contest, we all emigrated to London. I still recollect, with lively satisfaction, the many pleasant days we spent in the metropolis at the company's expense. There were just a neat fifty of us, and we occupied the whole of an hotel. The discussion before the committee was long and formidable. We were opposed by four other companies who patronised lines, of which the nearest was at least a hundred miles distant from Glenmutchkin; but as they founded their opposition upon dissent from "the Glenmutchkin system" generally, the committee allowed them to be heard. We fought for three weeks a most desperate battle, and might in the end have been victorious, had not our last antagonist, at the very close of his case, pointed out no less than seventy-three fatal errors in the parliamentary plan deposited by the unfortunate Solder. Why this was not done earlier, I never exactly understood; it may be, that our opponents, with gentlemanly consideration, were unwilling to curtail our sojourn in London—and their own. The drama was now finally closed, and after all preliminary expenses were paid, sixpence per share was returned to the holders upon surrender of their scrip.

Such is an accurate history of the Origin, Rise, Progress, and Fall of the Direct Glenmutchkin Railway. It contains a deep moral, if anybody has sense enough to see it; if not, I have a new project in my eye for next session, of which timely notice shall be given.

THE BARBER'S SUPPER

James White

Like the last story, "The Barber's Supper" was originally published anonymously in *Blackwood's Edinburgh Magazine*. The *Welleseley Index to Victorian Publications* reveals the author as Scottish author, James White (1803–1862), who wrote and translated for *Blackwood's* from 1828 to 1861 but is more or less unknown now.* White was a vicar until 1845 when he came into money and retired to the Isle of White to write historical tragedies. However, his work for *Blackwood's* was, predominantly, satirical, and often very silly. For example, "The Old Maid and the Gun" (1830) is narrated by a woman stuck in a cannon on board a ship. She is terrified that the sailors will fire the gun in honour of the Prince (who is on a boat nearby) but it turns out to be a prank.

"The Barber's Supper" is a sort of early anti-capitalist warning and revenge story rolled into one. The description of the merchant, Stephen Whiffle, who sets up a "private bank" as they were called and loses the townsfolk's money while enjoying his continuing wealth is delightfully malicious. He inevitably comes to a sticky end after a night of feasting and heavy drinking with his housekeeper. The escalating farce as the eponymous Barber comes to claim the symbolic fatted pig

---

* A complete version of the *Welleseley Index to Victorian Publications* can be found on archive.org.

from Whiffle's home is as grotesque as it is satisfying. White seems to have had a particular interest in "private banks" because he wrote another piece with a similar tone titled "The Murdering Banker" (1838). That tale bemoans the "well-fed" private bankers and hopes they were becoming a thing of the past in the wake of the new spread of larger establishments, but the story is more of a farcical account of mistaken identity than the revenge plot of "The Barber's Supper".*

* James White, "The Murdering Banker", *Blackwood's Edinburgh Magazine* (1838).

CHAPTER I

This is the age of speculations; but however promising they may be (and there is no lack of promises in any of their prospectuses that we have encountered), there is always a certain bitter in the midst of all their sweets,—always a lingering fear that their end may not be quite so flourishing as their beginnings, and that the dropping of the curtain may find the bubble burst, and the unfortunate speculator in jail. The absence of absolute downright certainty in any undertaking is a great drawback on its desirableness. How gladly would we pawn our last shred of property, yea, the very great-coat we have borrowed of our landlord, to realise money enough to become a shareholder in the joint-stock company for the working of the gold mines lately discovered in the mountains of the moon; or for the creation of antediluvian elephants by means of muriatic acid as discovered by Mr. Crosse; if we could only be *certain* that the gold would be plentiful and the elephants fit for work. Yet amidst all this uncertainty, it is very satisfactory to know that there is one speculation in which it is impossible to go wrong,—and which it requires nothing but a little observation and the use of one's own judgment to render quite as money-making a concern as a general balloon navigation company to all—except the original proposers. This speculation is—to fail; and there is but one art and mystery in it—to fail at the right time; not for a few paltry pounds, which are rigorously taken from you, but for a good slapping sum at once, enough to strike your creditors with reverence for your greatness, and respect for your misfortunes. At the very worst they will allow you a comfortable maintenance out of their own money, and perhaps present you with a silver dinner set in token of their gratitude for your allowing them to recover a shilling in the pound. And in circumstances like those there is always this comfort, that the remaining nineteen shillings enable you to fill the silver dishes with turtle and venison, and all things else in a concatenation accordingly.

There was once in a country town to the east of the Land's-end, and the north of the Isle of Wight, a merchant of the name of Stephen Whiffle, who, although he did not figure in the Red Book, had that very excellent and lucrative possession—a good name. In those days there were none of those multitudinous branch banks which now overshadow the land, but Stephen, with a desire to oblige that made him popular in all the neighbourhood, undertook to supply the place of one. He received all the savings of his friends and neighbours, and some were so delighted with this mode of investment, that they converted all their property into money, and gladly placed it in his hands. In fact, it was thought a great favour on the part of Stephen when he accepted the sums offered to him, and, of course, the favour was the greater the larger the amount. At last there was not a shilling in the town but what was in the custody of Stephen; the people returned almost to a state of pristine security; no door was bolted at night, there was nothing left to tempt the cupidity of thieves. The golden age revisited the borough town of Heckingham, and hogsheads of beer were quaffed every night by the happy inhabitants of the modern Arcadia to the health and happiness of Stephen Whiffle. But while all went gaily as a marriage-bell, and when the felicity of the population had reached to such a height that the tap-room of the Golden Lion could scarcely accommodate the ale-imbibing worshippers of the bestower of all this joy, and the pump in the market was forsaken as a useless implement, there came what is now called a crisis in the money market, but which we shall continue to call by its old name—a crash. Good gracious! can it be possible! The house of Osbaldiston and Tresham was a joke to this! Stephen Whiffle was a bankrupt; his property was found to be scarcely worth the dividing; his strong-box empty, his creditors broken-hearted, and the pewter mace, which on high days and holidays was carried before the mayor, was ordered by that official to be enveloped in crape in sign of the general lamentation. Stephen, however, continued to live in his old house; and the only change visible was an increased devotion and a marvellous tendency to grow fat. His attendance at chapel was regular as clock-work; his groans were heart-rending in the extreme, and no one could possibly help feeling compassion for his misfortunes when he began himself to adorn the pulpit, and preach on the perishable-ness of all earthly treasures. One consolation, however, remained to him, he used often to say in his discourses, and that was, that through the agency of his failure the Lord had turned the hearts of many from the Golden Lion, and opened their eyes to the superiority of the pump. The increase of sobriety was indeed remarkable, and the landlords of the different inns were untiring in their efforts to obtain a diminution of the duties on beer; the malt they did not care about, as having little connexion with it in the way of their business; but if the Bonifaces were untiring, the Chancellor of the Exchequer was unremitting, and so there was a Temperance Society established in the borough, on the most strictly involuntary principles. Among all those who owed the blessing of sobriety to the philanthropic and re-forming proceedings of the devout Whiffle, the person who seemed least grateful to his benefactor was one John Piper, the cor-poration barber. This ingratitude in John was extremely sinful, as he had not only to thank Mr. Stephen for having weaned him from strong ale, but also for the inestimable blessing of an appetite which might safely be called never-failing, seeing that he never had now the means of satisfying its demands. This unerring sign of health also was extended to his wife and six or seven children, so that John's obligations were certainly of the most powerful kind. But instead of looking with an eye of favour on Mr. Whiffle, he actually grudged that respectable gentleman every pound of flesh that adorned his ribs; his enormous breadth of back he considered a fresh theft of his property, and when a third chin began to develope itself, the indignation of the barber could no longer be restrained—his rage found vent in words, and he claimed the additional protuberance as his own. His claim was logically enounced—the produce of my money is mine; that chin is the produce of my money; *ergo*, that chin is mine. In the meantime Mr. Stephen had a life-interest in it as well as in all the other goods, chattels, and hereditaments of which he had so sagaciously possessed himself. But Stephen, though very devout, was not a little ostentatious; a combination you may perhaps have remarked on similar occasions if you are a person of observation; if not, take our advice, and watch, and you will see that the carriages of pious people who have abjured the world are always as gaudy as a lord mayor's coach. This rule is without exception. Stephen, we say, was ostentatious; but this vain-glorious spirit did not display itself in the trappings of his carriage, seeing that he contented himself with an occasional hire of a gig, but in the equally tangible form of a larder stuffed to the very roof; parcels of fish arriving every week from London, and the evolutions of a jack before the kitchen fire, which one might almost have fancied a specimen of the perpetual motion. One morning a sound as of the battle of Waterloo had alarmed half the town; deep groans and then high shrieks had filled the atmosphere for many yards around; there was neither earthquake nor eclipse; but when at last the horrific sounds had ceased, and "a solemn silence held the listening air," men looked at each other with faces that showed they knew the cause of the hurly-burly, and that Stephen had killed his pig! Such an enormous pig had never been fattened in Heckingham before by the ingenuity or the meal of man. Its sides swelled out like the mainsails of a three-decker in a stiffish breeze; its throat was imperceptible *quasi* throat, being rather a continuation of the prodigious body, and instead of being a narrow isthmus connecting two continents, it might have passed very well for a continent itself. Vanity indeed in such a possession was excusable in any one, and in Stephen the desire to show the lovely monster to his townsfolk was altogether irresistible. He therefore had it placed on the floor of his kitchen, which was visible to all the passengers, while he himself sat at the top of the stair which led down to it, to enjoy the wonder and admiration of the beholders. Oh, it was a sight worth seeing, the worthy Stephen Whiffle and his pig. At the first glance they might have passed for brothers; but a closer inspection, though it did not destroy the family resemblance, enabled one to perceive the different styles of beauty by which each was distinguished. Stephen had the ruddy glow of satisfaction diffusing its purple light, over the vast expanse of his chops—face we mean; whereas the other had that mild expression peculiar to the defunct of that species, which Lord Byron has called "the rapture of repose." Besides, what's the use of any more descriptions of the points wherein they differed? Stephen sat full-dressed like a worthy gentleman in his chair, whereas the other lay full length with his bristly coat around him on the kitchen-floor. Wherever a sight was to be seen, of course all the barbers of a town must be there to see it, and as our friend John Piper was the principal professor of the shaving art in the town of Heckingham, he came, saw, and cursed the proprietor with all his soul and with all his strength. On returning home, and reflecting on all the distress he owed to Mr. Whiffle—"how it was all along of he," as he expressed it, that very few people could now afford the luxury of a barber; that one of his best customers had put down his wig and his one-horse-chay the week after the failure; that baldness had become fashionable among the old; and long beards and moustaches among the young, ever since that eventful incident; when Piper, we say, reflected on all these things, he broke a good many of the commandments, among which we will only particularise the third and the tenth. What a wonderful thing hunger is! How it sharpens the wits!—how it teaches us logic, rhetoric, and philosophy!—how it makes us write books, or, at all events, publish them! Yes, hunger makes us do a great many curious things; and if you will wait for a very few minutes, you shall see what it induced the exasperated Piper to perform. It was indeed irresistible. Here was an opportunity to gratify at once his appetite and his revenge. "Wife!" he said, with a voice that portended strange things; "'tis past bearing, and I'll bear it no longer."

"What is it, dear John?" answered his helpmate, who was the most obedient wife that ever fell to the lot of a barber.

"What is it?—ugh—it chokes me. Why that infernal villain—that rascal, Whiffle, has killed the most beautiful pig I ever saw. The greedy, fat, dishonest, d—d intolerable beast—twenty score if he's an ounce—the cursed red-faced, pot-bellied, double-chinned impostor—besides liver and lights!"

"What is all this about?" enquired Mrs. Piper, who, in the strange jumble of her husband's ideas, could not exactly make out whether his descriptions were intended for Whiffle or the pig.

"I tell you 'tis mine! No power on earth shall persuade me that every inch of fat on both their carcasses is not my just and lawful property; and I'll have that pig this night as sure as my name's"—

"Steal it?"

"What do you mean, woman, by talking such nonsense? Steal! Isn't it my own? Haven't I paid a hundred and three pounds seventeen and twopence for it?—a good price—and haven't I a right, to bring it home?"

The good woman shook her head and sighed. John paused in mid career, and casting his eye mournfully round the room on the beds where all his children were sleeping—

"They will ask us for something in the morning, Letty, and we have nothing to give them:—no more credit, any where! The little ravens are fed in the fields, but we have nothing to put in the mouths of these little ones when they open them for food. Oh, cursed be he that cheateth his neighbours, and fattens his pig at other people's expense!"

Letty looked mournfully round, but said nothing. "Only think, wife," continued John, "in half an hour we could have the pig here;— a slice done on the gridiron would be delightful before going to bed. I would pawn some of my razors to buy some bread; we would waken the two elder ones to give them a taste, poor dears!—and to-morrow I would sell some of the bacon, and tell the rascal, Whiffle, I would give him a receipt for the value of the animal as part payment of his debt—eh! Letty?"

Letty could resist no longer. Her bonnet was on her head; the light, truck brought noiselessly from the back-yard to the door, and off the two set through the now deserted streets, for the clock had struck ten, and the watchmen had been asleep for an hour.

CHAPTER II

The day that Stephen Whiffle presented his fat pig to the admiring eyes of his townsmen was the happiest day of his life. His heart swelled with pride and exultation to such a degree, that he burst two of the buttons of his waistcoat. In a chair, conspicuously placed in the passage, in such a way as to command a view of the object of his admiration on one side, and the street on the other, with a pipe breathing perfume, and his ears wide open to hear the criticisms of his neighbours, from morn till noon, from noon till dewy eve, did Stephen labour, as we have said, without intermission in his effort to astonish the natives; and so persevering had been his labours, that his appetite on this occasion was increased to a pitch of sharpness that would have made an alligator ashamed of himself. But Dinah Prim, who on week days was his housekeeper, and on Sundays his fellow-worker in edifying the rebellious, in so far as she invariably groaned louder in her devotions than any of the unconverted have a right to do, had prepared a more than usually abundant supper, as if in anticipation of the exciting effects of her master's unwonted activity. An immense dish of stewed beef-steaks, accompanied with hot potatoes, and garnished with sundry pickles, sent up their savoury steams; a huge tankard, crowned with a diadem of foam, rested its precious cargo of exquisite home-brewed, at Stephen's dexter hand; Dinah Prim smiled with her sweetest smiles directly opposite; and a kettle "weaving its song of potatory joy," and breathing vows of ardent devotion to a pot-bellied bottle of gin which stood on the table, gave symptoms of an intention on the part of Mr. Whiffle to prove himself a patriotic subject by increasing the amount of the excise. But it is not to be imagined for a moment, that Stephen had sat all day exposed to the fresh air without some refreshment. Dinah had performed various voyages to the cellar, and returned laden with profound beakers of ale which her master had magnanimously tossed over the vast abysm of his throat with redoubled relish when he perceived that his happiness was witnessed by some hapless wretch to whom the flavour of John Barleycorn was one of the pleasures of memory, for Stephen was one of those Lucretian individuals to whom his own happiness was very much enhanced by a comparison with the misery of others. Supper at last was over; the tankard emptied; the gin poured into his tumbler, and over the huge expanse of Whiffle's countenance, now nearly blue from the quantity he had eaten, wandered an expression of self-complacent satisfaction that only the good can feel.

"What an excellent thing, Dinah, is a good conscience," snorted the almost somnolent Stephen, "and a contented mind. Them is the only things as is worth the search. All else is wanity and wexation."

"Truly; and if all blessings is used with moderation."

"What do you mean to hinsinivate?—That I ain't moderate?—Is not all things allowed to me as has repented?—Mayn't I heat a few beef-steaks?—"

"Yes, with humility—"

"Humble enough too for one as has reached such degrees as I have.—But you are yet at the houter wall.—You don't know nothink of true 'oliness, and that ere beef-steak hadn't half enough of innions.—So hold your tongue."

While this and similar conversations went on, the bottle got rapidly exhausted;—short broken grunts were all that proceeded at last from the meek lips of Mr. Whiffle, and with his head lean't back upon his chair, his nostrils wide distended, and his legs stretched out before him—to the eyes of one of the unconverted the immaculate Stephen might almost have had the appearance of being what the Gentiles call drunk. The unprofane would have considered him in a trance. There is no saying what visions were vouchsafed to him on this occasion, but it is probable they had some reference to the business of the day; for, muttering some unintelligible words about his pig, he made sundry efforts to rise.

"What do you want?" enquired Dinah, seeing his critical condition—"Better sit still for an hour or two, and sleep it off."

A growl, and reiterated attempts to leave his chair, were the only answer to this sagacious hint.

"Sit down, Whiffle; you'll expose yourself. *You* to be seen in this condition—for shame!"

A monosyllable energetically pronounced, which is generally appropriated to the female specimens of the canine tribe, showed that Dinah's eloquence was not of much weight with the self-willed Stephen.

"Sit still," she said at last, "you will hurt yourself if you attempt to move. The kitchen door is open, and you will never get down the steps."

"I will though," stuttered Whiffle, at last succeeding in his efforts, and staggering along the floor. "I will, I tell you. I'll go down and have one other look on him afore I tumbles in. Go to bed, Dinah; to bed, you jade, and I'll come this moment.—"

Two or three lurches hither and thither at length brought him to the door at the top of the stairs leading down to the kitchen, where the object of his veneration was extended. "Steady, steady," cried Dinah, as he swayed to and fro with the candle in one hand—"steady." But before she had time to reach his side, the step was taken,—crash, crash, down the stairs thundered the prodigious weight—a heavy fall at the bottom—a grunt as of the bursting of a bagpipe—perfect silence and thick darkness told Dinah that her worst fears were realised. In fear and trembling she searched for another candle, lighted it at the decaying fire, and went into the kitchen. There, at full length, lay the huge carcasses, Whiffle and his pig, lovely in their lives, in their deaths undivided. It needed a very slight observation to convince Dinah of the condition of the late Mr. Whiffle, and as soon as she saw that all chance of his resuscitation was hopeless, she displayed a degree of heroism and self-command, that would have done honour to a Roman matron. With the most delicate sensitiveness she spread a large table-cloth over the defunct, for Stephen, in order more fully to enjoy his supper, had stripped himself as far as decency would allow, and locking the kitchen-door, she proceeded to the parlour to make preparations for alarming the neighbourhood with the spectacle of her distress. For this purpose she finished all that was left in the bottle by way of a support under her great affliction, and then, wisely considering that no honest man can endure the idea of leaving the world in debt, she resolved to wipe off such a stain from the memory of her master by paying herself in full for all the services she had rendered him. His hoards were ransacked, and as between such friends the ceremony of counting the money might have the appearance of distrust, she transferred the grand total to her own trunk, along with all the articles of silver she could find, as "friendship's offerings" from the deceased. "All this," she murmured devoutly, as she closed the lid of her strong-box, "should have been mine, for many's the time he has promised to make me an honest woman—but he was a mean, selfish beast, and the Lord's will be done. I am resigned to every dispensation." When all these preparations were ended, she again unlocked the kitchen-door, threw on her bonnet in a mighty hurry, and sobbing and sighing as heavily as she could, she proceeded to alarm the neighbours, and call in the surgeon to her master's aid.

CHAPTER III

John Piper arrived at Stephen's mansion about five minutes after that worthy gentleman had performed the somerset which laid him on the kitchen-floor. Every thing was dark and silent. Dinah was busy in other parts of the house—the shutters were still unclosed, and John, knowing the locality too well to stand in need of a light, glided noiselessly in by the kitchen-window, felt his way cautiously along the floor, and kicking with his foot on the vast mass reposing beneath the table-cloth, concluded that he had discovered the object of his search. "How heavy the beast is!" muttered John, "I shall never be able to get him on the truck by myself. Here, Letty, come in and lend a hand!"—By incredible exertions, hauling and tugging by the table-cloth, the hungry pair managed to deposit the mighty burden on the little vehicle, and full of glowing anticipations of a smoking steak from the overloaded ribs, they proceeded to their dwelling. Happily without being observed by any human being, they reached their destination, bundled the prodigious carcase, still shrouded in the table-cloth, into their own kitchen; and while John went to the yard to deposit the truck, Letty made preparations for the approaching feast. The plates were laid on the table, the gridiron cleaned, the fire stirred up, and now nothing was wanting but the return of the husband to furnish the materials for Letty's culinary skill. John at last returned, took down a knife from the corner cupboard,—sharpened it for some time on the kitchen-dresser. "Now, Letty," he said, "off with the cloth, and let us have a slice out of the monster's rump."

"Hush," said Letty, somewhat alarmed, "I think I hear steps on the street."

"Only James Williams, the watchman, going home to bed—he

could not see any thieves in so dark a night, so what's the use of sitting up? Come, uncover, and I'll cut off three or four pounds."

"No—no—wait till the stops are past. Hark! they are stopping at Mr. Jones's the surgeon's—Don't you hear knocks at his door?—listen."

"They need not knock at Dr. Jones's—He has gone out of the parish to attend a rich woman at Melham—If they wants any one to be bled, they must come to our young man."

"Ah! poor fellow," said Letty, "I had forgotten him quite—and he hasn't had no supper this blessed night, nor no dinner as I know of—Ah! John."

This latter invocation was accompanied with a significant look at the table-cloth on the floor, which John quickly comprehended. "Surely, surely, Letty," he said, "when all is got right again we will ask Mr. Mason to join us. It will only be another slice or two, and Mr. Mason is a perfect gentleman, though his father, poor man, was ruinated like the rest of us by that infernal rascal old Whiffle. Off with the table-cloth till I dig the knife into him." But before this injunction could be complied with the noise came to their own door. A loud knocking began, which their fears magnified, with the thundering of a constable's baton. The knife was thrown down in terror, and John stood anxiously listening to the continued rat-tat-tat! "What's to be done, dear John?" cried Letty, almost hysterical in her alarm; "Oh that we had resolved to starve on, rather than steal the pig—they will take us up for the robbery!—my poor children!—oh dear, oh dear!"

"Hark!" cried John, "they are come for us already. They will break in the door. Put out the light, Letty; let us save ourselves if we can."

"Open the door, Mr. Piper," whined the voice of Dinah Prim, "it has pleased Providence to visit me with affliction. Is not there a doctor as lives in your upstairs?"

"Coming, Mrs. Prim, coming, madam," flustered John, now recognising the voice; "rather a late hour this, Mrs. Prim. What can I do for you?" he continued, cautiously opening the window.

"Oh he is gone! he is carried off," sighed the lady.

"Carried off! ahem—quite a mistake—good-humoured jest, that's all," said John.

"Jest! mistake indeed! No; he is carried off, I assure you; but I bows to the one as did it. It was done in kindness."

"Certainly, ma'am, no doubt of it," said the perplexed barber, not exactly knowing whether Dinah was aware of the truck adventure or not.

"If I had had any warning of it," continued Mrs. Prim, "it wouldn't have been so bad; but to be stolen away from me so momentaneously!"

"Why, yes ma'am," said John, more and more bewildered; "but ye see, ma'am, the truck is still in the back-yard, and your loss can soon be replaced."

"Oh, never, never," sobbed Dinah; "all things is for the best. But if you will tell the young doctor, as lodges here, it will be a great satisfaction if he will just cut my master's throat, that there mayn't be no chance of his being buried alive."

"Me, marm," exclaimed John, in the utmost surprise; "me tell Mr. Mason to come for to go for to cut Mr. Whiffle's throat, marm! No, he is an infernal old rascal, there aint no manner of doubt; but as to cutting his throat, it's vat no gentleman would condescend for to do, let alone the chance of being hanged for't; and who the devil vants to bury the old brute alive?"

"Come, Mr. Piper, we are wasting precious time. If you don't send the young doctor to me directly, I will carry my complaint to the Mayor."

"For any sake, Mrs. Prim, don't talk of the Mayor; I'll send Mr. Mason directly, marm; and if you wish it, I'll have my truck at your door in a moment."

"Oh, no, I want nothing of that kind—only the young doctor. Come with him yourself, you may be useful."

"Certainly, marm," said John Piper, as Dinah walked off; "but that 'ere idea about cutting the villain's throat is the rummest as ever I heard. Taking a little bacon aint nothing to that; but what can the old rascal want with Mr. Mason and me? Pr'aps to pay us our money? At any rate I'll go and tell him to his face that this here pig is my own, and that I aint ashamed of taking my own property."

With these and similar soliloquies, the magnanimous barber mounted the crazy stairs, and entered the room where Mr. Mason was still poring over his books by the light of one miserable candle. "Ask your pardon, Mr. Mason," said John, "but just as we was agoing to supper, Dinah Prim, old Whiffle's maid, came in to say that her master wished for to see you and me on very peticular business."

"Me! Mr. Whiffle to see me?" asked the young man in surprise, "Is he ill?"

"Can't exactly say. Mrs. Prim did talk in a hexeterordnary way about wishing you to cut his throat."

"Open a vein the woman means. I will take my lancet directly. He is plethoric, and is perhaps threatened with the premonitory symptoms of apoplexy. Follow me as soon as you can, there is no time to be lost."

"And if the old rascal says any thing about his loss to-night before I comes, tell him I take it in part payment."

But the young man hurried out of the room without enquiring into the worthy barber's exact meaning, and proceeded to the house of Mr. Whiffle on Esculapian thoughts intent. On arriving there Mrs. Prim was still greatly agitated, but whether from the circumstance of two or three tumblers of gin-and-water being insufficient to restrain her emotion, or from some other cause, Mr. Mason took no time to investigate. With a wave of her hand, which unfortunately extinguished the candle, she gave him to understand that his duty was in the kitchen—"You will find him on the floor," she hiccupped in the extremity of woe, and to the kitchen the practitioner accordingly groped his way. Stumbling down the steps, kicking his shins against tubs and chairs, he at last came to what he considered his patient; felt tenderly for the wrist, and was no little astonished to find he had hold of the trotter of a tremendous pig. Mr. Mason was not superstitious, but he had read of the metempsychosis.

"Bring a candle, Mrs. Prim; there is some mistake here."

That worthy lady, gathering all her energies once more, coaxed warmth enough into the fire to relight her candle, and staggered into the kitchen to the assistance of the surgeon.

"I s'pose he's quite cold, sir," she said, holding the candle with tipsy gravity over the gigantic porker; "there aint no chance of bringing him to life again, for he must have broken his neck half an hour ago."

"Who? Mrs. Prim—who must have broken his neck?"

"Why, the gentleman as you are feeling the pulse of. Do you think I don't know my own master."

"This, madam, this is a large sow or other animal of the porcina genus."

"A sow?—not my master?—then where can he be?" And the terrified woman looked all round for the body of the vanished Stephen. "I told him how it would be—the devil has carried him away—oh, dear—there, in this very spot I seed him land—put a table-cloth over him and all; and now he is spirited away. Don't you think you smell brimstone, sir?"

"Woman," replied young Mason, "you are either drunk or mad; you have played a most indecent trick in hoaxing a medical man. I know not what can have been your object, but I have suffered enough already from the villany of Mr. Whiffle not to be made the butt of your heartless jests."

The young man hurried home brim-full of wrath and offended dignity. He took no notice of the shivering barber's agitation as he opened the door. "You need not go to Whiffle's," he said, as he rushed up stairs "he is quite recovered and does not need any assistance."

"Heaven be praised; then my neck is saved from the gallows," ejaculated John Piper, as he again joined his wife, who had sunk into a chair, and was hiding her face in her hands. "Old Whiffle has got suddenly well again, and told Mr. Mason that he had no need for medicines. Let us to bed good wife—the fright has taken away my appetite, and I wish the old rascal much joy of his fat pig."

CHAPTER IV

The moment Mr. Mason had left the house to attend on Mr. Whiffle, the barber had gone into the kitchen where his wife was still busied in making preparations for the supper. "Now, Letty, lose no time," he cried, "the coast is quite clear. I shall be back before the steak is done. Off with the cloth, and let me cut them nicely!" The cloth was at last unwound, and it would be useless to attempt a description of the horror and surprise that fell upon the astonished pair, when in place of the portly chops of the much coveted pig they recognised the hated visage of the detested Whiffle.

"That rascal," cried John Piper, "will be the death of me, first by starvation, and then the gallows. Oh Letty, we shall both swing on the other side of the bridge, cheek by jowl with the murderer as was hanged last week."

"But we didn't murder him, John."

"What does the law care for that? We can't bring him to life again, and therefore we shall certainly be hanged."

"But we can take him back again."

"Impossible. That old woman has raised the alarm by this time. But how in heaven's name has the pig turned into old Whiffle?"

This was a complete puzzle.

"I'll swear it was a pig," said John, "when I laid it on my truck. It must have been Ingilby the conjuror, that was here at the fair, that turned a neck of veal into a goose and goslings. But what's the use of talking?" continued the barber. "All that won't save our necks. We must get quit of him."

After a moment's consultation, it was resolved to leave the unfortunate Stephen in the darkest part of the street, and rigidly to deny all knowledge of the adventure, if any enquiries were made on the subject. They accordingly again called the truck into requisition, and as the least suspicious place they could find, they laid him against the back of the watch-box of James Williams, the guardian of the streets of Heckingham, believing that that valuable officer had betaken himself to his couch. In this, however, they were mistaken, for that useful individual was sunk in a profound sleep within the very box against which they placed their burden. Silently the barber and his wife returned home;—waited the Doctor's arrival with no little expectation, and were relieved by the news he gave them of Mr. Whiffle's recovery. When James Williams the watchman had continued his slumbers far into the night, he resolved to alter the venue of the conclusion of them to his own bed at home. For this purpose he got up, but no sooner had he altered the centre of gravity of his box, by removing his own weight from the back part of it, than it yielded to the superincumbent ponderosity of the inanimate Whiffle, and falling—with hideous ruin and combustion—down it enclosed the scarcely awakened watchman in his own sentry-box, with such a mountainous weight above it that his efforts to extricate himself were for a long time unsuccessful. When at last he contrived to rear his prison, which enclosed him like a shell, and creep out on hands and knees, his efforts, and the persevering obstinacy of his overthrower, had irritated him to such a pitch of frenzy, that the first thing he did was to apply sundry thwacks of his baton on the body of his assailant, which Piper had reinvested in the table-cloth.

"I'll teach you," exclaimed the vengeful watchman, "to turn over my box—playing the ghost, too, you good-for-nothing vagabond, dressed up in an old sheet—I'll make you give up the ghost, I will. Who are you?" he continued—rather surprised at receiving neither an answer, nor any resistance to his attack. "Come, hold up your face to the light"—advancing the lanthorn, which had luckily escaped extinction in the *mêlée*. "Ha! gracious, Mr. Whiffle," he cried, starting back—"and dead, too—what shall I do:—these baton marks would hang me in any court!" But we need not trace the farther adventures of the hapless Whiffle, which were as numerous as those of the Hunchback in the Arabian Nights. We pass over how the watchman placed him against a physician's door—how the physician threw him into the river, and how finally he got into the hands of the confederates of the man who, the preceding week, had been hanged in chains for robbery and murder. Several days passed on—and still no news of the lost one. A sort of enquiry was instituted—Dinah Prim told her story. A report got abroad, which was industriously circulated by John

Piper, that the devil had carried away the defrauder of his neighbours; but those who did not go so far as this, believed that Mr. Whiffle had resolved to leave the neighbourhood, and that the housekeeper's story was the result of ignorance and superstition. In the meantime, John Piper took possession of the house, signing an agreement, to give it up on Mr. Whiffle's coming to claim it; and as his eloquence had been efficacious in persuading a good many people that there was something very mysterious in the Doctor feeling the pig's pulse instead of Mr. Whiffle's, and that there was a dreadful coincidence between the disappearance of the missing man and the continued presence of the "hanimal," few people objected to the Barber taking possession of the porker also, binding himself to account for it when its owner made the demand.

Dinah Prim also, in the first agitation of her alarm, had dropt some hints of the money she had taken, of which the watchful barber availed himself, to arrest it for the benefit of the creditors. Other discoveries of the places in which Whiffle had deposited his spoils were also made, and every thing was in a fair way to render the disappearance of Mr. Stephen one of the happiest circumstances which had happened in the town of Heckingham since the ever memorable period of his failure, when an unexpected incident occurred which increased the amazement of the inhabitants in a tenfold degree, and perhaps, if the truth were known, their satisfaction at the same time.

The Mayor of that eventful year was the most celebrated tailor that Heckingham had ever produced. He had made liveries for many years for the Lord-lieutenant of the county, and not many months before this time had made a shooting-jacket for the High Sheriff. When a man is at the top of his profession, and at the same time Mayor of his native town, a little pride may perhaps be excusable. There is indeed no denying that Mr. Clips was one of the vainest of men. He was vain of himself, of his shop, of his wife, of his children. He was vain not only of the beauties of his native town, but of every thing connected with it. He was not a little proud that Heckingham boasted of the smallest church and the largest prison of any borough town in England; but at the present moment the acme of his pride was the fact that during his mayoralty a malefactor had actually been hung in chains.

It was perhaps about a week after the mysterious disappearance of Mr. Whiffle, that the worshipful the Mayor of Heckingham, with a finely gilt chain dangling across his breast, a gold-headed cane in his hand, and gratified vanity ruling triumphant on every feature, accompanied an admiring stranger in an inspection of the curiosities of the place. "This here by the church-gate," began the Mayor, "is our stocks, and that there just opposite is the public-house—very convenient, you see, sir—the mealifactors haven't far to go. A little farther on is our prison. Excellent accommodation, and I am happy to say always quite full. The town-hall you have already seen. There is a little anecdote about that there figure of Justice over the door. Fine statty, aint it? Well, sir, you see we have a theatre here, and once when there was a row because Pizarro came on drunk, and give Rollo a bloody nose, the mob became uproarious and broke every thing they could find. Among other things they got hold of this here wooden statty—she was Thalia then, and had a very agreeable smile on her face—and knocked the upper part of her head all to pieces. Well, an idea came into my mind, and I bought it as old lumber; had a board—you see the board, sir?—nailed right over the top of her nose—because Justice, you know, is blind; hung a pair of wooden scales over her left wrist, and glued the right arm of Mars to the stump of her broken elbow—made a present of her to the town, and received the thanks of the corporation. She is painted green to keep her from the weather:—not quite so natral as red and white, but stands

243

the wear and tear much better." In this way the eloquent Clips paraded his visitor through the town;—and as the last and crowning wonder, "the bright consummate rose of the whole wreath," he conducted him to the other side of the bridge, and fixing his eyes intently on his friend to watch the effect of the spectacle, "There, sir," he said, "there is the glory of Heckingham,—the notorious Bill Swag—that robbed and murdered—no—murdered and robbed—the unfortunate old man on the great London road—a perpetual moniment of the watchfulness of Providence to detect a murder, and also of the horse-patrol. You see what a miserable care-worn, thin-looking rascal it is. No!—Heaven be over us! what is that?" and the Mayor's tongue ceased its office, though it still wagged, in vain attempts to reach the palate, the wide gaping of the mouth preventing all communication. The stranger looked astonished. "Sir," began the mayor, mastering himself by a strong effort, "this is the most wonderful thing that ever happened, and will make my mayoralty notorious to all future times. The fat man you now see on the gallows, sir, is not Bill Swag, but Mr. Whiffle—you've heard his story? There he is, sir—but this is too weighty a matter for delay. I must summon the Council forthwith."

In pursuance of this wise resolution the members of the deliberative body met in full conclave,—marched in solemn procession to the gallows to convince themselves of the fact, and returned to the town-hall to decide on farther proceedings. Opinions were long divided—some contending that it would be better to let things remain as they were—insinuating, at the same time, that the deceased was by no means unworthy of the situation he occupied. But the Mayor, rising with a dignity unknown to lower functionaries, addressed them in a speech which carried conviction to every mind. "As to old Whiffle finding his way to the gallows," said Clips in his oration, "with that we have nothing to do—because we know nothing about it, and he himself is not in a position to tell us. It is certain that by removing him, our beautiful town, gentlemen, will lose one of its proudest ornaments, for, let me tell you, it aint every town as can point to a murderer hung in chains;—yet, gentlemen, even this distinction I hope you will surrender for the sake of me, Thomas Clips, the Mayor of this town. It is not for the man's sake I wish him to be taken down—no—but when I tell you, gentlemen, that in this my year of mayoralty, I, the chief dignitary of this ancient borough,—with my own hands made the identical breeches in which he is now suspended—O! I feel certain you will not subject your principal magistrate to the indignity of having his handiwork disgraced upon the gallows!" The appeal was irresistible. It was unanimously agreed to act on the Mayor's suggestion, and Heckingham was robbed of the ornament which had rendered its inhabitants so proud.

Mr. Mason is now the principal surgeon in that part of the country, and the last news of John Piper, who is a rich man and flourishing perfumer, was, that he is the Mayor-elect for the next year, and threatens to put Dinah Prim in Bridewell, if she makes any disturbance by preaching on the streets. It is observed that John kills a fat hog every year, and distributes it to the poor—a sort of thank-offering for all the benefits he has experienced from his affection to that species of animal.

THE MARK OF THE BEAST

Rudyard Kipling

Rudyard Kipling (1865–1936) remains one of the most famous authors of the late nineteenth and early twentieth centuries. His poem, "If", remains one of the most popular and best-known pieces of British literature of all time. Kipling's complicated position on the colonisation of India in particular, as depicted in so many of his stories and novels, has made him a controversial figure in recent years. However, as Beetoshok Singha observes, "some of the works of Rudyard Kipling [...] reflect [...] the author's deep-seated anxiety and unease regarding the fate of the Empire in erstwhile colonies".* Singha goes on to argue that, although Kipling's fiction often supports the right of the "White man" to a racially-based priority in these spaces, "where the White man misuses his power [...] the ideology of White supremacy collapses and the rule is sustained by the exercise of brute force".† This brutality reveals colonialism and Empire for what they are, an unjustifiable and exploitative presence in another country or culture. In other words, Kipling's stories recognise the wrongs and damage of colonialism and Empire while at the same time problematically

---

* Beetoshok Singha, "Revisiting the Surfiction: A Study of Kipling's 'The Mark of the Beast'", *Labyrinth: An International Refereed Journal of Postmodern Studies* (2014).
† Ibid.

perpetuating some of the basic premises as essential rights. As previously mentioned, the gothic often usefully explores contemporary anxieties about social norms and ventures to transgress against those boundaries in order to challenge them. Sometimes known as "imperial gothic", this form of the weird tale is often torn between confirming biases and questioning the ethical and moral implications of colonisation.

As Deborah Denenholz Morse writes, "[p]erhaps the most frightening of the Kipling stories that negotiate the imperial encounter is 'The Mark of the Beast'."[*] It reminds the reader of the bestial origins and nature of the human. The drunkenness begins in some New Year festivities in an isolated outpost of India. The three British men involved stagger home and on the one way, one of them desecrates a temple, much to the horror of the other two. In the altercations with the worshippers that follows, the culprit is bitten on the breast by a "Silver Man". The next morning, Fleete begins to change and the results for him and for the "Silver Man" are a violent and horrifying indictment of the misuse of power in the Empire. Please note that there are scenes of torture and racist language in this story so take care of yourself as and after you read it.

*   Deborah Denenholz Morse, "'The Mark of the Beast': Animals as Sites of Imperial Encounter from *Wuthering Heights* to *Green Mansions*", *Victorian Animal Dreams* (2007).

Your Gods and my Gods—do you or I know which are the stronger?

NATIVE PROVERB

East of Suez, some hold, the direct control of Providence ceases; Man being there handed over to the power of the Gods and Devils of Asia, and the Church of England Providence only exercising an occasional and modified supervision in the case of Englishmen.

This theory accounts for some of the more unnecessary horrors of life in India: it may be stretched to explain my story.

My friend Strickland of the Police, who knows as much of natives of India as is good for any man, can bear witness to the facts of the case. Dumoise, our doctor, also saw what Strickland and I saw. The inference which he drew from the evidence was entirely incorrect. He is dead now; he died in a rather curious manner, which has been elsewhere described.

When Fleete came to India he owned a little money and some land in the Himalayas, near a place called Dharmsala. Both properties had been left him by an uncle, and he came out to finance them. He was a big, heavy, genial, and inoffensive man. His knowledge of natives was, of course, limited, and he complained of the difficulties of the language.

He rode in from his place in the hills to spend New Year in the station, and he stayed with Strickland. On New Year's Eve there was a big dinner at the club, and the night was excusably wet. When men foregather from the uttermost ends of the Empire, they have a right to be riotous. The Frontier had sent down a contingent o' Catch'em-Alive-O's who had not seen twenty white faces for a year, and were used to ride fifteen miles to dinner at the next Fort at the risk of a Khyberee bullet where their drinks should lie. They profited by their new security, for they tried to play pool with a curled-up hedgehog found in the garden, and one of them carried the marker round the room in his teeth. Half a dozen planters had come in from the south and were talking "horse" to the Biggest Liar in Asia, who was trying to cap all their stories at once. Everybody was there, and there was a general closing up of ranks and taking stock of our losses in dead or disabled that had fallen during the past year. It was a very wet night, and I remember that we sang "Auld Lang Syne" with our feet in the Polo Championship Cup, and our heads among the stars, and swore that we were all dear friends. Then some of us went away and annexed Burma, and some tried to open up the Soudan and were opened up by Fuzzies in that cruel scrub outside Suakim, and some found stars and medals, and some were married, which was bad, and some did other things which were worse, and the others of us stayed in our chains and strove to make money on insufficient experiences.

Fleete began the night with sherry and bitters, drank champagne steadily up to dessert, then raw, rasping Capri with all the strength of whisky, took Benedictine with his coffee, four or five whiskies and sodas to improve his pool strokes, beer and bones at half-past two, winding up with old brandy. Consequently, when he came out, at half-past three in the morning, into fourteen degrees of frost, he was very angry with his horse for coughing, and tried to leapfrog into the saddle. The horse broke away and went to his stables; so Strickland and I formed a Guard of Dishonour to take Fleete home.

Our road lay through the bazaar, close to a little temple of Hanuman, the Monkey-god, who is a leading divinity worthy of respect. All gods have good points, just as have all priests. Personally, I attach much importance to Hanuman, and am kind to his people—the great grey apes of the hills. One never knows when one may want a friend.

There was a light in the temple, and as we passed, we could hear voices of men chanting hymns. In a native temple, the priests rise at all hours of the night to do honour to their god. Before we could stop him, Fleete dashed up the steps, patted two priests on the back, and was gravely grinding the ashes of his cigar-butt in to the forehead of the red, stone image of Hanuman. Strickland tried to drag him out, but he sat down and said solemnly:

"Shee that? Mark of the B—beasht! *I* made it. Ishn't it fine?"

In half a minute the temple was alive and noisy, and Strickland, who knew what came of polluting gods, said that things might occur. He, by virtue of his official position, long residence in the country, and weakness for going among the natives, was known to the priests and he felt unhappy. Fleete sat on the ground and refused to move. He said that "good old Hanuman" made a very soft pillow.

Then, without any warning, a Silver Man came out of a recess behind the image of the god. He was perfectly naked in that bitter, bitter cold, and his body shone like frosted silver, for he was what the Bible calls "a leper as white as snow." Also he had no face, because he was a leper of some years' standing, and his disease was heavy upon him. We two stooped to haul Fleete up, and the temple was filling and filling with folk who seemed to spring from the earth, when the Silver Man ran in under our arms, making a noise exactly like the mewing of an otter, caught Fleete round the body and dropped his head on Fleete's breast before we could wrench him away. Then he retired to a corner and sat mewing while the crowd blocked all the doors.

The priests were very angry until the Silver Man touched Fleete. That nuzzling seemed to sober them.

At the end of a few minutes' silence one of the priests came to Strickland and said, in perfect English, "Take your friend away. He has done with Hanuman but Hanuman has not done with him." The crowd gave room and we carried Fleete into the road.

Strickland was very angry. He said that we might all three have been knifed, and that Fleete should thank his stars that he had escaped without injury.

Fleete thanked no one. He said that he wanted to go to bed. He was gorgeously drunk.

We moved on, Strickland silent and wrathful, until Fleete was taken with violent shivering fits and sweating. He said that the smells of the bazaar were overpowering, and he wondered why slaughter-houses were permitted so near English residences. "Can't you smell the blood?" said Fleete.

We put him to bed at last, just as the dawn was breaking, and Strickland invited me to have another whisky and soda. While we were drinking he talked of the trouble in the temple, and admitted that it baffled him completely. Strickland hates being mystified by natives, because his business in life is to overmatch them with their own weapons. He has not yet succeeded in doing this, but in fifteen or twenty years he will have made some small progress.

"They should have mauled us," he said, "instead of mewing at us. I wonder what they meant. I don't like it one little bit."

I said that the Managing Committee of the temple would in all probability bring a criminal action against us for insulting their religion. There was a section of the Indian Penal Code which exactly met Fleete's offence. Strickland said he only hoped and prayed that they would do this. Before I left I looked into Fleete's room, and saw him lying on his right side, scratching his left breast. Then I went to bed cold, depressed, and unhappy, at seven o'clock in the morning.

At one o'clock I rode over to Strickland's house to inquire after Fleete's head. I imagined that it would be a sore one. Fleete was breakfasting and seemed unwell. His temper was gone, for he was abusing the cook for not supplying him with an underdone chop. A man who can eat raw meat after a wet night is a curiosity. I told Fleete this and he laughed.

"You breed queer mosquitoes in these parts," he said. "I've been bitten to pieces, but only in one place."

"Let's have a look at the bite," said Strickland. "It may have gone down since this morning."

While the chops were being cooked, Fleete opened his shirt and showed us, just over his left breast, a mark, the perfect double of the black rosettes—the five or six irregular blotches arranged in a circle—on a leopard's hide. Strickland looked and said, "It was only pink this morning. It's grown black now."

Fleete ran to a glass.

"By Jove!" he said, "this is nasty. What is it?"

We could not answer. Here the chops came in, all red and juicy, and Fleete bolted three in a most offensive manner. He ate on his right grinders only, and threw his head over his right shoulder as he snapped the meat. When he had finished, it struck him that he had been behaving strangely, for he said apologetically, "I don't think I ever felt so hungry in my life. I've bolted like an ostrich."

After breakfast Strickland said to me, "Don't go. Stay here, and stay for the night."

Seeing that my house was not three miles from Strickland's, this request was absurd. But Strickland insisted, and was going to say something when Fleete interrupted by declaring in a shamefaced way that he felt hungry again. Strickland sent a man to my house to fetch over my bedding and a horse, and we three went down to Strickland's stables to pass the hours until it was time to go out for a ride. The man who has a weakness for horses never wearies of inspecting them; and when two men are killing time in this way they gather knowledge and lies the one from the other.

There were five horses in the stables, and I shall never forget the scene as we tried to look them over. They seemed to have gone mad. They reared and screamed and nearly tore up their pickets; they sweated and shivered and lathered and were distraught with fear. Strickland's horses used to know him as well as his dogs; which made the matter more curious. We left the stable for fear of the brutes throwing themselves in their panic. Then Strickland turned back and called me. The horses were still frightened, but they let us "gentle" and make much of them, and put their heads in our bosoms.

"They aren't afraid of *us*," said Strickland. "D' you know, I'd give three months' pay if *Outrage* here could talk."

But *Outrage* was dumb, and could only cuddle up to his master and blow out his nostrils, as is the custom of horses when they wish to explain things but can't. Fleete came up when we were in the stalls, and as soon as the horses saw him, their fright broke out afresh. It was all that we could do to escape from the place unkicked. Strickland said, "They don't seem to love you, Fleete."

"Nonsense," said Fleete; "my mare will follow me like a dog." He went to her; she was in a loose-box; but as he slipped the bars she plunged, knocked him down, and broke away into the garden. I laughed, but Strickland was not amused. He took his moustache in both fists and pulled at it till it nearly came out. Fleete, instead of going off to chase his property, yawned, saying that he felt sleepy. He went to the house to lie down, which was a foolish way of spending New Year's Day.

Strickland sat with me in the stables and asked if I had noticed anything peculiar in Fleete's manner. I said that he ate his food like a beast; but that this might have been the result of living alone in the hills out of the reach of society as refined and elevating as ours for instance. Strickland was not amused. I do not think that he listened to me, for his next sentence referred to the mark on Fleete's breast, and I said that it might have been caused by blister-flies, or that it was possibly a birth-mark newly born and now visible for the first time. We both agreed that it was unpleasant to look at, and Strickland found occasion to say that I was a fool.

"I can't tell you what I think now," said he, "because you would call me a madman; but you must stay with me for the next few days, if you can. I want you to watch Fleete, but don't tell me what you think till I have made up my mind."

"But I am dining out to-night," I said.

"So am I," said Strickland, "and so is Fleete. At least if he doesn't change his mind."

We walked about the garden smoking, but saying nothing—because we were friends, and talking spoils good tobacco—till our pipes were out. Then we went to wake up Fleete. He was wide awake and fidgeting about his room.

"I say, I want some more chops," he said. "Can I get them?"

We laughed and said, "Go and change. The ponies will be round in a minute."

"All right," said Fleete. "I'll go when I get the chops—underdone ones, mind."

He seemed to be quite in earnest. It was four o'clock, and we had had breakfast at one; still, for a long time, he demanded those underdone chops. Then he changed into riding clothes and went out into the verandah. His pony—the mare had not been caught—would not let him come near. All three horses were unmanageable—mad with fear—and finally Fleete said that he would stay at home and get something to eat. Strickland and I rode out wondering. As we passed the temple of Hanuman, the Silver Man came out and mewed at us.

"He is not one of the regular priests of the temple," said Strickland. "I think I should peculiarly like to lay my hands on him."

There was no spring in our gallop on the racecourse that evening. The horses were stale, and moved as though they had been ridden out.

"The fright after breakfast has been too much for them," said Strickland.

That was the only remark he made through the remainder of the ride. Once or twice I think he swore to himself; but that did not count.

We came back in the dark at seven o'clock, and saw that there were no lights in the bungalow. "Careless ruffians my servants are!" said Strickland.

My horse reared at something on the carriage drive, and Fleete stood up under its nose.

"What are you doing, grovelling about the garden?" said Strickland.

But both horses bolted and nearly threw us. We dismounted by the stables and returned to Fleete, who was on his hands and knees under the orange-bushes.

"What the devil's wrong with you?" said Strickland.

"Nothing, nothing in the world," said Fleete, speaking very quickly and thickly. "I've been gardening—botanising you know.

The smell of the earth is delightful. I think I'm going for a walk—a long walk—all night."

Then I saw that there was something excessively out of order somewhere, and I said to Strickland, "I am not dining out."

"Bless you!" said Strickland. "Here, Fleete, get up. You'll catch fever there. Come in to dinner and let's have the lamps lit. We'll all dine at home."

Fleete stood up unwillingly, and said, "No lamps—no lamps. It's much nicer here. Let's dine outside and have some more chops—lots of 'em and underdone—bloody ones with gristle."

Now a December evening in Northern India is bitterly cold, and Fleete's suggestion was that of a maniac.

"Come in," said Strickland sternly. "Come in at once."

Fleete came, and when the lamps were brought, we saw that he was literally plastered with dirt from head to foot. He must have been rolling in the garden. He shrank from the light and went to his room. His eyes were horrible to look at. There was a green light behind them, not in them, if you understand, and the man's lower lip hung down.

Strickland said, "There is going to be trouble—big trouble—to-night. Don't you change your riding-things."

We waited and waited for Fleete's reappearance, and ordered dinner in the meantime. We could hear him moving about his own room, but there was no light there. Presently from the room came the long-drawn howl of a wolf.

People write and talk lightly of blood running cold and hair standing up and things of that kind. Both sensations are too horrible to be trifled with. My heart stopped as though a knife had been driven through it, and Strickland turned as white as the table-cloth.

The howl was repeated, and was answered by another howl far across the fields.

That set the gilded roof on the horror. Strickland dashed into Fleete's room. I followed, and we saw Fleete getting out of the window. He made beast-noises in the back of his throat. He could not answer us when we shouted at him. He spat.

I don't quite remember what followed, but I think that Strickland must have stunned him with the long boot-jack or else I should never have been able to sit on his chest. Fleete could not speak, he could only snarl, and his snarls were those of a wolf, not of a man. The human spirit must have been giving way all day and have died out with the twilight. We were dealing with a beast that had once been Fleete.

The affair was beyond any human and rational experience. I tried to say "Hydrophobia," but the word wouldn't come, because I knew that I was lying.

We bound this beast with leather thongs of the punkah-rope, and tied its thumbs and big toes together, and gagged it with a shoe-horn, which makes a very efficient gag if you know how to arrange it. Then we carried it into the dining-room, and sent a man to Dumoise, the doctor, telling him to come over at once. After we had despatched the messenger and were drawing breath, Strickland said, "It's no good. This isn't any doctor's work." I, also, knew that he spoke the truth.

The beast's head was free, and it threw it about from side to side. Any one entering the room would have believed that we were curing a wolf's pelt. That was the most loathsome accessory of all.

Strickland sat with his chin in the heel of his fist, watching the beast as it wriggled on the ground, but saying nothing. The shirt had been torn open in the scuffle and showed the black rosette mark on the left breast. It stood out like a blister.

In the silence of the watching we heard something without mewing like a she-otter. We both rose to our feet, and, I answer for myself, not Strickland, felt sick—actually and physically sick. We told each other, as did the men in *Pinafore*, that it was the cat.

Dumoise arrived, and I never saw a little man so unprofessionally shocked. He said that it was a heart-rending case of hydrophobia, and that nothing could be done. At least any palliative measures would only prolong the agony. The beast was foaming at the mouth. Fleete, as we told Dumoise, had been bitten by dogs once or twice. Any man who keeps half a dozen terriers must expect a nip now and again. Dumoise could offer no help. He could only certify that Fleete was dying of hydrophobia. The beast was then howling, for it had managed to spit out the shoe-horn. Dumoise said that he would be ready to certify to the cause of death, and that the end was certain. He was a good little man, and he offered to remain with us; but Strickland refused the kindness. He did not wish to poison Dumoise's New Year. He would only ask him not to give the real cause of Fleete's death to the public.

So Dumoise left, deeply agitated; and as soon as the noise of the cart-wheels had died away, Strickland told me, in a whisper, his suspicions. They were so wildly improbable that he dared not say them out aloud; and I, who entertained all Strickland's beliefs, was so ashamed of owning to them that I pretended to disbelieve.

"Even if the Silver Man had bewitched Fleete for polluting the image of Hanuman, the punishment could not have fallen so quickly."

As I was whispering this the cry outside the house rose again, and the beast fell into a fresh paroxysm of struggling till we were afraid that the thongs that held it would give way.

"Watch!" said Strickland. "If this happens six times I shall take the law into my own hands. I order you to help me."

He went into his room and came out in a few minutes with the barrels of an old shot-gun, a piece of fishing-line, some thick cord, and his heavy wooden bedstead. I reported that the convulsions had followed the cry by two seconds in each case, and the beast seemed perceptibly weaker.

Strickland muttered, "But he can't take away the life! He can't take away the life!"

I said, though I knew that I was arguing against myself, "It may be a cat. It must be a cat. If the Silver Man is responsible, why does he dare to come here?"

Strickland arranged the wood on the hearth, put the gun-barrels into the glow of the fire, spread the twine on the table and broke a walking stick in two. There was one yard of fishing line, gut, lapped with wire, such as is used for *mahseer*-fishing, and he tied the two ends together in a loop.

Then he said, "How can we catch him? He must be taken alive and unhurt."

I said that we must trust in Providence, and go out softly with polo-sticks into the shrubbery at the front of the house. The man or animal that made the cry was evidently moving round the house as regularly as a night-watchman. We could wait in the bushes till he came by and knock him over.

Strickland accepted this suggestion, and we slipped out from a bath-room window into the front verandah and then across the carriage drive into the bushes.

In the moonlight we could see the leper coming round the corner of the house. He was perfectly naked, and from time to time he mewed and stopped to dance with his shadow. It was an unattractive sight, and thinking of poor Fleete, brought to such degradation by so foul a creature, I put away all my doubts and resolved to help Strickland from the heated gun-barrels to the loop of twine—from the loins to the head and back again—with all tortures that might be needful.

The leper halted in the front porch for a moment and we jumped out on him with the sticks. He was wonderfully strong, and we were afraid that he might escape or be fatally injured before we caught him. We had an idea that lepers were frail creatures, but this proved to be incorrect. Strickland knocked his legs from under him and I put my foot on his neck. He mewed hideously, and even through my riding-boots I could feel that his flesh was not the flesh of a clean man.

He struck at us with his hand and feet-stumps. We looped the lash of a dog-whip round him, under the arm-pits, and dragged him backwards into the hall and so into the dining-room where the beast lay. There we tied him with trunk-straps. He made no attempt to escape, but mewed.

When we confronted him with the beast the scene was beyond description. The beast doubled backwards into a bow as though he had been poisoned with strychnine, and moaned in the most pitiable fashion. Several other things happened also, but they cannot be put down here.

"I think I was right," said Strickland. "Now we will ask him to cure this case."

But the leper only mewed. Strickland wrapped a towel round his hand and took the gun-barrels out of the fire. I put the half of the broken walking stick through the loop of fishing-line and buckled the leper comfortably to Strickland's bedstead. I understood then how men and women and little children can endure to see a witch burnt alive; for the beast was moaning on the floor, and though the Silver Man had no face, you could see horrible feelings passing through the slab that took its place, exactly as waves of heat play across red-hot iron—gun-barrels for instance.

Strickland shaded his eyes with his hands for a moment and we got to work. This part is not to be printed.

*

The dawn was beginning to break when the leper spoke. His mewings had not been satisfactory up to that point. The beast had fainted from exhaustion and the house was very still. We unstrapped the leper and told him to take away the evil spirit. He crawled to the beast and laid his hand upon the left breast. That was all. Then he fell face down and whined, drawing in his breath as he did so.

We watched the face of the beast, and saw the soul of Fleete coming back into the eyes. Then a sweat broke out on the forehead and the eyes—they were human eyes—closed. We waited for an hour but Fleete still slept. We carried him to his room and bade the leper go, giving him the bedstead, and the sheet on the bedstead to cover his nakedness, the gloves and the towels with which we had touched him, and the whip that had been hooked round his body. He put the sheet about him and went out into the early morning without speaking or mewing.

Strickland wiped his face and sat down. A night-gong, far away in the city, made seven o'clock.

"Exactly four-and-twenty hours!" said Strickland. "And I've done enough to ensure my dismissal from the service, besides permanent quarters in a lunatic asylum. Do you believe that we are awake?"

The red-hot gun-barrel had fallen on the floor and was singeing the carpet. The smell was entirely real.

That morning at eleven we two together went to wake up Fleete. We looked and saw that the black leopard-rosette on his chest had disappeared. He was very drowsy and tired, but as soon as he saw us, he said, "Oh! Confound you fellows. Happy New Year to you. Never mix your liquors. I'm nearly dead."

"Thanks for your kindness, but you're over time," said Strickland. "To-day is the morning of the second. You've slept the clock round with a vengeance."

The door opened, and little Dumoise put his head in. He had come on foot, and fancied that we were laying out Fleete.

"I've brought a nurse," said Dumoise. "I suppose that she can come in for... what is necessary."

"By all means," said Fleete cheerily, sitting up in bed. "Bring on your nurses."

Dumoise was dumb. Strickland led him out and explained that there must have been a mistake in the diagnosis. Dumoise remained dumb and left the house hastily. He considered that his professional reputation had been injured, and was inclined to make a personal matter of the recovery. Strickland went out too. When he came back, he said that he had been to call on the Temple of Hanuman to offer redress for the pollution of the god, and had been solemnly assured that no white man had ever touched the idol and that he was an incarnation of all the virtues labouring under a delusion. "What do you think?" said Strickland.

I said, "'There are more things...'"

But Strickland hates that quotation. He says that I have worn it threadbare.

One other curious thing happened which frightened me as much as anything in all the night's work. When Fleete was dressed he came into the dining-room and sniffed. He had a quaint trick of moving his nose when he sniffed. "Horrid doggy smell, here," said he. "You should really keep those terriers of yours in better order. Try sulphur, Strick."

But Strickland did not answer. He caught hold of the back of a chair, and, without warning, went into an amazing fit of hysterics. It is terrible to see a strong man overtaken with hysteria. Then it struck me that we had fought for Fleete's soul with the Silver Man in that room, and had disgraced ourselves as Englishmen for ever, and I laughed and gasped and gurgled just as shamefully as Strickland, while Fleete thought that we had both gone mad. We never told him what we had done.

Some years later, when Strickland had married and was a church-going member of society for his wife's sake, we reviewed the incident dispassionately, and Strickland suggested that I should put it before the public.

I cannot myself see that this step is likely to clear up the mystery; because, in the first place, no one will believe a rather unpleasant story, and, in the second, it is well known to every right-minded man that the gods of the heathen are stone and brass, and any attempt to deal with them otherwise is justly condemned.

LINES INSCRIBED UPON A CUP FORMED FROM A SKULL

Lord Byron

Given the beautiful illustration on this book's cover, I could not resist including this poem by Lord Byron which was written about a real cup created for the writer. Byron described the discovery of the skull and his decision to make it into a cup to fellow writer, Thomas Medwin, who went on to publish a memoir about his conversations with the poet:

"The gardener in digging [discovered] a skull that had probably belonged to some jolly friar or monk of the abbey, about the time it was dis-monasteried. Observing it to be of giant size, and in a perfect state of preservation, a strange fancy seized me of having it set and mounted as a drinking-cup. I accordingly sent it to town, and it returned with a very high polish, and of a mottled colour like tortoiseshell [...] I remember scribbling some lines about it; but that was not all: I afterwards established at the Abbey a new order. The members consisted of twelve, and I elected myself grand master, or Abbot of the Skull, a grand heraldic title. [...] the *crane* was filled with claret and in imitation of the Goths of old, passed about to the gods of the Consistory, whilst many a grim joke was cut at its expense".*

---

* Thomas Medwin, *Journal of the Conversations of Lord Byron* (1824). With thanks to Jonny Davidson. You can read it on archive.org here: <https://archive.org/details/conversationsooomedw>.

Medwin goes on to say that he thought Byron "had a particular predilection for skulls and cross-bones" to which Byron replies enigmatically about the worth and power of particular bones, specifically those from the battlefields at Morat. Byron mentions the Battle of Morat in his famous narrative poem, *Childe Harolde's Pilgrimage* (1812–1818). Stephen Massett claims to have drunk from it in his 1860 essay "A Day at Newstead Abbey" in the American magazine *The Knickerbocker*. He visited the new owner of Newstead Abbey, Colonel Wildman, in the summer of 1858 and notes that it was "a very handsome goblet" which did not have the "terrific appearance of a death's head". He tells that the skull cup "was always produced after dinner when Byron had company at the abbey, and a bottle of claret poured into it".* The fate of Byron's skull cup is shrouded in mystery although a cup, which some claim to be the famous drinking vessel, was auctioned by Charterhouse in 2017.

* Stephen C. Massett, "A Day at Newstead Abbey", *The Knickerbocker* (1860), vol. LV, page 622.

Start not—nor deem my spirit fled:
In me behold the only skull,
From which, unlike a living head,
Whatever flows is never dull.

I liv'd, I lov'd, I quaff'd, like thee:
I died: let earth my bones resign;
Fill up—thou canst not injure me;
The worm hath fouler lips than thine.

Better to hold the sparkling grape,
Than nurse the earth-worm's slimy brood;
And circle in the goblet's shape
The drink of Gods, than reptiles' food.

Where once my wit, perchance, hath shone,
In aid of others' let me shine;
And when, alas! our brains are gone,
What nobler substitute than wine?

Quaff while thou canst: another race,
When thou and thine, like me, are sped,
May rescue thee from Earth's embrace,
And rhyme and revel with the dead.

Why not? since through life's little day
Our heads such sad effects produce;
Redeem'd from worms and wasting clay,
This chance is theirs, to be of use.

NEWSTEAD ABBEY, 1808.

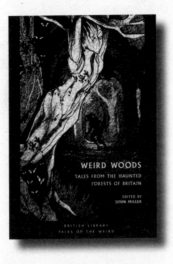

But foliage surrounded him, branches blocked the way; the trees stood close and still; and the sun dipped that moment behind a great black cloud. The entire wood turned dark and silent. It watched him.

Woods play a crucial and recurring role in horror, fantasy, the gothic and the weird. They are places in which strange things happen, where it is easy to lose your way. Supernatural creatures thrive in the thickets. Trees reach into underworlds of pagan myth and magic. Forests are full of ghosts.

Lining the path through this realm of folklore and fear are twelve stories from across Britain, telling tales of whispering voices and maddening sights from deep in the Yorkshire Dales to the ancient hills of Gwent and the eerie quiet of the forests of Dartmoor. Immerse yourself in this collection of classic tales celebrating the enduring power of our natural spaces to enthral and terrorise our senses.

*... and then the music was so loud, so beautiful that I
couldn't think of anything else. I was completely lost to
the music, enveloped by melody which was part of Pan.*

In 1894, Arthur Machen's landmark novella *The Great God Pan* was
published, sparking the sinister resurgence of the pagan goat god. Writers
of the late-nineteenth to mid-twentieth centuries, such as Oscar Wilde,
E. M. Forster and Margery Lawrence, took the god's rebellious influence
as inspiration to spin beguiling tales of social norms turned upside down
and ancient ecological forces compelling their protagonists to ecstatic
heights or bizarre dooms.

Assembling ten tales and six poems—along with Machen's novella—from
the boom years of Pan-centric literature, this new collection revels in
themes of queer awakening, transgression against societal bonds and the
bewitching power of the wild as it explores a rapturous and culturally
significant chapter in the history of weird fiction.

ALSO AVAILABLE

The whispering voice was very clear, horrible,
too, beyond all she had ever known.

"They are roaring in the Forest further
out... and I... must go and see."

From one of the greatest authors of twentieth century weird fiction come four of the very best strange stories ever written: "The Willows", "The Wendigo", "The Man Whom the Trees Loved" and "Ancient Sorceries".

Tightly wrought and deliciously suspenseful, Blackwood's novellas are quintessentially weird, pitching the reader into an uncanny space in which the sublime forces of primordial Nature still dominate, and in which the limits of the senses are uncertain. These are tales of forces beyond the frayed edges of human experience—tales which tug at the mind, and which prove as unsettling today as they first did over a century ago.

ALSO AVAILABLE

Where the indescribable thrills of music and the arts, piercing early psychology and terrifying supernatural beings find their meeting place, so dwell the startlingly original weird tales of Vernon Lee.

In this collection, fiction expert Mike Ashley selects the writer's eeriest dark fantasies: stories which blend the shocking, the sentimental, the beautiful and the unnerving into an atmosphere and style still unmatched in the field of supernatural writing.

From the modernised folktales "Marsyas in Flanders" and "The Legend of Madame Krasinska" to ingenious psychological hauntings such as "A Phantom Lover" and "A Wicked Voice", Lee's captivating voice rings out just as distinctively now as in her Fin-de-Siècle heyday.

For more Tales of the Weird titles
visit the British Library Shop (shop.bl.uk)

We welcome any suggestions, corrections or feedback you may have, and will
aim to respond to all items addressed to the following:

The Editor (Tales of the Weird), British Library Publishing,
The British Library, 96 Euston Road, London NW1 2DB

We also welcome enquiries through our Twitter account, @BL_Publishing.